THE MAYOR OF ROUND ROCK.

Warner glanced at Mrs. Roads and then at Laura. He said, "The desk clerk told me the mayor was up here."

"She is."

"Who is?"

"The mayor."

"What mayor?"

Laura indicated Martha Roads. He turned and stared at her. He said, "You're the mayor? Of this town? Of Round Rock? You sure you ain't the wife of the mayor—just a kind of stand-in mayor?"

She said, in her throaty voice, "My husband is the furtherest thing from a mayor you could imagine. He runs a saloon and whorehouse outside the city limits."

Laura suddenly laughed. Warner turned to her, feeling his face coloring. He said, "What the hell strikes you so funny?"

She pointed at him. "I wish you could see your face now. You look like you just swallowed something and you're not quite sure what it is."

"Giles Tippette is, quite simply, one of those gifted craftsmen whose skills cause others in the business to fall into a blue funk with the appearance of every new title bearing his name. . . . He writes with the soul of a poet. You could set the guy's words to music, such is the lyrical quality he possesses."

—Carlton Stowers, author of *Careless Whispers*
and *Innocence Lost*

PRAISE FOR GILES TIPPETTE AND THE HORSE THIEVES

MORE PRAISE FOR GILES TIPPETTE

THE BANK ROBBER

"A western in the Butch Cassidy vein. . . . Tippette walks a tragic-comic line."

—*Dallas Times Herald*

"Tippette can plot away the best of them. . . . The novel races to a whirlwind and unexpected realistic finish."

—*Dallas Morning News*

THE BRAVE MEN

"A tough, gutsy and fascinating book . . . for men who like to explore the root causes of human bravery. . . ."

—*New York Newsday*

"[Tippette's] insight into courage is the best I've ever seen and is alone well worth the price of the book."

—*El Paso Times*

THE SURVIVALIST

"A spellbinding tale of suspense by a fine Texas author."

—*Sunday Oklahoman*

"A penetrating, thoughtful novel of a man trying to escape the fear within himself."

—*Columbus Dispatch*

"[Tippette] can write rough and tumble action superbly. That remains a fact."

—*Chattanooga Times*

Books by Giles Tippette

FICTION

Slick Money*
The Horse Thieves*
Cherokee
Dead Man's Poker
Gunpoint
Sixkiller
Hard Rock
Jailbreak
Cross Fire
Bad News
China Blue
Wilson Young on the Run
The Texas Bank Robbing Company

Hard Luck Money
Wilson's Woman
Wilson's Revenge
Wilson's Choice
Wilson's Luck
Wilson's Gold
The Mercenaries
Austin Davis
The Sunshine Killers
The Survivalist
The Trojan Cow
The Bank Robber*

NONFICTION

I'll Try Anything Once: Misadventures of a Sports Guy
Donkey Baseball and Other Sporting Delights
Saturday's Children
The Brave Men

*Published by POCKET BOOKS

·SLICK· MONEY

GILES TIPPETTE

POCKET BOOKS

New York London Toronto Sydney Tokyo Singapore

This book is a work of fiction. Names, characters, places and
incidents are either products of the author's imagination or are used
fictitiously. Any resemblance to actual events or locales or persons,
living or dead, is entirely coincidental.

An *Original* Publication of POCKET BOOKS

POCKET BOOKS, a division of Simon & Schuster Inc.
1230 Avenue of the Americas, New York, NY 10020

Copyright © 1993 by Giles Tippette

ISBN: 0-671-79346-2

First Pocket Books printing December 1993

10 9 8 7 6 5 4 3 2 1

POCKET and colophon are registered trademarks of
Simon & Schuster Inc.

Cover art by Robert Tannenbaum

Printed in the U.S.A.

To Jessie Robbins—

Semper Fi

·SLICK·
MONEY

1

The bandits had come at him just as he was driving the four horses around a bend in the road he was following. They'd been hidden from sight at first because of a hill, but as soon as he saw the five of them he'd realized their intentions and realized the mistake they'd made by bunching up in front of him rather than fanning out in a semicircle so as to contain him and his horses.

In that instant when he'd recognized them for what they were, a number of thoughts had run through his mind. His first feeling had been one of anger, anger at himself for running the risk of driving the two-year-old Andalusian quarterhorse-cross colts to market in San Antonio rather than shipping them on the train as his partner, Laura Pico, had insisted he do. His second emotion had also been anger, but anger this time at the widow Pico for perhaps being right and then fear of what he'd hear from her if he lost the colts that had already been sold for $750 each. Why in hell had he been so hardheaded as to insist on driving them the 120 miles when he could so easily have loaded them on the train and left their responsibility for safe passage to the railroad? And that was not to mention the risk the bandits presented to the considerable sum of cash, over $500, that he, as a horse trader, habitually carried in his pocket. His final feeling had been anger at the bandits for putting him at such risk by being where they were at the same time he was there and for being there for the purposes of robbing him.

But even as those thoughts had flashed through his mind, and even as he'd started the motion to put spurs to the Andalusian he was riding, he'd taken careful note that only two of the bandits had drawn guns in their hands. It had made a strange spectacle to his eye—five robbers but only two guns, he hadn't taken an instant to dwell on it because, even in that blink of an eye, he'd seen a great deal more.

He'd seen that their clothes were worn and shabby and that the horses they were riding were of poor quality and that the men themselves looked neither particularly dangerous nor threatening. They did not look like road agents. They did not look like bandits or robbers. They looked like ordinary range workers who were about a business they didn't seem to have the slightest idea of how to handle.

He'd seen all that in a quick blink of an eye because he had what a friend of his described as "hunter's" eyes. When he'd understood what his friend had meant by it he had been surprised because he would never have thought of himself like that. He had always thought of himself as a man of a gentle nature who went about doing his job, respecting his neighbors, and trying to get along in the world. He knew he was good at what he did with horses and he knew he'd had some good teaching from his grandfather, but he would never, even though he'd seen a spot or two of trouble in his life, have thought of himself as someone having these so-called hunter's eyes. His friend, an ex-bank robber and gunman named Wilson Young, had said, "There's a great deal of talk about how fast a man is with a gun or what a good shot he is or how cool he is under fire, but I tell you that if a man ain't got the kind of eyes that can see everything—and I mean *everything*—in that first instant of danger, that first blink, he ain't going to last very long because he's going to get taken unawares from some quarter his eyes missed and that will be the end of him. A man that ain't got the eyes of a hunter, be he hunting game or other men, where he can see in every direction except straight behind him, ain't got no business carrying a loaded revolver because somebody is going to take it away from him and put a bullet hole through the top of his head by jamming the barrel of the gun up his ass."

So it had been his eyes that had caused him to react instantly and take the play away from the robbers and give him the advantage. The instant he'd sighted them and his mind had taken in all that he'd seen he'd yelled, *"Yiiihiii!"* to the valuable horses he was driving, causing them to surge suddenly into a fast trot, almost a lope, that halved the distance between himself and the would-be robbers long before they'd expected it.

Almost in the same second he'd drawn his revolver and, leaning forward over the neck of his horse, he'd carefully thumbed back the hammer of his weapon and fired at one of the two men holding drawn pistols. The slug had taken the bandit in the chest, knocking him backward and then down off the side of his horse. He had been cocking his revolver for another shot, his horses already starting to push in among the confused men, separating them and adding to their confusion. But even though there were no more than ten yards between him and the second man with a drawn revolver, his shot had been a bad one, due to the motion of his own horse and the way the bandit was sawing on the reins of his animal, obviously trying to turn him to flee. The bullet had hit the man in the arm, causing the cloth to fly, but he could tell it hadn't been a solid hit because the man's arm hadn't jerked. Just the same, the man had dropped his revolver like it had suddenly gotten red hot. None of the other men had made any motion to draw their guns. They seemed more intent on getting away now than taking his horses. He yelled, "Hold it, damn it! Stop! *Hands up, goddammit!"*

Now his horses were on past them and there was nothing between him and them except five or six yards of empty space. He said, "Get your damn hands up! *Now!"*

Very slowly, realizing they were facing a man with a loaded revolver who obviously knew how to use it, they dropped their reins and lifted their hands.

His name was Warner Grayson and, in that year of 1885, he was twenty-eight years old. He was a touch over six feet tall and slimmer looking than his 175 pounds in spite of his big shoulders and arms and hands. The rest of him was all horseman—slim hips and long legs and very little around the middle to hang a belt on. Horses had been his life and his livelihood ever since he'd started in trading them and gentling them and handling them under his grandfather's teaching. His parents had been taken by the fever when he was no more than six and his grandfather had had the raising of him until his grandfather had died when Warner was not yet eighteen. After that he'd tended to his own "bringing up," and while some might have argued with the results, especially a lady named Laura Pico, Warner was satisfied with the job he and his grandfather had done. His skill and touch and knowledge of horses and their care and improvement were almost legendary in South Texas, where he made his home on a small breeding ranch near the coastal town of Corpus Christi.

Warner was not a particularly handsome man, but he had a pleasant, open, friendly face that some people, to their sorrow in a horse trade, had mistaken for naïveté. Some people thought of Warner as stubborn. He wasn't stubborn, he was merely of the fixed opinion that he ought to be able to accomplish any matter that he set his hand to and bring it to a successful conclusion. He didn't like to be told he couldn't do something and he didn't like the word no and very specifically did not like people trying to push him around or play fast and loose with either his property or his person. Such attempts made him angry, and they made him dangerous.

Now he was appraising the four would-be bandits before him. They were sitting their horses, their hands in the air. Warner let his mount walk slowly toward them until only a couple of yards separated him from the men. He took a moment to look them over carefully. His first glance had been right; they looked rode down and rode over. He could see they were a ragtag outfit with second-rate horses to match. He said, evenly, "Get down off your horses. One at a time, beginning with you." He pointed his gun at a young-looking man in a slouch hat and a three- or four-day growth of whiskers. "And be damn sure you keep them hands up when your feet get on the ground."

The man Warner had shot in the arm was wearing a red

checkered shirt. Acting like he was in bad pain he said, "Mister, I got to—"

Warner said, "Shut up. There'll be time for talking later. Right now is the time for getting off your horses. Do it slow and careful. I got exactly the number of rounds left in this revolver that I need."

He watched them carefully as, one by one, they dismounted. Now that he had the situation in hand he found himself wondering about several matters. The first was why only two men had drawn guns and the second was why the others hadn't drawn and fired back when he'd shot two of their number. Their intent might have been to steal his horses or rob him, but they had gone at it in mighty poor fashion. With odds of five to one they could have surrounded him and left him no choice but to put his hands in the air and be disarmed. True enough, he had caught them off-guard with the sudden charge of his small herd of horses, but they should never have been so bunched up in the first place. And if they were going to commit armed robbery it would seem like a good idea that they all be armed. A man had to be awful poor at arithmetic not to know that five guns were better than two. He carefully dismounted, gun in hand.

Something was not right about the affair, but he didn't have time to sort it out. He had to get these would-be robbers to a jail and then get the horses he was driving into San Antonio. They were valuable horses, road horses bred to cover a lot of ground with a stylish gait. They were not for the man with a short pocket.

But now all the bandits were standing by their horses, their hands still raised. He took note that all the horses were ground reined, which meant that they were most likely cow horses. A cowboy working cattle didn't have time to find someplace to hitch his horse when he dismounted on the prairie, so a cattle horse was taught to stand with nothing holding him except his reins hanging down to the ground.

The checkered-shirted man Warner had shot said, "Cap'n, my arm is painin' me somethin' fierce where you put a ball through it. I wisht you'd let me lower it."

He ignored the man. He said, "Now, I want you all to take one hand, just one, and unbuckle your gun belts and let them drop on the ground. Anybody makes the slightest move toward the handle of a gun and I'm gonna put a hole through their lung and tell the law they died of pneumonia. You understand me?"

They nodded and began, awkwardly, to unbuckle their gunbelts with just one hand. The man that Warner had shot tried first with his wounded arm and then had to switch. Warner watched him without the slightest sign of sympathy. Normally Warner had such a boyish face that it was hard for people to take him for his age. But now his face was flat and hard. In truth Warner was a hard man inside. Most people only realized that when it was too late and then the realization came that they'd underestimated him.

When they were finally shed of their gunbelts he let them lower their hands and stand. On beyond them he could see his little herd of four horses were just off the road and grazing on the mesquite grass that was common to the country immediately south of San Antonio. His own horse was standing behind him, his packhorse's lead rope looped to the saddle horn. Warner said, "You, there on the end."

It was the youngest-looking one. Warner guessed his age to be no more than twenty, twenty-one at the outside. He said, "Yessir?"

Warner said, "I want you to take your lariat and cut it into four pieces. I'm going to tie your horses together stirrup to stirrup."

The young man looked unhappy. He said, "Mister, that's a mighty harsh way to treat a good lariat rope. That there's a Laredo sisal rope that was hand braided underwater and will make a loop stiff enough to roll along the ground like a kid's hoop. Cost me little over ten dollar."

Warner said, impatiently, "Then use the dead man's lariat. *He* ain't going to mind."

The young man said, "Well, thing of it is, his rope is pretty stiff just the same. Ain't goin' to cut into short snatches and will be hell to tie knots in."

"Goddammit!" Warner said. "There's some soft picket rope in my pack on my packhorse. Get it and do what I told you to do before you wear out my patience."

But as the young man started toward the packhorse the

wounded man said, "Cap'n, I reckon I'm bleedin' pretty bad. Reckon you'd let me take me a look at this bullet wound?" Because his checkered shirt was red it was difficult to see much blood, if any.

"Oh, hell!" Warner said in disgust. "We ain't ever gonna get started. Damn it, I seen the bullet when it hit you. It barely grazed you. Got you in the upper arm on the outside and I'll bet you won't be deep enough to bury a small cigarillo in."

The man stared at him. He said, "You tellin' us you *seen* the bullet hit me?"

"No, I don't mean I actual seen the bullet strike you, but I didn't see your arm jerk so I knew I hadn't hit you solid. I just saw the sleeve of your shirt kind of dance up."

The man looked around at the other two that were still standing there. He said, "I reckon we picked the wrong gent to invite to the dance."

Warner said, "One of y'all tear up a bandanna or some rag and bind him up before he gets himself to believing he's about to bleed to death. But don't nobody get in between me and anybody else. I want to be able to see all four of you at the same time. And get a damn move on."

He was slow but by then the young man had found the coil of soft rope in Warner's pack and now he stood, waiting. He said yes and nodded when Warner asked him if he had a knife. Warner said, "Then cut that rope in three six-foot lengths. Then take and tie the stirrup of one horse to the stirrup of the next."

The man looked at him in puzzlement. "Huh?"

"Oh, goddammit!" Warner said. "You road agents brought this on yourselves. Now you better commence to doing what I tell you or I'm going to get short of temper." He stepped closer and pointed. "Your horse is on the end. Tie one end of one of those six-foot lengths to your left stirrup. Then tie the other end to the right stirrup of the next horse. Then tie the left stirrup of that *same* horse to the right stirrup of the next horse. And so on. You reckon you can handle that?"

The wounded man broke in. "'Scuse me, cap'n, but we ain't no road agents."

Warner said, "You ain't no *good* road agents, but what else you want me to call men who come riding out on the road, blocking my way, with drawn pistols? Brand inspectors?"

The man said, "Ouch! Hell, Darcey, not so goddamn tight." But then he came back to Warner as his partner finished binding his wound. He said, "Mister, you never give us time to say what we *was*. Or what we wanted. First thang you done was let loose on Jake layin' yonder." He jerked his head where the dead man was laying facedown.

Warner laughed without humor. He said, "Was I supposed to let y'all shoot me down to make sure of your intentions? Listen, I reckon you better shut your mouth. I'm tired of listening to you."

The man who'd bound up the wounded man's arm, a short, stocky fellow who appeared to be a little older than the rest, said, "What you aimin' to do with us? What-all's this tying our stirrups together?"

"I'm stringing your stirrups together so you can't scatter and take your chances on me shooting one or two of you. This way you'll all stay together, and if you try to run, your horses will get to going all antigoggalin and out of gait. As to where you're going, you're going to jail. Where the hell did you think I was going to take you, to a church social?"

They looked at one another uneasily and then the short, stocky man said, "Mister, ain't they some way we kin git you to fergit about this? We ain't got much money 'tween us, maybe twenny-five, thirty dollar, but we'd give it if you could see your way clear to let us just ride on off. I mean, we ain't actually done you no harm."

For answer Warner nodded his head toward the dead man. He said, "Go load that feller across his saddle and tie him on tight. I don't want him falling off on the way into town. You there, in the chaps, give him a hand."

The man nodded. He hadn't said a word since Warner had first spotted the men. He was an ordinary-looking fellow who looked weathered beyond his years by wind and sun. Warner thought he had cowhand written all over him. He couldn't imagine what change would take him from honest work to the life of a thief. He kept his eyes down as if in shame. But after he'd taken two steps toward the dead man he stopped and turned. He said, "Mister, Jake's horse is lame. I reckon you ought to know that afore we load him up. Fact of the business that was why we—"

The stocky man, the one the wounded man had called Darcey, said, "Shut up, Les."

Warner stared at Darcey. He said, "Have you taken to managing affairs around here?"

The stocky man looked away. He was standing by the body of the dead man. He said, "No, sir. Jest don't figure we ought ta burden you with our troubles."

The dead man's horse was a brown-and-white pinto. Warner said, "Bring that horse over here. Lead him over here and then back off with the others."

Warner was careful not to let the horse get between himself and his view of the men. One by one he lifted the horse's feet. On the pinto's left front hoof he found an ugly bruise in the fleshy part inside the hoof. It was clear the horse had been poorly shod. It appeared that a sharp rock had made the sore. He said, dropping the animal's leg, "Horse has got a cut in the frog. Some fool cut the toe of his hoof too short and then shod him with soft land plates. Such shoes wasn't never meant to be worn in this rock country, especially if you're going overland. And y'all been going cross-country, haven't you? Avoiding the roads." He gestured at the young man in the checkered shirt. "Either give me your shirt or a dirty one or a pair of socks."

"My shirt . . . ?"

"Either that or something like it. I got to fix this horse's foot. It ain't but four miles into Hondo, which is where we're headed, but I hate to see an animal suffer. Now give me a big rag of some kind, damn it!"

It was Les who, moving carefully, went to his saddlebags and brought over a ragged flannel shirt. He said, "You'll be wanting to wrap it, raight? This ol' shirt ought to do it."

Warner gave him a look. He said, "You're a brave man. You stuck your hand in that saddlebag without seeing what my opinion on the matter might be. For all I know you might have been reaching for a revolver."

Les took off his hat and ran his hand through his hair. He was as sandy haired as Warner, though his hair was shorter. From some of the pale areas around his neck Warner could tell he'd just had a haircut. He said, "You want me to wrap that foot? I know how. You do it you'll have to put your gun down. It's a two-handed job."

"All right," Warner said. He stepped away. "Have at it."

The cowboy, for that was how Warner had began to think of him, took the pinto's foreleg between his knees like a farrier, facing backward, and used part of the shirt to fill the cavity inside the hoof and form a cushion between the cut and the ground. Then he tore the sleeves into thin strips and quickly and expertly tied the pad in place. He straightened up. "There," he said. "That ought to hold it fer a while."

Warner said, "Why didn't you do that in the first place instead of trying to rob me?"

He could see, by the glance that Les gave Darcey, that his shot had hit home.

Before they set out Les said, "Them animals you been driving is plain to see high-blooded stock, but I swear that horse you be riding, I don't believe I ever seen his like afore. Kin a man ast what breed you call them?"

Warner said, "Get mounted up. The bunch of you have held me up about as much as I'm going to stand for. I was doing fine tending to my business without your help."

Darcey said, with a cut of viciousness in his voice, "Well, you've kilt one of us. Thet ought to make up fer the trouble we've caused you."

Warner stared at the man so long that Darcey finally dropped his eyes. Then Warner turned to the cowboy wearing chaps. They wern't showy bat-wing chaps but leather leggings, the kind a working man wore in cactus brush country to protect his jeans and his skin. He said, "You take that lame horse on lead. We'll stick to the road and we'll be going at a slow pace. Take the bridle off him and cut you a lead rope off that soft picket line."

Before they got started Warner said, "Now, you will have taken notice I ain't tied your hands. And you may have a hideout gun somewhere about your person or your rig. And it may come to your mind that you might ought to take a chance and try and use that weapon. Just understand I'll shoot the first man that even looks like he is going to turn in my direction. Just face forward and ride on in to Hondo. We will be going to the sheriff's office, so stop when we get there. I'll tend to matters after that."

He sent the would-be robbers off first, riding in a line abreast with the horse carrying the dead man being led behind. Their stirrups were tied far enough apart that their horses didn't quite have to be in step, but there wasn't slack for much individual movement. Warner started the four horses bound for their new owners in San Antonio next. He'd been driving them for near a hundred miles and they were road wise and drove with almost no attention at all. Two of their main characteristics were their intelligence and their docility. It was what was causing them to be rapidly gaining popularity as horses for gentlemen or for people who had the price and wanted a horse that could cover ground and give no trouble.

His own mount was frisking along with his stylish sideways gait, crossing one foot over the other. It was no wonder that the cowboy named Les hadn't recognized the breed. So far as Warner knew there were only five others in the country, maybe in the whole of North America. His horse was an Andalusian, a Spanish horse that was known only in a part of Spain very near the Moroccan border. Or so he had been told. If anything, the horse favored the Arabian—a few of which Warner had seen—in looks and color, but his temperament was milder and he had more endurance and speed than the Arabian. What made him so valuable as a traveling horse was his walking gait, which was almost as fast as a quarterhorse's trot, and his lope, which was like a gallop on any other horse. The only difference was that the ride was so smooth you could almost sit on an Andalusian's back and drink a cup of coffee while he clipped off the miles at his ground-eating pace. He owned the horse that was between his legs and owned a sort of interest in the other five. When they had been imported from Spain some two years back, they'd cost $2,000 apiece, a startling price for anything except a Kentucky racehorse.

The other five Andalusian stallions belonged, on paper, to Laura Pico and were kept on his small breeding ranch near the Nueces River about fifteen miles south of Corpus Christi. Their previous home had been down on the Mexican border near the town of Del Rio, where Laura and her late husband had intended to breed the Andalusians to common range mares and produce a superior cattle horse.

Of course the idea had been so silly that nobody even bothered to tell the Picos that a cow horse could be fast or slow, nimble or clumsy, but the one thing it had to have was a headful of cow sense, and the Andalusians knew about as much about cats as they did about cattle. Laura had told him once, in her lofty, arrogant manner that made him want to grind his teeth, that she knew all that, but that the colts would get their horse sense from the range mares. He'd explained to her that that kind of thinking was about as hopeful as trying to roll a seven with just one die. But, since she hadn't known anything about dice, she hadn't gotten it.

Their partnership had come about in a strange way. A band of Mexican horse thieves had made away with the Picos' six Andalusians on a raid from across the river. They'd lost one, the one Warner was riding. On the bandits' next raid they'd come across Warner and his partner as they were heading for the border country with a little stock to trade and also to make the round of ranches in that country and get their remudas in top condition for the coming spring work. He and his partner had operated a custom horse-handling service. Most of the remudas got turned out in the winter when there wasn't any work to do, and most of the cowboys were let go to winter on their own. Warner and his partner made a business of passing from ranch to ranch taking the "bark," as they called it, off the big, rough ranch horses that had had three or four months of winter to get independent and spoiled. It saved wear and tear on the cowhands, and the ranch owner, who owned the strings of horses, could be sure the job would be done right.

But that had been his business only a few months of the year. The rest of the time was spent on his ranch in Nueces County breeding quarterhorses and Morgans and American saddlebred, breeding cowhorses and traveling horses and, for a few select customers, racehorses for the brush tracks and county fairs where horse racing over distances of a quarter of a mile on up to a mile was almost a religion. By the age of twenty-eight his reputation was such that the simple statement "That's a Warner Grayson horse" was enough to put the stamp of approval on an animal regardless of his type or use.

But on their second raid, when the Mexican bandits had

come across Warner and his partner, they'd killed Warner's partner, stole all their stock and money and guns and traveling gear, and then, after beating him half to death, had left Warner to die in an eighty-square-mile alkali flat where a rattlesnake couldn't make a living. Only Warner hadn't died. He had somehow walked for a day until, very close to collapse and not able to believe his eyes, he'd come across the very Andalusian he was riding. It had been the horse that had gotten loose from the Mexican bandits when they'd stole the Andalusians from the Picos. Warner had studied long and hard ever since how that Andalusian had come to be in the middle of that alkali flat. No animal was dumb enough to wander away from grass and water to desert and desolation, not even a horse. But that Andalusian had been there and he had saved Warner's life. Rather, they had mutually saved each other's lives because the Andalusian hadn't been in any too good shape. But he'd had enough left in him to carry Warner and himself to the Rio Grande and dump him in the water.

Warner had finally given up pondering over the set of circumstances that had brought the horse to his aid. He'd taken a piece of advice his grandfather had once given him and let the matter rest at that. His grandfather, who had been a strong soul for God and the Bible and Jesus Christ, though without benefit of the help of preachers, had told him, "Son, don't question why the Lord decides to send you a particular piece of good fortune. The Lord works in strange and mysterious ways and it ain't your business to wonder about the why of a thing. Just be thankful He thought enough of you to glance your way."

And that was all he could ever figure; that the Lord had chosen to glance his way on that occasion. Because, if he hadn't, Warner would have been a goner.

It made for a strange relationship between himself and the horse. Laura Pico actually named horses, and he knew other people who did the same thing. She claimed to "like" this horse or that one. Warner had never named a horse in his life for the simple reason that he didn't think the horse could remember it and he didn't think the horse would be interested in his, Warner's, name. So far as "liking" a horse, he had no idea what that meant. If a horse did his job and didn't cause trouble Warner gave him the best feed and care and training available and didn't ask for thanks. If the horse didn't do as he was supposed to, Warner got shut of him. He found his arrangement with horses very simple. He'd told Laura once, "Long as the horse understands I'm supposed to be on top and I make the choice of which way we go and when we go, then we get along fine."

But Laura was plain silly about horses and called them "baby" and "honey" and a lot of other idiotic names. Which was one of the reasons he still couldn't figure out how they'd come to be partners. When he'd been nursed back to health after his three days in the alkali country by Wilson Young he'd set out to find the bandits who'd robbed him and killed his partner and caused him so much trouble. In his determined fashion he had laid a trap for the *bandidos* and killed them all. He'd ridden the Andalusian on his hunt and had come to greatly admire the horse's qualities. Laura called him Paseta, but Warner didn't admire any horse enough to actually give it a name. In his pursuit of the bandits he'd managed to recover the other five Andalusians and return them to Laura. She had been widowed during the bandit's first raid, when her husband, showing a good deal more bravery than sense, had run out in the open and traded gunshots with them. Laura had proposed that Warner stay on at her ranch near the Rio Grande and go on with her fool idea of breeding the Spanish stallions to range mares. When he'd been able to get his face straight again Warner had proposed that she let him use the Spanish stallions to breed to Morgans and quarterhorses to make outstanding road horses and, maybe, the odd racehorse or two.

She'd agreed, but she'd come with the deal as a working partner, which meant that the only time they didn't argue was when they were in bed. And a man couldn't stay in bed all the time, even with a woman as exciting and hot-blooded as the widow Pico.

Laura wasn't beautiful, but she had deep butter-colored hair that sometimes showed a tinge of strawberry and a striking, slim figure with breasts the size of small canta-loupes and flaring hips. She was striking was what she was, Warner had decided. If she walked into a room people's eyes turned toward her, men and women alike. She had an air about her, stubbornness and plain orneriness, Warner thought, but some people said it was confidence. He supposed a lady couldn't ever be considered ornery, and Laura certainly was a lady.

Except in bed and in an argument. In both situations she went at you with everything she had, and didn't, as the phrase went, leave nothing on the wagon.

He considered that he was in his present circumstance directly due to the widow Pico's argumentative nature. Some few years past, the Texas & Rio Grande railroad had built a spur line from San Antonio to Corpus Christi because of the port's increasing trade. It had come on to be the second most important port in Texas after Galveston when the port and the town of Indianola had been blown away in the hurricane of 1882. Normally Warner would simply have taken the four horses he'd sold to a way stop at Calallen, which was only about five miles from his ranch, and shipped the horses to San Antonio in company and under the care of his top hand, Charlie Stanton. But one day he had made a casual remark, no more than that, about giving some thought to driving the four horses to San Antonio. He said that he'd been around the ranch too much and would enjoy a good long ride. Laura had immediately objected and that had naturally caused him to dig his heels in. He'd claimed the four colts were too fat and not fit and that a three-day drive to San Antonio was what they needed to get slicked up. Of course there hadn't been the slightest bit of truth in his reasoning and she had pointed that fact out—which had only made him the more angry. He had said that it was his reputation at stake on the horses, not hers, because she didn't have a reputation. At least not where breeding horses was concerned. That had got his face slapped for him and she'd packed her clothes, called for her buggy, and headed back for Corpus Christi. She did not live at his ranch. She stayed there sometimes, but her residence was in Corpus. When they had struck their partnership she had come down, looked over his ranch and his ranch house, and then had immediately gone back into Corpus and caused an opulent house to be built for her overlooking the bay and near the shops and other comforts of a port city approaching 10,000 in population. She came to the ranch sometimes on business and sometimes, when the mood was on her, just to see Warner. Sometimes she came and stayed two weeks, complaining all the while about the primitiveness of his house, and sometimes she came and only stayed the night. She handled the finances for the partnership and he handled the breeding and the training of the stock. At least that had been their original agreement, but while Warner had never felt the need to interfere in the business end of their affairs she couldn't seem to keep her hand out of the horse part. The problem with that was that she did, indeed, know considerable about horses, but she didn't know anywhere near as much as Warner. She knew, Warner had told her, enough to make her wrong a little better than half the time. Which was a percentage of error that wasn't acceptable in the breeding business.

It was early April and not quite noon. The air was soft and balmy and the mesquite was starting to come into bloom, a sure sign that the last frost had passed. People in that part of the hill country said that you could fool a peach tree or a willow or even an oak with a false spring, but you could never fool a mesquite. When it blossomed you knew the last of the freezing weather was over.

They appeared to be going along all right. The Andalusian cross colts were behaving themselves except for a playful nip one took at the neck of the other from time to time. His prisoners seemed resigned. After some initial trouble they'd finally struck a gait all their horses seemed agreed on and the jerky and balky going had smoothed out.

He still felt resentful toward Laura for this extra trouble. Except for her arguing he'd never have seen any of these men and certainly wouldn't have killed one. Not that he felt bad about that. The man had come at him with willful intent and Warner hadn't seen where he'd had much of a selection. He supposed he could have thrown his hands in the air and surrendered three thousand dollars' worth of horses, not to mention his own horse and the packhorse and the money he had in his pocket.

Still, the men drew his attention. They didn't look or act the role of road agents. They looked more like working men who'd fallen on hard times. But then robbers and bandits and road agents weren't born as such. They came to be outlaws and they came to be so by choice. A man could be an honest cowhand one day and the next day he could decide to stick up a stranger on a lonely stretch of road and rob him and perhaps leave him for dead. He would have crossed the line. He might still look like the cowhand on the outside, but, by his act, he had become an outlaw. He reckoned that was the case with the four men he had riding before him. Turning outlaw, he thought, was a good deal like getting hung—it didn't take but once.

The rooftops of Hondo were beginning to appear in the distance when the one called Darcey, who appeared to be their leader, called out, without turning in his saddle, "Mister, kin we have a word with you 'fore we git into town?"

"No," Warner said. "Keep pointed down the road and go to looking for the sheriff's office."

"Cap'n, I fear this might be a mistake fer the bunch of us, including yoreself." It was the wounded man in the checked shirt.

Warner said, "What's your name?"

"Quinn, cap'n, Otis Quinn."

"Well, Mr. Quinn, first of all I'm not a captain and—"

"Jes' a sign o' respect, suh."

"I wonder how much respect you'd show me if you had the gun and I didn't."

Quinn was silent.

Warner went on. He said, "You men are thieves and robbers and you come at me with drawn guns. Not only that but you are taking up my time. I was detouring through Hondo to visit an old friend before going on to San Antonio. Now, y'all have taken up so much of my time that my visit with a man who was a friend of my grandfather's will have to be a good deal shorter. That right there makes me mad as hell. And then there is the matter of coming at me with drawn pistols. I don't think you could have shot me because the both of you holding guns didn't look like you knew what you were doing, but you might have hit one of my horses and any one of those horses is worth more, in hard money, than the bunch of you put together is."

Without turning his head Les called back. He said, "Be a fair question to ast what them animals fetch on the market?"

"More than you could make in a year."

Les whistled.

Warner had been studying on a question for some time. It really wasn't any of his business, but now he decided to ask it. He said, "Why did you boys only have two guns out when they was five of you?"

Darcey called back, "What'll you give to know that? Would you give a drink of whiskey to some men ain't likely to see any in jail?"

Warner said, "Hell, I ain't that interested. It doesn't strike me that you folks are in much of a bargaining position."

Les said, "It was because we didn't have but four cartridges between us. Jake and Otis claimed to be the best shots so we give them the ammunition."

Warner said, "I've got a bottle of whiskey in my saddle bags. We'll pull up short of town and I'll give you all a good snort before we get to the sheriff's."

Les said, "That's damned decent of you, mister. But they is something I think you ought to know. We—"

Darcey said, loudly and viciously, "Goddammit, Les, keep your mouth *shut!*"

Warner said, "Darcey, you seem damned interested in me not finding out something. Why don't you tell me what it is?"

Darcey said, "Well, there's some smart thankin' fer you. If I'd'a wanted you to have knowed would I have been shuttin' Les up?"

Warner said, "Thought you wanted some whiskey is all. There's some smart thinking for *you.*" After a moment he said, "Even if three of your guns were empty why didn't you all make a show of it?"

The youngest of the three, the one who'd tied the stirrups together said, "Reckon you didn't take notice of what happened to Jake and Otis."

"You'd've still had a better chance of bluffing me down with five guns showing."

Les said, "Would you have bluffed down if we had?"

Warner said, "Them four colts are just the second crop of

18

a breed I'm trying to develop. Pretty nearly all my money is sunk in them. I honestly don't know what I'd've done."

Darcey said bitterly, "You didn't seem to have no trouble makin' up your mind when you shot Jake. An' then shot Otis. Otis, you damn fool, why didn't you git off a shot?"

"Goddammit, Darcey, I done what I could. They wadn't no time. The man was fifteen paces away and movin'. You reckon you coulda done better?"

"He hit you, din't he?"

Warner said, "The both of you shut up. You're both damn fools. I never seen such a botched job of robbin' in all my life. What brought you to such thinkin' in the first place?"

Les said, quietly, "We was desperate."

"Well, you're fixing to be a hell of a lot more desperate now than you was when you thought you were."

The youngest said, "Is bein' a road agent worse than robbin' a bank?"

Darcey said, "Shut up, Calvin. Goddammit, the whole bunch of you keep quiet."

Warner was watching the horse bearing the body of the man he'd shot. It was good that the town was close because the pinto was beginning to limp a little. Warner didn't have the slightest idea what Calvin had meant by the question and wasn't even curious. If this Darcey had some dark secret he wanted to keep, that was fine with Warner. All he wanted to do was get his prisoners in jail, go and have a visit with his grandfather's old friend, Tom Birdsong, and then get on the road the next morning and get his colts to their new owners.

2

He had stopped at the outskirts of Hondo, gotten the bottle of whiskey out of his saddlebags, and given it to his prisoners to pass around among themselves. While they were drinking he'd taken the remaining thirty-odd feet of soft lead rope and run it through the halter rings of the colts, tying it off about every five feet and then, finally, tying the end to his saddle horn. So far as he knew, the colts had never been to town before and while they might be as well-mannered as ever, he figured a handful of prisoners and a small herd of two-year-old horses might turn out to be more than he could handle.

He'd stopped in front of a glass-fronted office that said HARVEY PRUITT, SHERIFF. He'd gotten down and tossed the reins of his horse carelessly over the hitching post and then tied his packhorse and then the colts. In his mind he had almost said, "Paseta would be insulted if I was to tie him like a common horse," and then had given Laura Pico a good cussing for putting him in the way of calling a horse by name.

He'd dismounted his prisoners, let them tie their horses, and then marched them in to the jail office and bunched them to one side against a wall. A middle-aged man whom Warner took to be the sheriff was sitting at a desk in front of a door that obviously led back to the jail cells. The man was a little overweight and going bald on top. He had a heavy handlebar mustache and the look of a man who wished people would quit coming through his door and bothering him with their troubles.

Warner said, "Sheriff Pruitt?"

The man nodded slowly. He had his hands folded before him on the top of the desk. Behind him a big coffeepot was staying warm on a small wood-burning stove. Sheriff Pruitt said, "What's it about?"

Warner jerked his finger at the men. He said, "This bunch bushwhacked me about four miles outside of town. I need to put them in your jail for a couple of days."

Sheriff Pruitt blinked. He said, "What you mean, put them in my jail? You be chargin' them with something?"

"No," Warner said, "I'm not charging them here. I've got some business in San Antonio and I want to keep them under lock and key for a couple of days while I tend to my business."

The sheriff cocked his head. He said, "Be you a peace officer?"

Warner shook his head. "No."

"Are you askin' me to *board* them men?"

"I guess you could put it that way."

The sheriff jerked a thumb sideways. "Hotel is down that way about a block. Got good clean rooms."

Warner said, "Sheriff, I want these men under lock and key. Like I said, they jumped me on the road with drawn pistols and would have robbed and perhaps killed me."

Darcey suddenly said, "You're a damn liar! Was the other way 'round if it was anythang." He shot his arm out. "They's a dead man layin' 'crost his saddle. Wadn't none of us four shot him."

Warner looked at Darcey and then took a step in his direction. He said, "You call me a liar again and I won't charge *you* with nothing. I'll make sure you are out on the street and I'll even buy you some cartridges. You understand me?"

Darcey looked at him, but then his eyes wavered and he dropped his gaze. Warner turned back to the sheriff. He said, "I am willing to pay for their keep here. I'm not asking you or the county to be out anything. But I don't want to charge them here. I'm from Nueces County and I want to charge them there."

The sheriff looked up. He said, "You makin' some kind of accu—accus— some kind of insulting remark about the law around here? Meaning me?"

Warner said, "No, you're getting the wrong handle on this. I was driving some Nueces County horses to San Antonio and they attempted to take them Nueces County horses from me. And, for all I know, we was right at the extreme edge of Nueces County. I would have taken them back, but Hondo was closer and my business in San Antonio is pressing. I wasn't making any sort of accusation against the law here. I don't want to be making a trip back up here when they go on trial. Be easier all around. You won't be out the expenses of a court trial and I won't get taken from my business to come up here and appear against them."

The sheriff rubbed his jaw and looked over at the men. He said, "You say they is one of them dead? Outside?"

"Yes. And I need to get your local undertaker on that matter right quick."

"You say you kilt him?"

"I told you that." He turned and pointed at Otis Quinn and his bloody bandage. "And I winged that one. I reckon he ought to have a doctor take a look at the wound even though it ain't much."

The sheriff said, "Why am I supposed to take your word for all this? You come bargin' in here with a load of prisoners and go to telling me all kinds of tales. Will them men back up your story?"

Darcey said, "I damn sure won't. He kilt Jake in cold blood. Jake had already dropped his gun. Ain't that right, Otis?"

Quinn said, "Well, uh, yeah. I reckon." But he didn't sound very certain.

The sheriff looked at Warner and spread his hands. He said, "See what I mean? Looks like it's your word agin thars."

Warner said, "Do you know Tom Birdsong?" He knew, of course, that the sheriff would know his grandfather's old friend. Tom Birdsong was easily the biggest land owner in that part of the country and had been the past mayor and justice of the peace in Hondo.

The sheriff looked alert. He said, "You a friend of Mr. Birdsong's?"

Warner said, "I can call him by his given name. I used to call him uncle in younger days. I've known him for twenty-five years. He and my grandfather were partners in many a venture involving cattle or horses or land. His ranch house ain't a mile from here. Send a deputy out to fetch him in. Or I'll go myself if you'll hold these men here. I'll be staying with him tonight." He said the words knowing that Tom Birdsong more than likely still carried a good deal of power in the local politics.

The sheriff leaned back. He said, "Well, Mr. Birdsong is pretty good bono fides. What'd you say your name was?"

Warner told him. He said, "You can wire the sheriff of Nueces County about me. We are friends. I've sold him every horse he's rode for the last five years."

The sheriff sat forward. He said, "Are you that Grayson? The one that's famous about horses?"

"I'm Warner Grayson and I deal in horses. And have for the last fifteen years."

The sheriff said, "Hell, they say you can make a horse do everything but talk."

Warner jerked his thumb toward the street. He said, "Take a look at the four copper-colored colts I got tied up in front of your office. That's the horses I'm driving to San Antonio to their buyers. New breed I'm developing. They were bought sight unseen."

The sheriff got up and went to the front of his office and peered out the window. After a second he went to the door and stepped out on the boardwalk. He disappeared from sight, but then he came back in the door whistling. He said, "Whoooeee, that is what I call some horseflesh. Kin a man ast what horses like that sell for?"

Warner hesitated. Telling the price of his horses was a little like flashing a big roll of money in a border saloon. But he said, "The four of them have been bought for three thousand dollars."

The sheriff blinked and then shook his head slowly. He

said, "That is a power of money. What's that come out to apiece?"

"Seven hundred and fifty dollars."

The sheriff looked over at the four men lined up against the wall. He said, "When you boys set out to steal horses you set out to steal *some* horses."

Darcey said, "That's his story."

Before Warner could speak Les said, tiredly, "Aw, shut up, Darcey. You are just making things worse. Why don't you try and get on the man's good side instead of shooting off the ugly side of your mouth."

Darcey said, "Now, listen a goddamn minute you—"

The sheriff said, "Shut up. Both of you." He turned back to Warner. He said, "Now what all are we talking about here? You want me to hold these men for a couple of days. Is that it?"

"Two days, maybe three. Long enough to go to San Antonio, deliver that stock, get the money wired to my bank in Corpus, and get back here. And I need to get that dead man to an undertaker."

"County ain't gonna pay for that."

"I don't expect them to," Warner said. "I shot him, I'll plant him. Then I'll need to get their horses tended to."

The sheriff said, "That would have to be the livery stable. We ain't in the business of boarding horses."

Warner said, "How much money you need to get to hold these men for me?"

The sheriff looked off for a moment, scratching his head. He said, "Wall, seein' as this ain't never come up 'fore, I don't rightly know what to say. I know it costs us a dollar 'n' a half a day to feed 'em apiece on account that's what the café charges us. Now as to the price of a jail cell . . ." He stared up at the ceiling. Finally he said, "Hell, I don't know."

Warner said, "What about two and a half a day per head? That'd be ten dollars a day all around."

The sheriff nodded slowly. He said, "I reckon that would be all right."

Warner got out his money and leafed off two tens and laid them on the desk. He said, "There's for two nights counting tonight. Now, have you got a deputy I could pay to handle them other chores for me?"

"Got a depity," the sheriff said. "Don't know if he wants to work. He's back in the cells, takin' a nap I'd reckon." He turned in his chair and yelled, "Lonnie! Lonnie! Git out here!"

After a moment or two the door behind the sheriff opened and a lanky young man came out yawning and rubbing his eyes. He looked around the room, at Warner and the prisoners without interest. He said, "Yeah, shur'ff?"

Sheriff Pruitt jerked a thumb at Warner. He said, "This gent is a friend of Mr. Birdsong's. He's got some errands he wants run. You willin'? Says he'll pay."

Lonnie looked at Warner. "What kin' o' errants?"

Warner said, "I got a dead man draped over a horse outside. I need him taken to the undertaker's with instructions to plant him." He laid a twenty-dollar bill on the desk. "That ought to cover the undertaker. Then I need you to leave all five of their horses at the livery stable. What do they get, Sheriff, about a dollar a day?"

"I'd think."

Warner put a ten-dollar bill on the table and followed it with a five. He said, to Lonnie, "The five is for you if you can handle this business for me."

The sheriff said, "Five dollars! Fer that little bit? Hell, *I'd've* done it fer that."

Warner said, "I intend to pay you for your time and trouble, Sheriff. Look, I don't feel hard toward these men. Will you let them have a drink from time to time?"

The sheriff shrugged. "Long's they don't get rowdy and cut up ugly."

Warner put down another five. He said, "That's for a little whiskey and tobacco." He looked at Lonnie. "You willing?"

"Shore!" the deputy said. His eyes had never left the roll of money Warner had in his hand.

Warner said, "Sheriff, their handguns and gun belts are in my pack. They didn't have a rifle between them. If Lonnie will get them out of my pack I'll leave the weapons with you."

"On my way," Lonnie said.

The sheriff got up and turned to open the door. Warner sensed rather than saw or heard the movement. He whirled, drawing as he did. The *clitch-clatch* as he cocked his revolver made a loud sound in the jail office. Darcey stopped three feet short of the door that Lonnie had left open. He stood there, his back to Warner, and slowly raised his hands.

Warner said, "Back up, Darcey. And then turn around. Sheriff, I reckon you better pen this one first."

Darcey never quite got turned around. The sheriff hustled across the office and grabbed him by the collar and said, "Goddammit, if you are goin' to be thet way we'll jest have to tend to you the way you act." As he went by Warner he said, "By gawd I won't put up with no lallygaggin' around in *my* jail. Git in there, you!"

Warner waited until the sheriff had locked up each man. As Les passed him he said, "Much obliged for the tobacco and whiskey." The rest of them didn't say anything.

Lonnie came in with the prisoners' revolvers and gun belts. He said, "Somebody got some of the damndest purtiest horses I ever laid eyes on. You ought to see 'em, shur'ff."

"I have," the sheriff said. "I swear, Lonnie, a wagon could fall on you an' you'd not notice. Didn't you see that prisoner coming out right behind you?"

Lonnie looked surprised. "Naw! Prisoner tried to get away?"

The sheriff said to Warner, "Wakes up in a new town ever' mornin'." Then he sort of squinted his eyes and gave Warner a long look. He said, "I thought it was hosses you was supposed to be so good with."

"I work 'em, yes. Why?"

"You had that gun out and in business in one hell of a hurry. Only seen one other feller operate that sudden. Wilson Young. Heared of him?"

Warner smiled slightly. "Used to sell him horses. Still do as a matter of fact. Good friend of mine."

"He give you some larnin' with that sidearm?"

Warner shook his head. "It happened that way that one time. Usually I'm like molasses in cold weather."

The sheriff looked at him oddly. He said, "Yeah, I'll bet. I bet them prisoners tell a different story. I got the feelin' they are right sorry about who they selected to hold up."

Warner said, "Well, if we're straight I'm going to get out to Tom Birdsong's. I'll be spending the night there if you need me for anything. Then I'm leaving early in the morning for San Antonio."

The sheriff jerked his thumb back toward the cells. He said, "They'll still be here."

He'd had a good visit with Tom Birdsong, though he'd been saddened to see how the man had aged since their last visit. But that was, he reckoned, to be expected. His grandfather had died at the age of fifty-four when Warner'd been eighteen. It had been a heart attack that had carried off the rough-hewn old sage. Tom Birdsong, Warner figured, was in his sixties, but he somehow seemed older. He was crippled and stiffened with arthritis, yet his mind was as sharp as ever. He had been much interested in Warner's new venture, but had strongly urged him not to stray too far from the meat and potatoes of the horse business, cattle horses. He'd said, "Of course there's a call for good road horses, but there's getting to be too many ways to get around now. The roads are running nearly everywhere and you can carry your family and goods in a wagon. And there's more stage lines and every time I pick up a newspaper they are building another railroad. But there will always be cattle and there will always be a need for good cow horses to work them with. They ain't going to fetch the prices of these fancy breeds you're coming up with but they are sure money, money in the bank. And that's the kind of money to count on."

As far as Warner was concerned, his grandfather and Tom Birdsong had been the two most educated men he'd ever met who'd never spent a day in school. Both had read every book they could lay their hands on and Tom still had a personal library of over a thousand volumes. Either one of them could talk with you on any subject from mathematics to the newest model of hay mowers. Both of them took a great deal of their wisdom from the Bible. Warner's grandfather had said, "It ain't just a book for heaven, it's a mighty good guide for how to arrange your life on this temporal orb." When he'd asked his grandfather what a temporal orb was he'd been told to go look it up. One of the first things Tom Birdsong had asked him, even after all the intervening years, was if he'd ever found out what "temporal orb" meant.

Tom Birdsong, when he'd heard the story, had also been curious about the five men who'd jumped Warner with four cartridges among them. He'd said, "They must have been in a hell of a hurry to take a chance like that, especially as inexperienced as you make them out. Wonder who was chasing them or who they was chasing. They could have laid up a day and doctored that horse's foot and gone on their way without resorting to road agentry."

Warner shrugged. "Beats the hell out of me. I think a couple of them want to tell me something, but the bully boy of the bunch won't let them."

"Split 'em up. Get him away from the others."

"To tell you the truth I'm kind of figuring to turn them loose when I get back. They didn't really cause me no harm and one of them did get killed and another wounded. Right now I reckon they are sweating bullets about pulling some years in the state prison. That ought to be enough."

Tom asked, gently, "Is that fair to your neighbor?"

"You mean do I reckon they'll try it again?" He shook his head. "No, I don't reckon. I don't figure it's in them. I know the good book says I'm my neighbor's keeper, but I don't reckon this instance fits the case."

Tom said, "They've cost you money."

Warner thought a moment. "Right now I ain't out but thirty-five dollars. Of course, that don't count the cost of burying the dead man. I could take his horse in payment, I reckon, but he's a worthless pinto. Not worth much over seventy-five. Of course, he might have next of kin who would claim the animal and I reckon they'd have the right. But, hell, Tom, I can't go on keeping these boys in jail. It's running fifteen dollars a day, counting their horses. If it was only the bully boy and the smart-talking one I might think otherwise and bring charges. But a couple of them seem like all-right fellows. I'll give it until I get back from San Antone.

One, I reckon, is a hand off some ranch, maybe out of work and hard pressed. But I know I didn't take them boys to raise, good neighbor or not. I'm doing fairly well in the horse business, but I'm not planning on taking over the county's job of jailing prisoners and paying for their upkeep. They ain't criminals, just out of work right now and hard pressed."

Tom had said softly, "Being hard pressed ain't never been excuse for robbery or pointing a firearm at your neighbor."

Warner had left the subject with a promise to Tom to give the matter a good deal of thought on his trip to and from San Antonio.

He made an early start next morning and by a little before noon had the four colts safely penned at the San Antonio Mule and Horse Auction House, which was the biggest equine market in all of the Southwest. When he walked into the office of the broker who had handled the account, Royce Bell, Royce said, "The money is here. Arrived yesterday. Got it in my trading account right now. If you'll take a seat I'll write you up a draft for twenty-eight fifty. That's three thousand, less my five percent commission."

"I know that," Warner said. He liked Royce Bell even if he did wear town clothes. Royce had sold the horses on Warner's reputation to a gentleman rancher in Mexico. Warner had figured that had to be some rich kind of *caballero* to pay that kind of money just to be able to ride around his land at greater ease and show off more at fiestas. Of course, he knew that the Mexican would use the colts for breeding purposes, breeding them to his own stock. The first batch of colts he'd get would be pretty good, but they'd start getting watered down as the Mexican bred them to more and more inferior mares. That was one reason nobody ever stole horses in Mexico and drove them back to Texas. Good horses were hard to find in Mexico because the Mexicans didn't seem to understand that the dam was as important as the sire in getting a good animal.

But it was no concern of his. He sat down on a little divan and picked up a copy of the local newspaper, the *San Antonio Express News.* The paper was a couple of days old, which didn't make much difference to him. He generally stayed about a week behind on the news. As he started to read, an article halfway down the page jumped out at him. It said:

BANK IN ROUND ROCK ROBBED

ROBBERS FLEE WITH $ 30,000

In a daring daylight robbery five armed men held up the Mercantile Bank of Round Rock and escaped with what bank officials said was more than $30,000 in cash and gold.

Bob Thomas, president of the bank, said the robbers struck just after the bank had opened and apparently timed their robbery as money was being taken from the open vault and transferred to the tellers' cages. Mr. Thomas said, "It was over in a very few moments. I'm glad there were no customers present who might have been injured. We didn't get a good look at the men because they were armed and were wearing kerchiefs over their faces."

No shots were fired within the bank but a number of bystanders on the street observed the five robbers riding out of town and firing their revolvers into the air.

The article went on to give a description of the men from the half a dozen bystanders who'd seen them near the bank and then had seen them ride away shooting off their pistols. As Warner read the descriptions the hair on the back of his neck began to rise. One was surely Darcey, short and stocky and described as vicious looking. And one wore a red-checkered shirt. That, Warner thought, would be Otis Quinn. One was wearing leather leggings. Les. The other two were described in less telling detail but Warner had read enough. He was staring off into space when Royce got up from his desk and came around and handed the bank draft to him. Warner took it, not even glancing at the amount, and stuffed it into his pocket. Royce said, "Something wrong, Warner?"

Warner looked up. "Huh?" he said.

"You looked like you had left town, staring off like you was seeing ghosts."

Warner stood up. He said, "Wasn't ghosts I was seeing. It was money."

In the last paragraph of the article the bank had stated they were offering $500 a man for the robbers dead or alive.

Royce said, "You just put the money in your pocket. It ain't over there in the corner."

Warner said, "I told the widow Pico that there was profit in driving those colts to market instead of shipping them. She disagreed. Wonder what she'll say now?"

Royce said, "What the hell are you talking about, Warner? I never knowed you to be a morning drinker."

"What?" He focused on the broker. "Oh, nothing. Just thinking out loud."

"How about I buy you a bite of lunch?"

Warner shook his head. He said, "Naw. Appreciate it, though. I got to get moving. I'm fixing to make twenty-five hundred more on those horses."

The broker looked startled. "What? What are you talking about? Those horses are sold."

"Never mind." Warner said. "I'm taking your paper, if you don't mind. It's two days old."

"Yeah, but—"

He walked out of the office, leaving the broker staring after him.

He stayed in San Antonio only long enough to go to a bank where he was known and arrange to have the amount of Royce's draft wired to his bank in Corpus Christi. After that he turned the Andalusian horse for the town limits and the road to Hondo. He'd left his packhorse at Tom Birdsong's, so as soon as he was good on the road, he put the Andalusian into his ground-eating canter and set out. It was not quite twenty miles to Hondo and he expected to make it in less than three hours.

As he rode he did some thinking and figuring. Round Rock was a good-sized town of six or seven thousand souls on the northeast side of Austin, about seventy or eighty miles away. In his mind he visualized the location of all the towns that would come into play. The bandits had headed south, no doubt heading for Mexico. They'd passed on the east side of San Antonio and had come across him south of Hondo. And the time fit. They had jumped him on the third

day after the robbery, which would figure out about right for
the distance of perhaps a hundred miles they would have
had to have traveled to intercept him on the road to Hondo.
There wasn't the slightest doubt in his mind that the men he
had in custody were the bank robbers. No wonder they'd
had to try and steal a horse to replace the one that was going
lame. They would have been afraid to go into a town,
especially a small one, to buy another horse. And they might
have been taking an equal risk in going into a big city like
San Antonio. There was law to spare in San Antonio. The
city attracted more than its share of unsavory characters
and the town fathers made sure there were enough peace
officers around to keep the peace. And they wouldn't have
gone into Austin; that was way too close to Round Rock.
Besides, the horse might not have been lame by then. He'd
been lamed, as Warner had figured, by their fleeing across
the rocky hills and avoiding the roads.

He smiled a little. Now he understood why Darcey kept
telling everyone to shut up if they so much as offered a clue
to any other business they'd been up to outside of attempted
horse stealing.

A sudden thought hit him. Where was the money? They
certainly hadn't had it on their persons or in their gear. He'd
had a good look through that. And no four men alive could
hide that much money in their clothes, especially, as the
paper had said, when some of it was in gold.

Upon returning to Hondo, he went straight into town and
to the sheriff's office. He came through the door and Sheriff
Pruitt was sitting exactly where he'd been when Warner had
left. He wondered if the man had moved. Warner said,
"How is my livestock keeping?"

Sheriff Pruitt said, "If you're talking about the prisoners,
they seem to be on the right side of the fence. Except that
Darcey fellow. He's disputing your word."

"But they haven't caused you any real trouble?"

The sheriff shrugged. "Don't see how they could. They
inside and I ain't. Ain't much kin come through them bars
will do a body on the outside much harm 'less they got a gun
and I don't generally allow prisoners to have such. You come
for 'em?"

"Not just yet," replied Warner. "It'll be at the earliest

tomorrow before I'm ready for them." He got his roll out of his pocket and took off a ten and laid it in front of the sheriff. He said, "That's for the extra trouble."

The sheriff looked down at the money, uncertain. He said, "I ain't sure I ought to be taking this. Might look like a bribe."

Warner said, "Use it any way you want. Jail improvements. Whatever. How can you be bribing a man you've already made a deal with?"

The sheriff nodded. He said, "Well, yeah, that would be true." He picked up the ten and folded it carefully and put it in his pocket. "If you look at it that way, might be a few things I could use it for around the jail that the county don't pay for."

"Maybe another chair," Warner said.

"Yeah, that er somethin' else."

Warner said, casually, "By the way, you ain't had any wanted paper come in here lately, have you?"

The sheriff yawned. He said, "Matter of fact I did. Got a little bundle off the train yesterday afternoon. Ain't had time to look it over yit. Why?"

Warner said, "Oh, no special reason. I was just wondering if any of my birds might have got his likeness drawed or his picture took."

The sheriff pulled open a drawer and took out a thin sheaf of wanted posters. They were still in their original paper wrapping and tied with a string. He broke the string and took off the brown paper and handed to posters to Warner. He said, "He'p yourself."

Warner went to the side of the room and sat down on a little bench. He looked at the first poster and laid it aside. The second was also not of interest to him. In the third poster he found what he was looking for.

WANTED

THE FIVE DESPERADOES WHO HELD UP
THE BANK AT ROUND ROCK
ON THE MORNING OF APRIL 4TH

REWARD OF $500 EACH WILL BE PAID
FOR THESE MEN DEAD OR ALIVE

There followed a brief description of the five men and the horses they were riding.

Warner read through the descriptions several times and looked up, puzzled. The descriptions were vague enough to fit any five men you cared to name. And there was no mention of Otis's red-checkered shirt or Les's leather leggings or the paint horse that Jake had been riding and that had gone lame. It had been in the paper, but it wasn't in the wanted poster. He got out the newspaper and read it again to be sure. He thought it passing strange that such a wanted poster would be put out, but he was no less sure that the five men who had jumped him were the five who had robbed the bank. They had obviously hidden the money during their getaway, but that was none of his concern. He was interested in the reward. He got up and returned the posters to the sheriff.

"Find anything to take your interest?"

"Naw, not really." Warner said. He thought a minute. He said, "Wonder if you'd mind bringing out the one they call Les. I'd like to have a few words with him."

"You wouldn't rather talk to him back there?"

"I'd rather get him alone. Might get more out of him that way."

"I'll fetch him," the sheriff said. He got up and took a ring of keys off the wall and opened the door to the cells and walked back. Warner could hear him say, "Les! You there, Les! Git up offen that cot. Man wants to talk to you."

He heard the rattle of keys and then he heard Darcey's voice, threatening, "You keep your mouth shut, Les. You hear me! Shut tight!"

Les said, "Oh, go to hell, Darcey. We wouldn't be in this mess it wasn't for you."

Les came out of the hall blinking his eyes, though it didn't seem to Warner that the cell area was that much darker than the jail office. The sheriff followed Les and locked the door behind him and then hung up the keys.

"I don't reckon you'd mind if I take Les here out on the street to have a little talk, do you?"

The sheriff blinked. "You want to take that prisoner *outside?* Jest to talk? We don't do thet as a reg'lar thang."

"Well, Sheriff," Warner said, trying to put it diplomatically, "he is kind of my prisoner."

The sheriff was wearing his hat. He pushed it back. He said, "Wall, yeah, I reckon that's true." He scratched his balding head and looked worried. "Still an' all, I ain't exactly shore this is all straight an' proper."

"Sheriff, this man ain't going nowhere and you don't want him for nothing. And ain't I paying for his keep? And ain't I paying for the upkeep of the jail while they're here?"

The sheriff still looked puzzled. He said, "Yeah, I reckon all what you say be true. Still, I can't seem to get no handle on it. You reckon this kind of thang ever been done before?"

"Well, I don't know about that," Warner said. "Of course I ain't never been what you'd call an official law officer, just a member of the Nueces County Mounted Posse."

Which was a lie. The closest he'd ever come to the Mounted Posse was selling its members horses. And the only official duty he'd ever seen them perform was to ride in the Fourth of July parade.

But the sheriff's brow instantly cleared. He said, "Oh, wall, that makes all the difference in the world. Hell, you're a law officer. Practically the same as my depity. I jest remembered you sayin' you wadn't."

Warner said, "I reckon that was because I didn't want to make it sound like I was a *regular official* peace officer like yourself. I wouldn't want you to have thought I was putting on airs or claimin' to be something I really wasn't."

The sheriff looked much relieved. He said, "Why, hell, I'da never thought no sich a thang. Day may come when I'll need me a favor outten the Nueces shur'ff's office an' right there you'd be."

Warner thought to himself that he hoped that day was a long time in coming. But he said, "So, it'll be all right if we step outside?"

"Shore, shore. Want me to have Lonnie come along with a scatter gun?"

Warner looked at Les and smiled slightly. He said, "I don't reckon so."

When they had stepped out onto the boardwalk that ran along between the stores and the street Warner said, "Well, how's jail?"

Les shrugged. He said, "The eats are better'n what we been used to and we are obliged to you fer the tobaccer and whiskey, but it's still jail. I reckon if they sent in a passel of dance hall girls it would still be jail. If you can't leave when you want to it gits kind of confining."

There was a bench in front of the jail window and Warner indicated they should sit there. He said, as they were getting settled, "I don't have to warn you about getting any ideas, do I?"

Les half smiled. He said, "I don't reckon so. I figure jail is bad, but dead is worse."

Warner studied the man's face for a moment. He calculated they weren't that far apart in age, but Les's face showed years of hard times and hard usage. He said, "Whose idea was it to jump me?"

Les turned his head away and spit a slight stream of tobacco juice into the street. He wiped his mouth with his sleeve. He said, "They is some of that bunch I like and some I don't. But that don't make any difference. I ain't cuttin' nobody out as the *honcho*. We is all growed men. We knowed what we was doin'. Well, maybe Calvin is a little young." He spit again. He said, "But we didn't jump *you*. We jumped the first lone man we seen had an extra horse. You had five extra ones countin' your packhorse, but we still wouldn't have taken but the one and we'd've left you Jake's to make up fer it. Though now I see it might not could have been considered a even swap." He smiled slightly. "Not considerin' them horses you was drivin'." He shook his head. He said, "I been cowboyin' since I was fourteen year old as a reg'lar thang an' them was the purtiest horses I ever seed."

Warner said, casually, "How come y'all was in such an all-fired hurry that you'd take to robbery to get a fresh horse? Or is that a regular line of work for your bunch?"

"Not me!" Les said vigorously. "Onliest thang I ever stole before was a apple or pear offen somebody else's tree."

"Then what was the rush?"

Les looked uncomfortable. He said, haltingly, "Well, uh, we was, uh, hustlin' to git down south. We'd heard they was some work down thar."

"How come you wasn't already on somebody's payroll? You look like a likely enough hand to me."

"I was hurt," Les said. "Got hurt in late January. Horse fell with me. By the time I got to where I could get around good all the ridin' jobs was taken. I was gettin' a little day work first this place and that, but what with this mild spring the calvin' was nearly over an' nobody needed no extra hands."

"Where was this?"

Les shrugged. "Oh, up north."

"Up north where? North of Austin?"

"Oh . . ." Les looked uncomfortable again. "Oh, up around Waco. In thar."

"How come y'all didn't just go in the first town you come to after the horse went lame and buy another one? That horse wasn't hurt all that bad. You could have fixed him up to make enough miles to get you into Hondo. I seen you do it."

Les spit again. He had the look on his face of a man being crowded into a corner. He said, "Fact of the business is that we jest didn't have the money."

Warner said, calmly, "That ain't true, Les. I think you've got more money than Darcey let on. I think you got considerable more money than you are letting on you've got."

The cowboy bit his lip. He said, "Mister, I swear to God we ain't got much more'n what Darcey was trying to offer you. We had a few dollars a couple of days ago but, what with one thing and another . . ." He shrugged. "We ain't got much left."

"What one thing and another?"

Les smiled slightly. "Them one things and anothers that you find in a cathouse in San Antone. Women and whiskey and crooked card games."

Warner wasn't willing to believe that they had gone through $30,000 in a whorehouse in one night, but he was willing to believe they'd spent what they'd taken out of their stash and were trying to get back to it, wherever they had hidden it.

He had the paper he'd gotten in San Antonio in his back pocket. He took it out. He said, "Les, can you read?"

The cowboy nodded. "My ol' mother seen I had me a little edjecation. I kin read an' write an' do sums."

Warner held the paper out. He said, "It says in here that you five robbed the bank in Round Rock."

Les went pale under the weathered tan of his face. He said, with vigor, "We never! I swear we never!"

Warner thrust the paper at him. He said, "Then read what it says about five men who did. Says one was wearing a red-checkered shirt. Says one was wearing leather leggings. Says one was riding a pinto horse. That struck me as kind of dumb, Les. Though y'all didn't come at me in the smartest way I've ever seen. But a pinto horse does tend to stick out. That and a red-checkered shirt."

Les was looking miserable. He said, "I swear we never done it."

"Les, what do you want to lie for? You was there! You were seen riding out of town firing your guns into the air. Was that where all your cartridges went? Whose damn-fool idea was that?"

Les looked down, the same miserable expression on his face. He said, "It don't make no never mind. You ain't gonna believe me no matter what I say."

"Is that how come Calvin asked me which was worse, bank robbing or stealing horses?"

"We seen the paper, mister. Seen it in that cathouse in San Antone. That's what spooked us. That's what sent us tearin' acrost the rocks and the hills and stayin' off the roads. We seen that paper an' we knowed we was in a world of hurt. We was headin' fer Mexico. That was all we could thank to do."

"Where'd you hide the money, Les?"

"Shit!" Les said. "We never had no money. We got fifty dollars apiece was what we got."

"Paper says you got thirty thousand. More than thirty thousand, I believe it says."

Les spit again. "Thutty thousand dollars. Shit. Ain't that much money in the world. I wouldn't know what three hundred dollars looks like, let alone thutty thousand."

"Where's the money, Les? You give the money back they liable to go easier on you. You ain't going to believe it but I'm trying to help you."

Les gave him a direct look. He said, "Naw, it's you ain't doin' the believin'. We never robbed no bank. Never even set in to rob no bank. Wouldn't have the nearest idea how to rob no bank."

Warner tapped the paper. He said, "It describes the robbers right here. It fits you and the others to a tee. How do you explain that?"

Les stood up. He said, "I cain't. Whyn't you take me on back in 'fore Darcey figgers I'm telling you more'n what he wants knowed and I have to fistfight him."

Warner said, "So that's it. You are afraid of Darcey."

"'Fraid of Darcey? Shit. I'll whip his ass any day he picks. I jest don't want no trouble in that jail. You git in trouble in a jail, don't make no difference who starts it. The jailer takes it out on the lot. I don't need no more trouble'n what I arready got."

Warner put out his hand. He said, "The bank's offering a reward, Les. Five hundred a man."

"We seen that in the paper, too." He looked away. "Might as well be you as gets it seeing we put you to considerable trouble. And you be already out the money I seen you payin' the shur'ff. Don't make a hell of a lot of difference to me. Going to jail fer bank robbery or road robbery. Prison's all the same no matter what got you there."

"They'd go easier on you, I'm telling you, if you'd give them back the money."

Les looked at him and then shook his head. "Money? Shit. Mister, you jest don't understand."

"Then make me understand."

Les shook his head again. "I cain't. It shames me I was such a damn fool. I was a damn fool twice over, three times over. Hell, I di'n't have to stay with that lot. Di'n't have to agree to come at you on the road. I could have cut loose from that bunch. Taken off by myself."

Warner asked, "You got family?"

Les hesitated. "I reckon. Got two sisters. My ol' maw lives with one of 'em."

"That's why you won't say where the money is. You figure

you're caught anyway so y'all intend to get word to your families where you've hid the money."

Les hung his head. He said, "Mister, you been more than square with us. They ain't no money! An' we never robbed no bank."

"Lot of folks think you did."

"Like I say, it's all one to me. I'm goin' to prison anyhow. All I'm doin' right now is hopin' it don't come out what a damn fool I was. Mister, I swallowed a hook would have landed the biggest sucker in Dallas county. You'd be doin' me a favor you let me go back in now."

But he stopped at the jail office door and turned back, looking into Warner's face. It was the face of a man, he thought, that he could have worked with or for or taken a sociable drink with or trusted at poker. He said, "Even if I told you what happened about that bank robbery it would jest be the word of some worthless saddle tramps. Ain't nobody goin' to believe us. That's 'bout the only thing I agree with that damn Darcey on—keepin' our mouths shut."

Warner nodded, accepting the man's decision. "Anything you need?"

Les smiled slightly. "A good horse and a day's head start."

Warner smiled back. "'Fraid I can't do that. You're worth five hundred dollars to me, Les."

Les made a sound. "Not even as much as one of them high-bred colts you was takin' to market."

"Yeah, but I didn't have to feed and train you for two years."

They walked into the office. Warner said, "Here he is, Sheriff. I managed to bring him back."

The sheriff yawned and got up to get the keys. He wondered to himself how he'd ever had any doubts about this young Grayson. Where had his eyes been? Hell, one look made it clear the man was a peace officer, even if he was only a reserve deputy. Authority stuck out all over him. He opened the door and shepherded Les through and put him in his cell and then came back, locked the door, and hung up the keys. "What's your plan now?" he asked. "You be takin' them boys out in the mornin'?"

"I don't know," Warner said, thoughtfully. "Right now I

need to do a little studying. I reckon I'll ride on out to Tom Birdsong's and give the matter some thought. You mind if I take a few of them posters with me? Just to have something to study on?"

The sheriff opened the drawer and pitched the package back on top of the desk. "Naw. He'p yourself. I've heared of men who've studied them things and actual made reward money out of it."

"Is that a fact?" Warner said.

Tom Birdsong had never been a very big man. From earlier days Warner had remembered him as being not much taller than Warner had been at fifteen. But he'd always been wiry and leathery and amazingly strong. Warner could remember his grandfather saying that pound for pound, Tom Birdsong was as strong a man as he knew.

Now age had withered him and gathered him in so that he looked much smaller. Warner didn't reckon he weighed much more than 125 pounds and he was so stooped that he stood barely over five feet. But he still had a head of white hair and most of his own teeth, and his dark brown eyes were as quick and sightful as ever. Two Mexican women saw to his needs in his big rock and frame ranch house, and a Mexican foreman ran his considerable-sized ranch where he grazed a thousand head of whiteface and Hereford crossed cattle on a little over 15,000 acres. He had a mama cow–type operation, selling off the calves as fast as they were weaned. It was an unusual method of ranching but Tom Birdsong was an unusual man. He ran a cow-calf operation because the land was poor and he couldn't have grazed a thousand cattle on the amount of acreage he had, much less with their offspring added. So he supplemented the feed of his mama cow herd and got at least four calves out of a cow before he sold her and then started over with a new heifer in the old cow's place, the old cow having gone to market as beef.

It was also unusual to have a Mexican foreman giving orders to white men. But that didn't matter. He said, "It's my ranch and I hire whoever I want to as my foreman. They don't want to take orders from Meskin Joe they don't got to. But if they want to draw wages on this ranch they'll do what he says or they can roll their gear and ride out the gate. He's my foreman because he's damn good at his job. He could be an *Irishman* for all I care if he gets the work done."

Now they sat at supper, eating stew and biscuits and fresh-churned butter and iced tea. There was an ice-making plant in San Antonio and they delivered big lots of it to an ice house in Hondo where it could be bought by hundred-pound blocks. Laura Pico had introduced Warner to the practice of putting lime juice and sugar in his tea and he'd been trying to get Tom Birdsong to try it.

Tom said, "Hell, I'm still getting used to the tea being cold. What in the world would I want to mix the taste up with all that other stuff for? I'd bet my last piece of pecan pie that they is a woman behind this notion."

Warner said, grimly, "Sometimes I wonder."

"What?"

"Laura. If she's a woman. Sometimes I think she's about half bear-cat."

"Why don't you quit fighting with that woman and either marry her or run her off? My second wife was like that. Goddamn, what a bronc. In or out of bed she could outbuck anything I ever got astraddle of. Whew! Always tryin' to get a halter on me. Would have put a ring in my nose given the chance." Tom shook his head. "But in that bed . . ." He sighed and let out his breath. "Well, best we don't talk about that. Not at my age. Just thinkin' about Molly makes my heart go to ripping around more than it ought."

"She was the one that was kicked by the buggy horse?"

"Wasn't no more a buggy horse than I am. *She* was gonna make it a buggy horse. Was a half-broke bronc. Kicked her right between the eyes and knocked her colder than a well digger's ass. Never opened her eyes again. Lingered for two days. I miss that woman to this good day, but she was a handful. Never saw such a willful woman in all my born days."

Warner said, "Tom, there's something that has always confused me. How you and my grandfather come to be such close friends. You don't mind my saying it, you was kind of known as a hell-raiser and a ripsnorter. And Granddaddy— well, you know he set great store by the Bible though I don't reckon he was much for church. It just seems an odd combination to me."

Tom Birdsong put his fork down and clapped his hands for the women to come and clear away the supper dishes. He said, "Carver Grayson was the most honest, truly good man I have ever known in my life. Ain't a day goes by I don't miss him. But if you've got some idea in your head that just because Carver believed in the good book and the Lord and tried to follow the Commandments that he was some sort of wishy-washy pushover, then you got the wrong end of the stick. Now, he *would* turn the other cheek, but you'd better git your best lick ready because that would be all you'd get. He played honest and he played fair and he expected the other man to do the same. If he didn't . . . Well, I've seen a few wished they had. You never saw Carver in his prime. I'm seventy now and we was passing close in age so if you did see him at his best you was seeing him as a baby. He was as tall as you, but thicker, more muscled up. For that matter so was your daddy. I reckon you get that slim look from your mother's side. But if Carver thought he was right about a matter he went straight ahead. It didn't matter if the whole county, hell, the whole country, thought contrarywise, he still went straight ahead. Carver didn't have no trouble making up his mind about matters. Right was right and wrong was wrong. It was that simple."

They had coffee and peach pie and Warner slowly began to tell Tom Birdsong what he'd learned about the five men that had tried to hold him up on the road. He said, "So it appears I was wrong, last time I talked to you, about maybe just turning them loose. Now I understand why they needed a fresh horse so bad."

"They was running from that bank robbery. Heading for Mexico with their winnings they taken off that bank."

"But, Tom, they ain't got the money."

"Of course they ain't got the money. They'd hide it somewhere until matters cooled down and then go back and collect it. Besides, might be kind of hard to prove was them without the money actually in hand."

Warner handed the wanted poster and the San Antonio paper across the table. Tom had to send for his spectacles before he could read either one. It took him a few minutes to read the newspaper article and to study the poster. He laid them down and took off his glasses. He said, "You sure them are the men?"

Warner smiled slightly. "What do you reckon the odds are about being held up by five other men, one wearing a red-checkered shirt and another looking mean as hell and a third wearing leather leggings and one riding a pinto horse?"

"I reckon those are the men."

"What you think I should do?"

Tom Birdsong squinted an eye. He said, "Well, first thing is to wire the bank and advise them you are pretty sure you have their robbers. Ask them to send down a lawman and a couple of eyewitnesses to identify the robbers."

"What about the reward?"

Tom Birdsong said, "Hell, you don't give them the robbers until you get the twenty-five hundred dollars. They advertised it, you caught the men, the reward is yours. The sheriff they send won't have no authority in this county. And they are your prisoners. You don't give them up until you get your money. You are the one paying for their room and board. I'll have a word with Harvey Pruitt and kind of prop him up. He ain't made out of the stoutest wood you've ever come across. But he'll hold to the law as soon as I make sure he understands it."

Warner got up. He said, "Well, I reckon I ought to go into town and get me a hotel room. Like to leave my packhorse out here for the time being."

Birdsong was shaking his head. "They is four bedrooms in this house and I only sleep in one. Ain't no use you laying out money for no hotel room. Or are you deliberately setting out to insult me?"

Warner smiled. He said, "Well, *Uncle* Tom, far be it from me to do something like that. I'll stay the night and then get that telegram off in the morning. But after that I'd kind of like to stay in town, close to my prisoners."

Tom Birdsong said, "I can kind of understand you wantin' to close herd 'em. Five hundred a head ain't bad for any kind of cattle, even the two-legged variety. Well, c'mon, let's have a few games of checkers and a little whiskey before bed. I'm gonna pin your ears back with that checkerboard, young man."

"You wouldn't be a gambling man, would you?"

"I have been known to accept a light runnin' wager in my time."

"Dollar a game be too stiff for you? I know you need to save your money for a good rockin' chair, but—"

"Make it five a game and you better be carryin' cash. Ain't takin' no IOUs from the likes of you."

But while they were setting up the checkerboard Tom Birdsong said, "Didn't it strike you they wasn't much description of the five men in the reward poster?"

"Yeah, I taken notice of that. Same thing with the newspaper. Only people seemed to give any description were bystanders. I guess them bankers couldn't see nothing but the bore size of the revolvers the robbers were holding on them."

Tom Birdsong finished setting his checkers in place. He said, "I'll let you have red. You can go first."

"Don't do me no favors. I'd just as soon you went first. Give you a chance to make a mistake quicker."

Tom said, "Would you ride a pinto horse on a bank robbery?"

"Not if I was in my right mind."

"Ain't ten pinto horses in this part of the country."

"Maybe that was all he had to ride."

"Would you leave town firing in the air? Sounds like they wanted to make sure ever'body in town knew they'd robbed the bank."

Warner sighed. He said, "It is all passing strange. I especially don't like it that the reward poster don't give no description. Maybe there's a reason. It don't feel right to me, but I'll wait and see after I send the bank a telegram."

"And meanwhile you are paying room and board on some

46

men who may be bank robbers and may not. But then, according to you, you was maybe going to turn them loose anyway. You still feel that way?"

"You going to play checkers or try to get my mind so loaded down I can't think straight?"

"That wouldn't be no chore. You learned to play from Carver and I bought this ranch with what I won off him playing checkers."

Warner said, "Old man, you better quit tellin' them pwhoppers. You can go to hell for lying just as quick as you can for drinkin' whiskey. Especially that rotgut you set out for company."

"Then quit drinkin' it. Don't touch another drop."

"Move, damn it. I'm about to go to sleep over here."

The next morning Warner rode directly to the telegraph office at the depot in Hondo and got off a wire addressed to the president of the Mercantile Bank in Round Rock. It said:

AM HOLDING THE FIVE MEN BELIEVED ROBBED YOUR BANK STOP SEND YOUR LAW OFFICERS ALONG WITH EYEWITNESSES OR WHO YOU CHOOSE FOR MAKING A SURE IDENTIFICATION STOP WILL NOT RELEASE SUSPECTS HELD IN CUSTODY TO YOUR CUSTODIAN UNTIL REWARD IS IN HAND STOP WIRE THE UNDER-SIGNED CARE OF THE HONDO SHERIFFS DEPARTMENT STOP

He signed it with his full name, paid the goggle-eyed telegrapher a dollar and forty cents for its transmission, and then rode down to the jail office, dismounted, and went inside. He had been wondering how he was going to give the news to the sheriff and what sort of arrangement they could reach. By rights he owed the sheriff nothing. They were his prisoners and he was paying for their upkeep and the reward should be wholly his. But Tom Birdsong had recommended that it might be good politics to keep Harvey Pruitt sort of sweetened up. They'd discussed it and had arrived at a figure of $300. Tom had said that Harvey made $90 a month. He'd said, "That'll be better than three months' wages for him and will give him good reason to get some backbone when that Round Rock sheriff goes to trying to get him to release the prisoners on the basis that the robbery occurred in his jurisdiction and, by rights, they are his prisoners."

Warner had said, grimly, "Yeah, and look for the reward in the next mail."

Tom had said, "Or until hell freezes over. You need Harvey on this so you got to make it worth his while. There's a fine point of law here that could go either way if the matter went to court."

"But right now we got nine-tenths of the law. I got the prisoners."

"Yeah, but they're in Harvey's jail."

"You reckon three hundred is enough?"

"You give him more than that an' he'll go to believing he actually went out and captured them men himself. Three hundred is just fine."

He went in to find Harvey sitting where he usually was. Hondo was a quiet town close enough to San Antonio that anyone who wanted to do any hell-raising didn't have far to go to find anything he was big enough to handle. Sheriff Pruitt's stock in trade generally consisted of the odd domestic squabble or an occasional disagreement about the ownership of an unbranded calf or stray cattle getting into some town lady's garden. There were saloons in the town and an average number of drunks and fistfights, but it could hardly be compared to a border town or a place like San Antonio or Fort Worth.

Pruitt looked up as Warner entered. He scratched his head and yawned and nodded back toward the little stove. He said, "Jest put the coffee on."

"I've had plenty," Warner said. He took the reward poster out of his pocket along with the newspaper and laid them on the desk in front of the sheriff. He'd drawn a circle around the article with a pencil. He said, "Take a read of these and then let's talk."

It took him a moment to go over both pieces. Warner saw nothing in his face. Then he picked the reward poster up with his left hand as if tilting it toward the light would bring greater revelation. He looked at it for a long moment and then read the newspaper article again. Finally he stared off in space for a moment or two. Warner stood, waiting patiently. The sheriff turned around and looked at the door that led back to the cells. Then he looked at Warner. His eyes were starting to get big and round. He said, "You don't reckon . . . ?"

Warner nodded.

The sheriff's mouth dropped open. He said, "Wings on pigs! I'll be dogs! You mean it's *them?*" He rattled the paper. "Them as is wrote about here?"

Warner nodded again.

"Grease the doorknob, Tilly, I'm acomin' home!" He got up out of his chair and took the keys and let himself into the run between the four cells he had in the back.

Warner called after him, "Don't say nothing."

"Nary a word! I jest want to look!"

Warner half smiled. The sheriff's reaction mirrored that of the telegraph clerk when he'd read the words Warner had written on the telegram blank. This sort of thing didn't happen in a sleepy little village like Hondo. Five bank robbers in the jail? Go on! Who you joshin'? Yeah, an' ol' man Smith is givin' away free canned goods at the mercantile.

The train stopped in Hondo on its southbound run out of San Antonio three days a week. Outside of an occasional revival preacher or a medicine show coming to town, it was the biggest event that broke the daily routine. And now this business about five actual bank robbers being down at the jail. Would miracles never cease?

Warner figured it wouldn't be more than an hour before word would be all over town and the windows of the jail office would be crowded with the curious. A few of the more important citizens would find a way to actually come in the jail office, but most would be content to look through the office windows and hope to get a look at something interesting. A few would go around back and try to see through the barred windows, but they were ten feet off the jail floor and, unless somebody got up enough nerve to plant a ladder against the side of the jail and climb it, they weren't going to catch sight of the prisoners.

The sheriff came back and sat down in his chair, slinging the big ring of keys on his desk. He got out a big bandanna and wiped his face. He said, "I'll jest be go to hell! Four of 'em and they in my jail!" He looked up at Warner and said, "Well, what's to be done?"

Warner told him about the telegram and about what he and Tom Birdsong had talked about. He said, carefully, "Sheriff Pruitt, I think, because of your cooperation, that you should have a part of that reward. Tom Birdsong has suggested three hundred dollars as fair."

The sheriff blinked and then wiped his neck with the bandanna. He said, "Three hun— Three hundred dollars?" His voice almost squeaked. "All in one chunk?"

"All in one chunk."

He said, "But I ain't done nothin'. I mean, who am I to say no to a piece of money like that? But I ain't done nothin' 'cept cooperate with a feller lawman."

Warner said, "You've been a big help, Sheriff Pruitt. I was obliged for the smooth way you handled matters. You and your deputy. I'm going to see he gets a little something."

"Wall, now, wait a minute. I don't want you to go to spoilin' Lonnie. He's lazy enough fer two white men as it is. Naw, I'd want to thank on that."

Warner said, "That three hundred would be just between me and you, you understand."

The sheriff nodded vigorously. "I'd be much obliged for that. People talk, you know. Git the wrong idee. Naw, them's your prisoners. You caught 'em an' you brung 'em in fair an' square an' you been payin' they room and board." He suddenly frowned. He said, "Come to think of it, the way this thang has fell out, I don't see no need fer this jail to be chargin' you fer the upkeep of them robbers."

"That's all right," Warner said hastily. "I'm glad to do it." In fact, he was more than glad to do it. He didn't know what points of the law might come up in future but he wanted to be able to show clearly that the men had been in his care if not his direct custody. To back up his words he got out a twenty-dollar bill and put it on the sheriff's desk. He said, "That ought to get me a little ahead."

The sheriff adjusted his hat, frowning. He said, "Hell, it jest don't seem right. You makin' the town famous an' all. Hell, they liable to put *us* in the San Antonio paper an' that ain't happened since the midnight fast freight derailed jest outside of town. Hell, it wasn't even *in* the town." He looked up to see a half a dozen young boys staring in the window. He said, "Now what in hell do them little pissheads thank they are gapin' at?"

"Does the telegraph office have a messenger boy?"

"Why shore."

"Don't you reckon he's got a mouth?"

"Yes, an' been runnin' it, I'll wager." The sheriff got up and started for the front door. "School may be out, but I reckon it is still paddlin' season."

The boys scattered before he could open the door.

The sheriff said, "Whyn't we go back there and have a talk with that bunch? Make 'em out with the truth."

"I've already had a talk with the most reasonable of the gang, the one I took outside yesterday. He won't say anything and I don't think any of the rest of them will either. Besides, they answer the description. We got what they advertised for. I don't see where it's our responsibility to get a confession out of them. Let the Round Rock sheriff take on that chore."

"That's right," the sheriff said. "That's damn sound thankin'. Ain't none of our affair to git 'em to tell us." But the look he cast back toward the cells was that of a man who's left the dinner table not quite satisfied.

Warner saw it and felt what the sheriff was thinking. He knew the sheriff would like to play the hero by getting a confession out of the prisoners and being able to crow over his counterpart from Round Rock. But there was the chance, in Warner's eyes, that the sheriff might get carried away and get too rough. He said, "Another thing . . . right now they don't figure they are in much trouble so they ain't cutting up rough. They think we don't know about the bank robbery. But you bring that up to them and they are likely to get out of hand. Go to screaming for lawyers and a judge to set bail and who knows what all. Remember, they stole thirty thousand dollars. That kind of honey will draw a lot of lawyers. Some of them out of San Antonio. Big-city, slick lawyers."

The sheriff licked his lips. He said, "By gawd you're right. That be sound thankin'. I don't know what passed through my mind. We need to keep this on the qt." He put his fingers to his lips. "Ain't no use to start stirring the pot till the stew goes to stickin'."

"Good thought, Sheriff."

But Sheriff Pruitt looked up. He said, "But hell! Ever'body in this town knows what we got by now. You seen them kids at the window!"

"But the prisoners don't know that we know. Set Lonnie out at the back so they can't get to the cell windows and yell things in."

"Damn right," the sheriff said. "He be next door at the café. I'll roust his sorry ass out right now. He wasn't the mayor's kid brother he'd never got the job inna first place."

But then he stopped with his hand on the doorknob and looked back at Warner. "What are we supposed to be doin'? I mean besides putting Lonnie back thar to keep nosy pokers 'way from the winders."

Warner folded his arms. He was wearing clean jeans and a shirt that one of Tom's housekeepers had washed and ironed for him. The shirt and the jeans were blue but his $29.50 10X beaver Stetson hat was a light brown. He said, "Nothing."

"Nothing?" The sheriff rattled the knob. "With five desperate men back there?"

"Four."

"Four? But they was five robbed the bank."

"I shot one."

"Aw, yeah." As if that answered his original question about what they should be doing, the sheriff opened the door and hustled out to find his deputy. Warner half smiled and shook his head. There really was nothing to do but wait, though privately he didn't expect it to be a long wait. He expected a return telegram before the day was out and certainly one by the next day. Of course, bankers being what they were, they'd probably have to have a board meeting and talk the matter to death before somebody woke up and said, "Wait a minute. Hadn't we ought to send the sheriff down to gather them boys up?"

He had deliberately not mentioned that one of the robbers was already dead. Banks being what they were and bankers' thinking being what it was they might decide that it would be wasteful to pay a reward on a bank robber who was already dead even though their reward poster had advertised dead or alive. He knew they'd try to argue the matter, but his position was firm. He'd caught five bank robbers, in differing conditions, and he expected to be paid for five bank robbers. Hell, for all he knew they might want to knock off a hundred dollars on Otis Quinn because he was wounded and therefore damaged goods. Which caused Warner to remind himself that that was another five dollars he was out, the five dollars being the price the doctor had charged to bandage up a wound that was no worse than a briar scratch.

When the sheriff came back he looked gloomy and preoccupied.

"Couldn't find Lonnie?"

"Aw, yeah. Lonnie ain't hard to find. The café or the saloon. I sent him round back to keep watch."

"You look kind of down in the mouth."

"Wall, I was jest thankin'."

"About what?"

"The mayor." The sheriff went around behind his desk and sat down.

"What about the mayor?"

The sheriff grimaced. He said, "Wall, knowin' that son of a bitch, havin' growed up with the bastard, you kin jest bet he's agonna hear about these here prisoners an' the reward."

"So what?"

The sheriff looked up. "You jest watch. He'll be over here tryin' to figure him out a way to cut hisself in, that's so what."

Warner said, "Those are my prisoners."

The sheriff nodded vigorously. "I know it," he said. "An' you know it. But that goddamn Elton Pomroy has got the biggest goddamn nose in Jim Wells County."

Warner said, "I reckon we can get Tom Birdsong to settle him down if it comes to it."

The sheriff shook his head sadly. He said, "He's servin' the last year of his fourth term. Can't run no more. Town law. An' the idjit ain't got sense enough to know that Tom Birdsong can make things mighty warm for him in other ways. Mr. Grayson, he is dangerous because he is as dumb as a gopher hole."

"Well, what can he do? How in hell can he horn in? You don't work for him, you're an elected county official. Ain't got a damn thing to do with the town of Hondo. Hondo is just the county seat."

The sheriff sighed. He said, "I don't know. But you can bet he'll be over here soon's he get hisself a plan with the city marshal claimin' them prisoners."

Warner shrugged. He said, "We'll deal with it when we have to. Right now all we can do is wait to hear from Round Rock. For all we know they got a law officer on a train right now heading this way. Them prisoners could be out of here before your mayor wakes up from his nap."

The sheriff said, "Wall, I'll be mighty pleased if they was to hurry."

Warner waited until the afternoon of the second day since he'd wired Round Rock and then he got off an overnight telegram to the bank asking why they hadn't responded to his first wire either by telegraphing their intentions or by dispatching the witnesses and law officials he had originally requested. He again stated that he was certain that he had in his custody the men who had robbed their bank and again requested that they send witnesses to confirm this fact and law officers to take them in custody.

He was puzzled by the bank's attitude, but not alarmed. After all, they were the ones who had lost $30,000, and he reckoned their depositors would see that they followed up on every lead. Maybe it was simply that the bank was trying to get itself reorganized after such a loss and hadn't had time to act on his message. Though it did seem like somebody, anybody at the bank, could have found a few minutes to wire him back and say they'd got his telegram and to sit patient. But he was not accustomed to the whims and ways of bankers and therefore could hold no solid opinion.

On the morning after he'd sent his second telegram he was sitting in the jail office drinking coffee with Sheriff Pruitt when Mayor Elton Pomroy and his town marshal came marching in. Pomroy was a little banty rooster of a man wearing a starched collar, a four-in-hand tie, and gabardine trousers, a skinny runt except for his ample potbelly. Warner guessed him in his early forties, very near the age of the sheriff. The marshal was a dried-up little man who was wearing a sidearm, but the holster was so old and cracked that Warner reckoned it hadn't been used in ages.

The sheriff was about to take a drink of coffee. He set his cup down and a look of distaste came over his face. He said, "What the hell do you want, Elton?"

The mayor raised his right arm like he was about to deliver a speech and said, "I want the custody of those outlaws in this jail. This jail is city property and I demand that those bank robbers be turned over to the jurisdiction of the city marshal at once."

Warner was sitting in a little wooden chair he had leaned back against the wall. He let its front legs drop to the floor with a thump. Both the marshal and the mayor gave him a quick look, but then they brought their attention back to the sheriff. The mayor said, "This is not a request, Harvey, this is by order of myself and the city council."

The sheriff sighed. He said, "Elton, you was a horse's ass when I first seen you in grade school an' you are still a horse's ass."

"Your opinion of me ain't shared by the majority of the voters in this town, praise the Lord. But that ain't the point. They is a substantial reward for them robbers and that money can do a world of good for this town."

The sheriff said, sourly, "In case the town was to ever see any of it."

The mayor acted like he hadn't heard a word. He said, "Them prisoners is lodged in this jail, which is on city land in a city building. You will surrender responsibility of them forthwith."

Sheriff Pruitt said, "Oh, horse shit, Elton. County rents this jail from the city an' you know it. And the rent is paid up. Now git outten here before I throw you inside what you claim to be your jail."

The mayor raised his hand again, index finger pointed. He said, "I am telling you as mayor of this city that—"

Warner said, "Hold on, feller."

The mayor turned to give him a look. "I am not a 'feller.' I'm the *mayor* of this town and you'll keep that in mind when you address me."

Warner said, "You keep running your mouth about *my*

prisoners and I am liable to address you *and* stamp you *and* mail you out of town. I don't know if those men are bank robbers or not. And neither do you. But I do know they jumped me down the road and tried to rob me of my life and some livestock. And the jurisdiction they are under is me. And if they go anyplace it is going to be Nueces County on a serious charge. Meanwhile, *I* am paying for their upkeep and the upkeep of their horses. Not the county here, not the sheriff, not the deputy, and damn sure not you."

The mayor had stiffened with every word. He said, "And just who the hell are you?"

The sheriff answered for Warner, saving him the lie. He said, "He's a Nueces County peace officer and he's within his rights."

The mayor said, "Well, by gawd, if he's keepin' prisoners in the city's jail the city is going to have the say over them."

Warner said, quietly, "I'm going to give you a piece of advice, Elroy—you figure on messing with them men in my custody you better do some more figuring. I would not take kindly to that at all."

The mayor drew himself up and began sputtering. He said, "Are you threatenin' me? Me! By gawd, I think you are." He turned to his marshal. "George, arrest that man."

George gave Warner an apprehensive glance and said, "What fer, mayor?"

"Fer threatenin' my life, what the hell you think fer? You deef?"

George gave Warner another look. He said, "I don't recollect him prezactly *threatenin'* you, Mayor. I—"

The sheriff said, "Oh, get the hell out of here, George. And take that fool thinks he's the mayor with you."

They left, but the mayor went out the door shaking his finger at both the sheriff and Warner. He said, "You jest wait, Harvey Pruitt! Jest you wait!"

"Aw, git outten here or I'll fire Lonnie."

When they were gone the sheriff said, "And I would, if me and the mayor wasn't in-laws once removed."

Warner blinked. "What? In-laws once removed? I never heard of that kind of kin before."

"Aw, his sister is married to my brother. Don't worry

about him. He's a windbag. He come in huffin' and blowin', but that's all it'll amount to."

Warner was far less worried about the mayor than he was about the silence from Round Rock. On the third day since he'd sent the first telegram he rode out to talk to Tom Birdsong about it.

He went in the late afternoon, in time for to have a few drinks with Tom and a little talk before supper. As he rode he admired the rolling country, dotted with mesquite and cactus and cedar and post oak. It was the beginning of the hill country and was not soft country as he was used to further toward the coast. It was rocky and full of crags and outcroppings and sudden gulleys. It wasn't the best cattle country in the world, but it was good to look at with the sun going down and the harsh features of the land softened by the fading light.

Tom Birdsong's house was halfway up the side of a small hill, looking big and white against the greening grass and the row of evergreen cedars that grew behind it. Riding, he noted that Tom's mama cows and new calves were doing good, though he thought that Tom's remuda could stand a little upgrading. 'Course Tom would argue, and rightly so, that it didn't take real cattle horses to handle a mama-cow cattle operation. But he could argue back that Tom's *vaqueros* would appreciate it and that they were probably tired of getting outrun by a pregnant cow.

When they got sat down to a tumbler of good whiskey each, Warner told his friend about the visit from the mayor. He finished by saying, "I think he nearly scared his town marshal to death."

Tom Birdsong laughed so hard the cords stood out in his leathery neck. He said, "Oh, Elton. He's a good example of just how useful a mayor is to this town. He's like a lazy mule. He might not do no work but at least you don't have to worry about him gettin' in with your mares. If I was a mean-spirited soul I might send him in word that you're my grandson and remind him that I'm still the county tax assessor. And Elton's got a lot of acres to assess. They ain't worth watered-down milk, but a mean-spirited assessor might just see them as a good deal more valuable and place a higher tax evaluation on 'em."

"If you was mean-spirited."

Tom smiled slightly. "Yes. If I was. But I will have to say, though it ain't in my nature, it ain't no chore of work to get mean-spirited where Elton Pomroy is concerned. I sometimes wonder if the good Lord had taken Elton Pomroy into account when he laid down the Golden Rule."

Warner took a sip of whiskey and got out a little cigarillo. He didn't smoke much, and when he did, it was a sign he was either worried or concerned about something. He said, "Well, the hell with the mayor. It's that damn bank I can't figure out. They've had damn near seventy-two hours to reply to my telegram, the first one, and better than a day since my second one. If your bank had been robbed, wouldn't you have some interest in a wire from somebody claiming to have the culprits in hand?"

Tom Birdsong nodded. He said, "It is passing strange. They advertised and you answered. Do you reckon they might already have five men they think done the deed?"

"Hell, even if they do they ain't got a copper-bottomed cinch because I *know* I got the ones what did it. And even if they are holding what they think are the men, don't you reckon they owe me a telegram just out of plain common courtesy?"

Tom sighed. "I'd think that and you'd think that. But everybody didn't think alike. For all we know they ain't a soul in Round Rock that can call themselves sane. Been a time since I was in the town so I can't speak firsthand."

"Well, it's a puzzle to me and it's just about to start making me mad."

Tom Birdsong said, "Now, now. You recollect what your grandfather used to say. Gettin' angry never made a horse any smarter or a woman any gentler. Or was it the other way around?"

Warner smiled. But he said, "Nevertheless, I'm in a quandary about what to do. I can't keep on sitting here on my dead ass. I got work at home needs tending to. But that is twenty-five hundred dollars and I've earned it fair and square and I intend on having it. And that's something else my grandfather might have said."

Tom nodded. "Yes, he would agree with that. Only thing I can say is, if you ain't getting no satisfaction by telegram, you might have to go to the trouble and expense of going there yourself."

Warner grimaced. "I hate to do that. I trust the sheriff and all, but I trust myself more. For the time being I don't want to go off and leave those prisoners."

Tom Birdsong said, "I could slide into town and give them a looking over whilst you was gone."

Warner shook his head emphatically. "No sir," he said. "I ain't in the habit of visiting good friends with my trouble. Besides, you are in your busy season getting your calf crop ready for market. I noticed riding in that some of your mama cows are already setting out to wean their calfs."

"The mayor will not be any trouble to you. I can guarantee that."

"It's not the mayor and it's not the sheriff. It's that kid, Lonnie, the mayor's brother. He might turn them over to the mayor or they might just flat get away from him. Harvey Pruitt has got him sleeping up there at night, supposedly standing guard, but I wouldn't let him watch a dead horse for me."

Tom rubbed his chin. He said, "You've got a point there. I'm damned, then, if I know what the answer is."

Warner said, grimly, "The answer, I'm afraid, is to involve my partner. She's gonna demand half the money anyway so I might as well make her work a little for it. I'll send her to Round Rock. See what she can find out."

"Isn't she the one you described as being made out of barbed wire and thistles?"

"Listen, you need about four *u*'s in ugly to describe that woman."

Tom looked surprised. He said, "I thought you told me she was a right comely woman. Handsome. Fetching."

Warner said, "Oh, yeah, but that's her looks. I'm talking about the way the woman acts. Bossy ain't the word for it. She tries to boss everything and everybody. She'd boss a barn door if she could get it to listen."

"And you reckon to send a *woman* into this kind of a situation? Confront a bunch of bankers and such? Maybe even the law?"

"I reckon to send *this* woman to handle the matter, yes. They liable to pay her the reward out of hand just to get shut of her. Never mind the robbers I got here."

"Did you tell me if they had admitted it or not? I disremember."

Warner grimaced. "No, they keep saying they haven't robbed a bank. At least the only one I talked to said that. But there's something funny about the whole matter. I swear there is a piece missing. First glance you think you got the whole pie and then you take another quick look and something ain't right."

"You ain't making yourself very clear."

"That's because I can't. Can you explain to me why the bank didn't put a description of the robbers in their reward poster? There was, according to the newspapers, a whole raft of people out on the street who saw them riding away. Why didn't they put those descriptions in the poster like they was in the paper? Hell, the way the reward poster reads it could be anybody. I understand the bankers were scared and nervous and less interested in studying the robbers than they was in getting shot, but they ought to have noticed something!"

Tom Birdsong said, "Like one of them riding off on a spotted pinto horse."

"Maybe they didn't stick their head out the door. But you have to believe that the sheriff or the town marshal circulated around amongst the citizens and come up with some ideas about what they looked like."

Tom sighed and got up and poured himself out another tumbler of whiskey. He offered the decanter to Warner, but Warner shook his head. "It just makes me itch inside. Something is going on here and I damn well intend to find out what."

"Now you sound like your grandaddy. That was one man that could not stand for somebody to try and play him. I don't care if it was a cattle deal or marbles when we was kids, or a horse not being shod the way it was promised. He'd go to Jericho to square accounts, even if it wasn't over ten cents. By the way, he'd also go just as far to make the other feller's end even. I've read that about Lincoln, but I've *seen* your granddaddy do it."

"I don't know whether to talk to those men I got in jail or not. I don't know but what it might confuse me more."

Tom Birdsong said, "Why don't you quit thinking about it for the time being? I can hear the sizzle of steaks coming from the kitchen. Let's have a good meal and a few more drinks and play a little checkers and then you get a good night's sleep. Think on it tomorrow."

Warner stayed over the night as a relief from his bed at the hotel. He'd stayed in a hundred hotels like the Hondo Hotel. It wasn't any worse than the rest, but neither was it any better. Twelve or fourteen rooms with either a sour-faced or ignorant desk clerk, a rickety washstand and chair, and a bed with a lumpy mattress. Usually he was more comfortable out on the prairie.

Next morning, as he had before, he rode into town and went straight to the telegraph office. His telegram to Laura was, by necessity, a long one. He began by explaining, as best he could, the situation as he saw it. Then he directed her to take the next train out of Corpus Christi and go straight to Round Rock and straight to the officers of the Mercantile Bank and confront them with her information and inquire why they had not replied to his telegrams. He ended by saying:

SOMETHING IS FISHY STOP SUGGEST YOUR BEST APPROACH IS JUST TO ACT YOURSELF STOP WIRE ME ANSWERS SOONEST STOP

Warner could see the eager look on the telegrapher's face. Here was the chief player in the biggest drama the town had seen for years. He was full of questions, but, of course, duty forbade him to give voice to them. However, if Warner cared to make some comment . . .

But Warner ignored the telegrapher other than to pay the two dollars the wire cost and to instruct him to get it off immediately. Then he went back outside and mounted the Andalusian and rode him down to the livery stables and had him put up. There was no need for the horse to stand out in the sun all day when he wasn't going to be needed.

He walked toward the sheriff's office, running matters through his mind. He had no idea how long it would be before he heard from Laura. If she wasn't off somewhere she should have his telegram in hand within a few hours. But he seriously doubted she'd pick up and go right then and there. There might not even be a train leaving. He figured it would be the next day before she'd depart. The train would put her into San Antonio within four hours. He knew that because he'd ridden that selfsame train. It left at nine in the morning and got into San Antonio around twelve-thirty, give or take half an hour for freight stops.

But from San Antonio he had no idea how long it would take her to get to Round Rock. There was a train, any number of trains for that matter, that ran between Austin and San Antonio. But whether one went on to Round Rock or she'd have to change or lay over or even go by coach, he had no way of knowing without going back down to the depot and asking the passenger agent.

He figured that the best he could hope for, once she was

on the ground in Round Rock, was some word within seventy-two hours because, once she was in Round Rock, little time would be wasted finding out just what the hell the Mercantile Bank was up to.

Harvey was in his accustomed position when Warner walked in. He yawned and asked Warner how Tom Birdsong was. Warner smiled and told him what Tom had said about reminding the mayor he was also the tax assessor.

The sheriff laughed, enjoying the thought. He said, "Yes, and I'm the official tax collector. Tell Mr. Birdsong I'd be happy to enforce any tax rate he cared to hit Elton Pomroy over the head with."

Warner sat down in the wooden chair by the wall. He said, "How the hell does a little frog like Pomroy get elected?"

"Hell, he's kin to half the town. And them he ain't kin to believe his lies. Besides, ain't that much to choose from. We don't get a man like Mr. Birdsong to stand fer office all that often."

They fell silent for a few moments, each with his own thoughts. Warner lit a cigarillo and thought about going down to the saloon for a whiskey. He was not normally a morning drinker, but he thought maybe the drink would take the edge off the restless impatience he was feeling.

Harvey Pruitt said, "Boy, that bank in Round Rock." He had his hands folded in front of him on his desk top. He shook his head, slowly. "Grandma was slow but she was old."

"If it was my bank," Warner said, "I know I'd be ginning around and looking under every rock."

"*And* answering ever' damn telegram that come in concernin' the matter." He said it with the air of a man who'd just delivered a great truth. He nodded. "*Ever'* little word what come in. If I got me a letter from a half-wit girl name of Doris with a wooden leg I'd still go and see what she knew."

"Yeah," Warner said. He wasn't going to tell the sheriff about the telegram to Laura Pico, first, because he didn't want to explain about Laura, but mainly because it was his nature to not tell any more about his business than he had to. Warner wasn't a close-mouthed man; he'd make small talk all day long and could be as good company as a man, or a woman for that matter, could want. But when it got down to serious matters he tended to do more thinking and watching and listening than talking. When matters of weight were at hand he said exactly what he meant to in as few words as possible so there'd be less chance for a misunderstanding. If he set a man in a position and told that man not to move or he'd shoot him it was to that man's best interests to give serious thought even about blinking his eyes. He was not a man given to repeating himself and that was a major complaint of his about Laura Pico—everything was an argument. He had told his friend, Wilson Young, when he and Laura where just beginning their love-hate business relationship-affair, "Goddammit, she just won't stay put. You turn your back on her and she's either moved off in her mind or in her body. That damn woman changes her mind more times in the course of a day than most women change their dress during a lifetime."

But his patience and reluctant acceptance of such behavior began and ended with Laura. It extended no further, with the possible exception of the deaf and the blind. Other than those very narrow categories he expected whoever was hearing him to understand that he meant what he said.

He suddenly sat forward in his chair. The restlessness was beginning to get his goat. He felt like he had to do something, advance the matter in some way, even if it was the wrong thing to do. He said, "Harv, I believe I'll take another run at talking to one of them robbers."

"Now you're atalkin'," the sheriff said. He got up. "Which one you want? That young one, Calvin, might be the ticket. He's startin' to git a little jail fever."

Warner said, "Naw, I think I'll take a run at Darcey. Clint, ain't that his given name?"

The sheriff frowned. "Yeah, but he's the hardest case of the lot. He's been cuttin' up pretty ugly. Nearly scared Lonnie to death last suppertime. Tried to hit him with the tin tray Lonnie had carried his supper to him on."

"That's just it—the rest of them are afraid of him. Ain't no use talking to them because they're afraid Darcey will get at them somehow. Besides, you got that young man in the same cell with him. Now that I think of it, I wish you'd separate them. One to each cell. Put Darcey and Otis Quinn each in the two cells on the left and split off Les Russel and Calvin into the two cells on the right. Maybe that might make them a little less spooked."

The sheriff frowned again. He said, "Thing about it is that the first cell to the right don't work so good. Lonnie sleeps in there of a night and takes his naps there. He's slammed that door so many times the lock is all afoul."

"Well, if you could at least get Darcey away from the others."

"I can do that."

"All right, bring him on out."

Warner stood up and waited while the sheriff let him into the cell area. He heard the jangle of the keys as Pruitt unlocked the cell. The sheriff said, "You stay back there on that bunk, Calvin. You ain't wanted. Git on up here Darcey, an' don't git no fancy idees. I ain't wearin' no gun but they's a gent outside is and knows how to use it."

Then Warner heard the jangle of heavier metal and heard the sheriff say, "Stick your hands out. You well and good know what these here irons is fer."

Warner stepped quickly to the door to the cells. He said, "Sheriff? Sheriff."

Pruitt was on the point of putting wrist manacles on Darcey. He looked around. "Yessir?"

"Them irons won't be necessary."

Pruitt frowned. "You sure?"

"Yeah."

"This sumbitch thanks he's 'bout half mean."

"We'll get along. Just bring him on out."

Warner was watching Darcey coming out of the end cell to Warner's left. The last cell on the right was occupied by Les Russel and Otis Quinn. Les was standing up, motioning to Warner. He said, "Mr. Grayson, Mr. Grayson." He was waving his hand back and forth as if in a warning motion.

Warner said, "What, Les?"

But before Les could answer, Darcey growled at him. "Lester Russel, you better shut your goddamn mouth if you knows what's good fer you." Warner could see him giving Les a hard look.

Les grimaced. Warner said, "You want to say something, Les?"

But Les just sat down, still grimacing, and slowly shook his head.

Warner shrugged and stepped aside as Darcey came down the cell run in front of the sheriff. He gave Warner a look but didn't say anything.

The sheriff came out and turned and locked the door to the cells. He said, "Wall, thar he be. If you want to talk to him in private like I kin go down to the café."

Warner said, "Naw, I thought I'd take him outside and we'd sit on the bench." He looked at Darcey. "You wouldn't mind a little fresh air, would you, Clint?"

Darcey gave him a sneering look. "Whar you reckon it comes out to be fresh air, setting by you, Mr. Big Shot?"

Warner smiled. He said, "You are just thoroughly convinced that you are the toughest thing ever walked the earth."

"You take that gun off an' gimme a clean lick at you we'll find out damn quick who's tough an' who ain't."

Warner laughed. He said, "Naw, I don't want to play. Walk on out the door. There's a bench to the left. Take a seat. Remember, I'm right behind you."

He followed the squat, muscular shape of Clint Darcey as he walked to the door, jerked it open, and then stepped outside. Darcey had left his hat in his cell and Warner could see he was going bald on the crown of his head. He could also see that Darcey's khaki pants were worn and stained, as was his shirt and vest. Either they didn't have a change of clothes or nobody had brought them one. He made a mental note to ask the sheriff about it and to make some arrangements for the prisoners to get some kind of bath. Warner himself was neat in his habits and dress and felt uncomfortable when he couldn't have a wash and a shave.

Darcey's remarks hadn't bothered him. He reckoned that he'd feel the same way if the positions were reversed. But he had no intentions of wrestling around with the chunky man for the sake of proving nothing. He didn't fight for fun. When he did fight it was with the intentions of winning as quickly and thoroughly as possible.

The bench was six feet long. Darcey sat down almost right in the middle of it, causing Warner to sit closer to the man than he'd wanted. There was more space at the other end of the bench but that would have put his right side next to Darcey, the side where his revolver was.

When they were settled he offered Darcey a cigarillo. The scowling man took it and accepted a light from Warner, but he said, "Ain't no little cigar buyin' you shit. You had a lick o' sense you'd turn the bunch of us loose 'fore you make more enemies than you want."

Warner put his left elbow up on the back of the wooden bench. It made a sort of barrier between himself and Darcey. If Darcey tried a sudden move he was in a position to hold him off while he either hit him or drew his gun. He had his right hand resting on his right thigh, only a few inches from his revolver. He said, "You boys robbed that bank in Round Rock, Darcey."

Darcey leaned forward and spat over the narrow boardwalk into the dusty street. He said, "You fulla shit, you know that?"

"Whatever I'm full of ain't what you're gonna be full of for the next fifteen or twenty years and that's prison grub. I hear it ain't too good. Where'd y'all hide the money? You turn that up I'd reckon it would go a long ways in the eyes of a judge when it come to sentencing you. You didn't kill nobody so you got that in your favor."

Darcey said, "You gimme half a chancet an' I know me one sumbitch I'd kill." He gave Warner such a look of hate that there was no doubt who he meant.

Warner said, "I'm trying to talk sense to you, Darcey, but I can see it is a waste of my time. So far you've managed to scare the others into keeping their mouths shut, but that can't continue. Now I'm going to explain it to you one last time and then I'm going to give up on you. I reckon you will draw less of a sentence from that bank robbery if you give the money back and admit it than you will from the charges I'm going to bring against you. And I'll be bringing those charges in my home county where I'm known and where I know some people such as judges and whatnot. I'll charge you with attempted horse theft, attempted murder, and road agentry. They'll stack them charges up until your sentence will be plumb over your head. But you give in on this bank robbery and I don't see a judge being that hard on you."

Darcey's eyes glittered at him. He said, "What the fuck you keer happens to us?"

Warner said, "Because the bank put up a reward of five hundred a man on you and I intend to collect it. You make it easier on me to do that and I'll make it easier on you. You too dimwitted to understand that kind of thinking?"

Darcey said, "You really thank you sompthin', don'cha? Big horse owner, big blooded-stock owner. Clean clothes, new hat. Aw, yeah, you really think you are shit on a stick. Well, you might not be as well off as you thank."

Darcey coughed and bent over with the effort. Warner didn't see his left hand slide inside his boot. His first warning was the glint of steel in Darcey's left hand as he drew the arm back and then thrust forward at Warner, swiveling his body as he did.

It was the position Warner had his left arm in that saved him. If it hadn't been there, and if he hadn't reacted instantly, the knife would have gone into his chest and perhaps found his heart.

But as Darcey swung the knife in a short arc toward his chest Warner had suddenly jerked his left arm down, knocking Darcey's arm down and in, causing the knife to go into Warner's left side.

The searing pain of the cut caused him to come stumbling to his feet, lurching to his right as he clawed at his right side, reaching for his revolver. The knife was still sticking out of his side, just a few inches up from his belt. He got a look at Darcey's face. He could see the indecision. The man didn't know whether to grab the knife out of Warner and have another try or to flee. He could see Warner staggering backward until he was out of reach. He jumped down from the boardwalk and began running down the street.

Warner still couldn't seem to get his balance. He finally stopped his backward movement and took a step forward. But his boot heel caught in a crack in the boardwalk and he stumbled forward, drawing his revolver as he did. But he was already off balance and his next step unexpectedly took him off the boardwalk and he fell forward, catching himself on his knees and with his left arm. If he had fallen full face he would have rammed the knife in even further.

But now he was on his knees, his revolver in his hand.

Darcey was twenty yards away and running hard. Warner's side was burning like fire. He couldn't imagine what vital organ the son of a bitch had hit. He thumbed the hammer back and sighted as best he could on the back of Clinton Darcey as he ran straight down the middle of the street. He didn't bother wasting any of his breath on calling for the man to stop because he knew he wouldn't. Darcey was looking for the first horse that wasn't tended or tightly tied, but trying to put some distance between himself and Warner before he stopped for the horse.

Warner's hand was trembling slightly. It surprised him. He supposed it was the shock of the knife attack, but he was having a hard time holding on the center of Darcey's back and the distance was increasing with every second. But his stance, on his knees and bent forward on his left hand, was an awkward one. It put a strain on his right shoulder that traveled down his arm and to his hand. He was dimly aware of people all up and down each side of the street. It was important to shoot at Darcey before he cut to one side or the other.

He fired, the shot making a loud *boom* in the suddenly quiet street.

Darcey immediately spun around and fell on his side in the dust, then flopped back on his chest. At first Warner thought he'd hit him where he'd been aiming, in the middle of the back, but then he could see Darcey writhing around and clutching back at his right side and hip.

But he knew he'd hit him someplace hard and someplace vital and that the man was not going to be getting up. At least not without help. He holstered his gun and then turned painfully to his left and reached for the handle of the knife that was sticking out of his side. He'd expected to have difficulty pulling it out, but it almost fell into his hand. It had been hanging there, held mostly by his shirt. Either he'd joggled it loose when he'd fallen off the boardwalk or the knife hadn't gone in as far as he'd first thought. All he knew was that it was still hurting like hell and that, as far as he was concerned, meant a serious wound.

He got slowly to his feet. Around him he became aware of a hubbub and people talking. He saw several men running into the street toward Darcey. He wanted to call to them to stay away, that the man might still be dangerous. But just then he heard behind him the booming voice of Harvey Pruitt. "You people stay away from that man, goddammit! This is law work! Somebody run for the doctor. And be quick about it! *I said stay away from that man, Thorton! I got to whisper it in your damn ear?"*

Then the sheriff was beside Warner. He said, "How you doin'? Din't I tell you not to trust that bastard? How bad you hurt? *Somebody go get the goddamn doctor!"* He took Warner under the arm. "We better get you set down."

Warner said, "He had a knife in his boot. He'd 've got me dead center, and I mean *dead* center, if I hadn't blocked him off with my elbow."

They looked down at the dust of the street. The knife was lying there. The sheriff bent and picked it up. He said, "Hell, this ain't nothin' but a common kitchen knife. It come from the café. That goddamn Lonnie is supposed to make *damn* shore he counts the tableware when he picks up they trays and plates and whatnot. That dumb son of a bitch! I'm gonna have a piece of his ass for this."

Warner was holding his side. The blood was still pumping out. Some had run down his pants as far as his knee. He said, tightly, "Damn sure don't look like no table knife. Looks like a dagger. Look at the point on that thing."

The sheriff said, thoughtfully, "The sonbitch ground him an edge on it on the floor of his cell. It's concrete. And this soft metal won't keep an edge, but he didn't need it to. That son of a bitch. This here is a dangerous weapon."

"I know." Warner said. He was beginning to feel a little faint. He said, "Sheriff, I reckon I better sit down somewhere."

For the first time the sheriff seemed to become aware of Warner's condition. He said, "Good Lord! You are bleedin' like a damn stuck hog." He yelled at the crowd that was surrounding the fallen Darcey. He yelled, *"Get that doctor over to my office an' I mean right now!*

Then he took Warner firmly around the shoulders and helped him across the street and into his office. There was a bench there and Warner gratefully lay down on it. He said, "I could use a shot of whiskey. But you ain't got none."

Harvey said, "Ain't got no whiskey? Me? Hell, I got more whiskey than a saloon. I thought you was a teetotaler an' wouldn't approve."

"I approve," Warner said faintly. "I approve. Just hurry."

"You want corn whiskey or rum?"

"Goddammit, Harvey . . ."

5

The wound in Warner's side was more a rip than a stab or a cut. The point of the knife hadn't actually penetrated because Warner's quick move had disturbed the arc of Darcey's left-handed slash. The damage had been done by the jagged edge of the knife. The young doctor who'd washed it in grain alcohol and then put half a dozen stitches in it to hold the edges together had said it looked more like somebody had gotten after him with the teeth of a hand saw than a knife. Of course, the burrs on the edge had been caused by the uneven grinding job Darcey had done on the concrete floor. He'd managed to get a needlelike point on it, though, and if that had reached his ribs, the doctor had cheerfully told Warner, it would have gone on through to his lights and liver like, well, like a sharp knife through flesh. The doctor had speculated that the pain had been caused by the ragged way the knife had torn through the skin. He'd said, "You take a good sharp knife and run it through a man, why, he'll generally not even notice it till later. Maybe too much later." He'd explained that Warner had lost so much blood because the human body had a great many blood vessels up near the skin and the slash had cut quite a few of those. But, the doctor had said, imparting all this while he was busy sewing up Warner's side, "Few steaks and a couple nights' rest and you'll be good as new. Little stiff for a time, but you'll be able to get around. I'd stay quiet the balance of the day, though, and get to bed early tonight. This might leak a little blood, but it ought not to commence pouring out again 'less you rip them stitches loose."

White-faced and sweating after the stitching was done, Warner had sat up on the doctor's treatment table and assured the doctor he wasn't about to do anything that would cause the doctor to have to do any more sewing.

The doctor had offered Warner a small bottle of laudanum for the pain, but Warner had declined. He said, "I've had it before. It helps the pain, but it leaves me kind of fuzzy-headed and I ain't got the luxury of being fuzzy-headed right now. I'll stick with whiskey."

The doctor had agreed that laudanum would make your thinking a little woolly, but some preferred it to the feel of the stitching needle or the scalpel.

Darcey had not gotten off very lucky. The doctor had already examined the robber before he'd seen to Warner, correctly judging that Darcey was in much worse shape. While Warner was buttoning up his shirt and gingerly tucking it into his belt over the bandage on his left side, the doctor explained that Darcey would have been much better off if Warner's bullet had caught him square in the back and killed him. He said, "You hit him in the right hipbone and it busted everything to hell. I've got him doped up while I try to figure out what to do, but he's in a hell of a mess. The bullet is still in there, buried in his pelvic bone, if you can imagine that. It's going to be one hell of a job digging it out and I'm not even sure it's worth the effort. I don't think the man is going to live. A wound like that will get infected every time and there's just not anything to amputate to stop the spread of the infection. Of course, I'll douse it with alcohol and keep an alcohol drip going into the wound, but there's always some little nook or cranny you can't reach and that's where the infection will start. Don't have to be no bigger than a pinprick at first, but it will kill you just the same.

"And even with the laudanum it's going to cause him one hell of a lot of pain when I start gouging around in there for that bullet, or them pieces of bullet. I think the slug fragmented, and there's bone splinters everywhere." The doctor sighed. "Hell," he said, "I'm damned if I know what to do. Even if he don't die he'll never walk on that hip again."

Warner said, "Doc, all you can do is do your job the best you can."

The young doctor gave him a look. "I wish you'd done yours better. This man ought to be over at the undertaker's."

Warner gave him a flat look. He said, "Thirty yards is a hell of a distance for a revolver. And my hand was shaking. Maybe if you'd come out right then and give me some of that laudanum I'd of made the kind of shot that would have made your job easier."

The doctor shrugged and dropped his eyes. "I'm sorry. I shouldn't have said what I did. I'm just feeling sorry for the man in there."

"Would you have felt as sorry for me if I hadn't deflected his hand?" Then he said, quickly, "Never mind that question. I feel sorry for the poor bastard. But, if it's any consolation to you, he was as mean as sin and would happily dig a bullet out of your hip whether there was one there or not. And with a pickax, not a scapel."

But later he told the sheriff, "Harvey, that's what comes of getting cocky and careless. I dread when Tom Birdsong hears about this. Think I'm hurting now? He'll have the skin off me."

"He won't hear it from me."

Warner started to laugh and then stopped abruptly at the pain in his side. He said, "He probably already knows about it. And now I've got to explain why I took a dangerous prisoner outside all by myself with no help."

"You couldn't have known he had that knife. And I am still gonna turn Lonnie inside out about the matter. If he's been told oncet he's been told a thousand times to count the knives, forks, and spoons when he picks up after a meal. And if one is missin' to call me right then an' thar. Dumb son of a bitch."

"I should have been expecting anything."

The sheriff said, "By the way, Les Russel knowed about the knife Darcey had. That was why he was callin' to you when we was takin' Darcey out. He was tryin' to warn you.

But then Darcey told him to shut up. They's all scairt of Darcey. He'd promised that the man that told on him would never see another mornin'. Mean bastard."

Warner smiled slightly. "Yeah, I can testify to that."

"Wall, he's got up to his last bit of devilment."

Warner looked grim, and not just from the pain. "I made a mistake, Harvey, a bad mistake. I underestimated the opposition. My grandfather said if you made a mistake in a bad situation and got out alive you've made a profit. What he meant was you had better profit by that mistake and not make another or else you ain't going to live to spend the gain you lucked out with." He smiled thinly. "And at the time he was only talking about taking the bark off broncs. Dangerous enough work, but ain't shucks with dangerous men." He looked over at the sheriff. "Harv, I come within a quarter of a second of using up all my credit, let alone the profit. If I'd been a quarter of a second slower . . ." He let the thought hang there.

"Warner, it's over. Whyn't you let it lay?"

"I wasn't trying to be a smart aleck by telling you not to put those manacles on Darcey. I had a reason. I wanted to make a trade with him and I figured he'd be easier to deal with than if he was humiliated by wrist irons. I should have listened to you."

"Whyn't you jest leave it alone? Hell, look on the bright side. He's one less you got to feed and house here in the jail. Think on that."

Warner smiled without humor. He said, "Yeah, you've got a point, Harvey. How old are you anyway?"

The sheriff pushed his hat back. "Was forty my last birthday."

Warner said, "I hope someday I can say that. Way I'm going I might not get the chance. But, what the hell— Why don't we go next door to the saloon and I'll buy you a birthday drink."

Harvey was out of his chair in an instant. He said, "If you be waitin' for me you are already behind."

6

Warner left town that evening and rode out to Tom Birdsong's to spend the night. His bed at the hotel was bad enough, but with the wound in his side it would be well-nigh unbearable. The off side to that was that he'd have to give Tom Birdsong all the details of a situation he'd only heard the top of. And the details of how he came to get cut was not a subject Warner cared to discuss, especially with Tom Birdsong.

But his grandfather's friend, now his friend, made surprisingly little out of Warner's carelessness. He did, however, insist on seeing the wound and strongly recommended a poultice of turpentine and tobacco cud. Warner had declined, saying he was already hurt as bad as he wanted to be, but Tom had said, "You can't put no stock in these here modern doctors. Where they learn their doctorin'? In some school. That ain't where you learn to help folks that is hurt or shot or broke down. Listen, I've seen men give up for dead, shot through and through, and make it back to the land of the living with country doctorin'. I guarantee you a poultice of well-chewed tobaccer cud and turpentine will take the swellin' and the redness out of that wound in twenty-four hours."

Other than that he'd left the subject alone and they'd

mainly talked, or speculated, about what was up with the Round Rock bank and how much longer Warner could afford to keep fooling with a mess that was getting messier all the time.

"Not much longer," Warner said. "It depends on what I hear from the widow Pico. If it ain't pretty strong I am going to turn them boys loose and head on home and try to recoup what I've lost with a little hard work."

"You including your checker losses in your balance sheet?"

"You ain't three dollars ahead of me. And I'm still convinced you slipped a man back on the board on me that last game you won."

"I don't have to cheat to beat you. You ain't as good as your granddaddy and I won enough off him to buy this ranch and stock it with five hundred head of cattle."

"Last time it was enough to buy the ranch. Now you've thrown in a herd of cattle. What more you gonna add, the first month's wages for your hired hands?"

"Actually it was more like the first six."

During supper Tom said, "If that bank don't pay pretty soon, why don't you take what robbers you got left and send them back up there to rob the bank again? Likely they've got the hang of the job by now."

Warner looked up. He said, "That ain't a bad idea."

"Warner, I wasn't serious. You can't send to rob a bank. That would make you as much a part of it as if you was on the scene."

"I didn't mean *actually* send them to rob the bank. I ain't gone loco. But what if I was to send that bank a telegram threatening to turn them outlaws loose and point out the road back to Round Rock? They don't know that two is dead. Or one dead and maybe one dying."

Tom shrugged. "I don't know," he said. "Might give 'em something to think on. Might get their attention. Nothing else seems to have."

Warner sat back in his chair. "I've about half a mind to do that. See what happens."

"You gonna wait until you hear from your gal?"

"She ain't my gal. And I'm damn glad she wasn't here to

have heard you say it. I'd hate to see an old man like you scratched to death. Yes, I'll wait to hear from her, but I'm not real hopeful. I don't see what she can do. I don't see what I could do if I was there. I've sent them word on everything I know by telegram. Short of loading up thet last three and shoving them through the front door of the bank, I don't see what else can be done."

"Well, quit dawdling over your supper. I'm ready for some pie an' you ain't half through your plate. And it ain't got nothin' to do with you being hurt."

Before he went to bed that night Tom Birdsong handed him a bottle of whiskey for his bedside table with the flat remark that he could figure on needing it before the night was out.

But it was worse than that. Before the night was out Warner was extra sorry that he'd turned down the laudanum the doctor had offered him. The whiskey took a little off the edge of the pain, but not much. His side throbbed until he could almost swear it was moving. A few times during the small hours before dawn he was reduced to either walking the floor or biting his pillow. Finally, between the whiskey and sheer exhaustion, he fell into a restless sleep just before morning. When he awoke it was good light. He sat up in bed, wincing as his side bit him, and fumbled around on the bedside table until he found his watch. With a start he saw that it was nearly nine o'clock. He couldn't remember ever being in bed at nine o'clock in the morning in his entire life. He looked at the bottle of whiskey and noticed, with a start, that he had drunk more than half of it during the night.

The surprising fact of the matter was that no one had come to wake him up. He couldn't imagine Tom not sending up one of the Mexican women to hurry him down for breakfast when he hadn't shown up on time.

He sat on the bed and slowly pulled on his jeans, wincing with every effort. Leaning over to pull on his socks and then his boots left him pale and sweating. For a second, as he sat back up, he thought he was going to pass out, but he grabbed the whiskey bottle and took a quick gulp and then sat very still until the feeling passed.

Finally he got his shirt on and tucked in. With every step

he felt like the stitches the doctor had put in were straining to tear loose. But he got the door open and started down the stairs. The house was very quiet. He figured Tom was out and about his business and the Mexican women were busy with their work. He headed for the kitchen, hoping there was still some coffee on the stove. The kitchen had a swinging door and he opened it. The two women were busy at the sink and the stove and Tom was sitting at the kitchen table drinking coffee. He said, "Hello, sunshine. What are you doin' up so early?"

"Ain't no use being sarcastic, Tom. I'm ashamed enough already. If my grandfather were here he'd have a few choice words to say to me. Why didn't you call me?"

"'Cause you're supposed to still be in bed. Any damn fool knows the body heals itself faster when it's restin'. You *claim* to know this and that 'bout horses—you work a horse when he's hurt or you let him lay up and rest?"

Warner eased himself into a chair, wincing as he did. His side was much sorer than it had been the day before, but he'd expected that since the knife wound was not the first insult his body had suffered at the hands of other men or different broncs or cattle. He said, "I seldom have a horse to deal with that's just been in a knife fight so I'm not on sound ground on the matter. Naturally, I got you here to keep me straight."

Tom picked up his coffee and blew on the top. He said, "And a damn good thing, too. You ought to go back to bed after you've had some breakfast and I ain't funnin' about that. You might need to be at your best here right quick, so you need to heal up fast as you can."

One of the Mexican women put a big cup of coffee in front of him. He nodded gratefully at her and managed to burn his lips on the first sip. "Damn!" he said.

"Son, you are a danger to yourself. That's clear as spring water. Dorcita, put some brandy in this young man's coffee. Cool it down for him before he hurts his mouth again. You'll get yourself cold-jawed you keep scalding yourself like that and that widow Pico will have to put a spade bit in your mouth."

"I don't want to hear about the widow Pico this early in

the morning, you don't mind. And she ain't never got close to getting so much as a halter on me, much less a bit, spade, or chain."

Tom chuckled. He said, "No, I reckon she don't need either. I reckon you neck rein for her right nicely."

Warner gave the old man a look but didn't say anything. He was fond of Tom Birdsong. In many ways Tom had come to replace his grandfather. There had been times, in his younger days, when he'd come to the old man for advice and counsel just as he used to go to his grandfather. They reminded him of each other, Tom and his grandfather Carver. Not in size, because his grandfather had been much the bigger man, but in the way they approached a situation and looked at it from all sides, the way they kept their head, and the determination along with goodwill that could be seen in their eyes. Warner had once heard his grandfather described as the best neighbor a man could have but the worst enemy the wrong kind of man deserved. Warner could see that in Tom Birdsong. He was glad to have the help of Tom handy during this latest little patch of trouble. Of course, there was a price. The old man had a pitchfork for a tongue and he'd jab at you every opening you gave him. Right then Warner was content to drink his brandy-enriched coffee while his ham and eggs cooked and try to forget about the pain in his side. Now that Tom had discovered the widow Pico was a delicate sore spot with him Warner could expect the old man to jab at her every opportunity he got. Well, it was his own fault. The old man was sly. He'd let you talk on, a mile a minute if you was so inclined, until he found out some of your more vulnerable secrets, then he'd wade in and get out the vinegar and salt and give your scratches a good rubbing. Of course, all that was just in fun. Tom Birdsong, like his grandfather, never joked a man about his serious business. And you'd better not joke Tom Birdsong about his or you'd wish you hadn't.

Warner said, "I want to move around a little this morning, see if I can't keep this side from stiffening up too much. I'll get it some rest this afternoon."

"When's that doctor gonna take them stiches out?"

"He didn't say."

Tom sipped at his coffee. "Let me know, will you? In time

to be there. The only hollering I ever heard that was louder than a woman givin' birth to twins was a man getting some stitches pulled."

Warner gave him a disgusted look. He said, "You really are a mean old man. How come my granddaddy chose to take up with the likes of you I'll never understand."

He contented himself with walking around the ranch that morning, never straying more than a couple of hundred yards from the main house. He could clearly see how Birdsong's cow-calf operation worked. The vaqueros were bringing in the calves as fast as they were weaned. Sometimes in twos and threes, sometimes in bigger bunches. They were penned near a large barn and fed in a long trough on grain mixed with cow's milk. The milk made them not miss their mama's so much and the grain mash gave them quicker strength so they'd be able to travel sooner. They were all headed for northern grazing ranches where they'd be fattened up as yearlings and then either sold as slaughter cattle or put through another year of fattening on the rich grazing of the northern ranches in Wyoming, Montana, and the Dakotas. Birdsong held some of the female calves back to let them graze his own ranch and eventually become mama cows to replace his breeding stock that was getting too old.

Warner stayed another day and night. On the morning of the third day since he'd been slashed he felt almost back to normal. The Mexican women had fed him steak and eggs and stew and some enchiladas and potatoes and every kind of canned vegetable that was to be found. He figured it was time to get away from the place before his pants quit fitting. Some of the swelling had gone down in his side and the wound didn't look so angry, though it was still an odd sight to look down and see his skin sewed up like he was a piece of yard goods. The wound still hurt and he had to be careful of his movements, but his strength had mostly returned. Since he hadn't left word of his whereabouts he was anxious to get back to town to see what had transpired and see if a telegram had come from Laura. Certainly there'd been enough time if she'd got about the business promptly, but he was not going to count on that as a sure thing.

He stayed for lunch and then Tom had the Andalusian

saddled and brought around to the front porch for him. As they stood watching the copper-colored horse being led up, the old man said, "I guess you still don't want to sell that horse."

"What would you do with a horse like that? You'd ruin him in a week. Just stick with these old plow horses you've got your vaqueros believing are cow ponies. Besides, you can't afford a horse like that."

Tom Birdsong said, "You are still going to stand there in the sight of God and the assembled company and claim that horse is worth two thousand dollars?"

"No," Warner said, "I never claimed the horse was *worth* two thousand dollars. I said that's what he *cost*. He's worth considerable more."

"I see now that that blood you lost has addled your brain."

Warner clapped Tom on the shoulder and walked down the steps and mounted Paseta. He said, "I've got to go, you old crook. I'm obliged for the hospitality. Whyn't you come into town before I leave and let me buy you some dinner?"

Tom Birdsong said, "Why should I ride two miles to eat slop when I got the best food in the county right here?"

Warner nodded—the old man had a point. He turned the Andalusian and put him in his half lope, half gallop gait and started for town. It was a good afternoon, warm and balmy with a hint of rain to give an extra softness to the air.

He left his horse in front of the sheriff's office and walked through the door. He said, "Harvey, have you been out of that chair since I left?"

The sheriff yawned and pushed his hat back. "I might've gone to supper once or twicet. I forget."

Warner sat down in his accustomed chair against the wall and lit a cigarillo. "I think you've growed to the damn thing."

The sheriff looked over at him. "How you feelin'? Least you ain't pale as death."

Warner shook out the match he'd used to light his cigarillo and dropped it in a spittoon. He said, "Pretty good." But then his face darkened and he said, "But if I'd had that bastard to hand a couple of nights ago at about three in the mornin' I'd've shot him in the other hip. For a wound that didn't do much more than bleed me out a little, this son of a bitch has hurt an uncommon amount. Still stiff as hell. I drop something I wait for somebody to come along and pick it up."

The sheriff got a slight smile on his face. "Speakin' of Darcey—the mayor come in an' claimed him fer the city. Said he was in the doctor's infirmary and that damn shore was city property even if it was private. Said he was goin' to wire the bank fer the reward."

Warner pulled on his cigarillo. "He did, huh?"

"Yeah." The sheriff smiled a little more. "Come in here mealy-mouthin' around wantin' to know what bank to wire."

Warner laughed. "What'd you tell him?"

"Told him I thought it was the Cattleman's National Bank in Fort Worth."

Warner laughed until his side warned him to stop. He said, "Oh, yeah, I reckon that ought to come as a surprise to the bankers at the Cattleman's National. I'd want a company of cavalry to try and rob that place. Of course, the telegrapher down at the depot knows which bank."

"Be worth his job if he told."

Warner twirled the cigarillo with his fingers. He said, "Well, I reckon the mayor is shit out of luck. Unless you want to tell him?"

"Not me."

"Me neither."

The sheriff said, "By the way, your bank robbers want to talk to you. Seem right anxious." He jerked his thumb back toward the cells. "Seems Darcey's absence has had a right pleasing effect on them."

Warner glanced toward the back. "Wonder if I ought to talk to them one at a time or all in a bunch?"

"They asked in a bunch. Didn't no one of 'em slip up on the qt to me and whisper in my ear. By the way, they's a telegram for you up at the depot. Want me to send Lonnie after it?"

Warner got up. "Naw, I'll go myself. I might need to send a reply back." He wondered if it was from Laura or the Mercantile Bank. "Whoever brung word say who it was from?"

The sheriff shook his head. "Naw. Jest a kid. I give him a dime."

"Probably make himself sick on candy." He started for the door. "Tell those men back there I'll talk with them when I get back."

He passed on outside and mounted up and rode toward the end of town to the depot. The telegrapher must have seen him coming for he handed Warner the telegram the minute he came in the door. It was from Laura and said:

SITUATION HERE VERY COMPLICATED STOP UNABLE PUT DE-
TAILS IN WIRE STOP VERY FISHY STOP SUGGEST YOU GET YOUR
BEAST OF BURDEN HERE SOON AS POSSIBLE STOP HAVE ALLY IN
MAYOR STOP DON'T FORGET YOUR WEAPONS STOP BRING ANY
HELP YOU CAN STOP

He read the telegram twice and then once again and was as puzzled as the first time he'd read it. How could the situation be complicated? He'd sent her up there to uncomplicate it. And what difference did it make if she'd made an ally out of the mayor? What help was *he* going to be about the reward? And she was practically warning him to expect trouble. He turned away from the telegrapher's counter muttering to himself. As he started for the door the telegrapher cleared his throat. Warner looked back. "What?"

The telegrapher cleared his throat again. He was a thin, dried-up little man wearing a green eyeshade and sleeve garters. He said, "Uh, Mr. Grayson, this ain't none of my bid'ness . . ."

Warner knew the man had been dying to question him from the first day. He said, "Go ahead, I ain't gonna bite you. What do you want?"

"Uh." The telegrapher shifted his eyes. He said, "Uh, well, you jest didn't strike me as the kind of feller would have a donkey."

Warner stared at him, puzzled. "What? A donkey?"

The telegrapher motioned toward the telegram in Warner's hand. He said, "Whoever sent that telegram said fer you to get your beast of burden up there."

Warner smiled. "I don't own a donkey. She meant it in the biblical sense."

"The biblical sense?" The telegrapher looked puzzled. "I don't reckon I git that."

"What's a beast of burden referred to as in the Bible?"

"Why—" the telegrapher said. "Why—" He thought a moment. "Onliest thing I kin think of is a—" He stopped and turned red. "Ass! Mr. Grayson, she can't send a word like that over the official telegraph wires!"

Warner said, "Looks like she just did."

He was laughing as he left the telegrapher's office, but his mood was dour as he came into the sheriff's office and threw the telegram on his desk. He said, "Take a look at that, Harv, and tell me what you think."

While the sheriff furrowed his brow and pursed his lips, making his way, word by word, through the telegram, Warner went and sat down. When the sheriff was finished he said, "Yessir?"

Warner flung out an arm. He said, "Well, hell, Harv, she tells me the situation is very complicated, she sees it as very fishy, she tells me there might be trouble by recommending I bring my *weapons*. Well, goddamn, I already knew all that. Shit, I didn't have to send her clean to Round Rock to figure that out. I knew all that about one telegram ago. I sent her down there to straighten matters out. I—"

"'Scuse me," Harvey said. "You keep sayin' 'she.' Is this here wire from a lady?"

Laura had not bothered to sign the telegram. Warner said, "Well, there's some question about that. You might better describe her as a rawhide quirt wrapped in lace with a silk bow around it. But for all the lace and silk they is still a quirt inside. She's my partner. I thought I explained all that to you."

"Well, no, you didn't."

Warner waved his hand. "Doesn't matter. It just makes me damn mad is all."

The sheriff smiled faintly. He said, "She ain't bashful about telling you to git your ass up there."

"That's funny. The telegrapher didn't get it."

"Amos Stringer? Hell, he's a pillar of the Baptist church. I think he's the one got the key to the front door."

"Then a churchgoer like him ought to get it before a sinner like me."

"I don't thank he figures he's allowed to think on such things. I reckon he says donkey when he comes to that word in the Bible."

Warner said, "So that leaves me right back where I started. Why does this have to get so snarled up? That bank got robbed. They advertised a reward. I caught the damn robbers. Why don't they pay me what they owe me?"

Harvey cocked his head. He said, "Maybe they don't know you as well as some others."

"What's that supposed to mean?"

"Means," Harvey said, "if I owed you twenty-five hunnert dollars or twenny-five cents and I had it and you made demand I'd pay you. That's what it means. I seen enough to convince me they are not makin' too wise a choice."

Warner sat there with a sour look on his face. "Why don't you get out your bottle and pour us out a drink and then I'll go see what the boys in the back rooms want to tell me. I'm about half mad, you know that?"

Harvey said, "I'm pourin' as fast as I can. I wisht the mayor would come in right now. I've always figured Elton would piss his pants under the right circumstances."

When they'd finished their drink the sheriff unlocked the door to the cells. He pointed to the fact that the upper half of the door was covered with bars and could, therefore, be heard through. He said, "I kin go outside. Or go next door to the café."

Warner said, "Let me see if they mind if you hear. If it's something they want to tell me in private we'll keep our voices low. I ain't gonna see you run out of your own jail."

He stepped into the runway. Les Russel was alone in the first cell to his left and Calvin and Otis Quinn were in the back cell. As soon as they saw him they all three got up and came crowding against the bars. Les said, "Mr. Grayson, we've been talking it over and they's some matters we'd like to git straightened out. Somethin' you ought to've been told way back at the first."

"Except for Darcey?"

Les grimaced. "Yeah, him. But also a kind of shame on our parts."

"Is this something you don't want the sheriff to hear? I got to tell you I've cut him in on the reward so I figure he ought to know what I know."

From the back cell Otis Quinn said, "We don't mind him hearin'. In fact we'd druther. Might make it quicker fer us to git out of these damn cells."

Warner said, "I don't know about that. But I'll hear you out." He turned and called to the sheriff. "Harv, you might as well come along. I would imagine this will concern you also."

Warner walked into the cells until he was opposite Les Russel but with Calvin and Otis crowding to the corner of their cell so that he was mostly facing all three. The sheriff stayed in the doorway. As small as the area was he could easily hear what was being said. Warner lounged back against the bars of the empty cells behind him and crossed his arms. He said, "All right, go ahead. You got my attention."

Les said, "You think we robbed that bank in Round Rock, don'cha?"

Warner said, "I don't *think* you robbed it, I *know* you robbed it."

"Yeah?" It was Otis Quinn. He said. "We been in here a pretty good many days. How come you ain't took us back thar er how come the law from there ain't come to fetch us? Les said you told him there was a five-hunnert-dollar reward a man on us. You shore as hell wired off for that, di'nt ya?"

Warner said, uncomfortably, "These matters take time. What's y'all's rush? You ain't goin' nowhere."

Les said, "I bet you wired an' you ain't heared nothin' from that bank."

"What makes you so sure of that?"

The youngest, Calvin said, "'Cause we never robbed that bank, that's why. That'n 'er any other'ns."

From the doorway the sheriff shook his head wearily and said, "Shit! Jest once I'd like to git somebody in this jail who will actual admit they done the thang they is accused of."

Warner said, "Then how come the description by the bystanders outside gives such a clear picture of the five of you?"

Les glanced over at his cellmates for an instant. Otis

87

Quinn seemed to nod his head. Les came back to Warner. "Because," he said, "that was the only place they saw us. I don't know if that bank was robbed or not. I don't know if we was jest used as a blind whilst the real robbery was goin' on. All I know is that they wasn't a man one of us ever in that bank. Not us three."

"Never," Otis said. "Never stepped foot in the place. Wadn't in the town more than an hour at the outside. Rode over early that mornin' from Austin, done our business, and got the hell out."

"What business? Damnit, you are talking in circles." He looked at Les. "You told me once you were ashamed."

"Embarrassed. Embarrassed at bein' suckered like we was."

"All right. If you didn't rob that bank, then who did?"

Les shook his head. "I don't know. All I know is we never stepped foot in it and we *damn* shore ain't never seen no thirty thousand dollars. Or even three hundred."

Calvin said, "Whyn't you go ahead and spit it out, Les? Shit! We was played fer calves an' we should've seen it comin' 'cept we didn't. Now we pay."

Warner looked at Les. "Well?"

Les hung his head. He said, "We was hired—at least me and Otis and Cal was hired for fifty dollars to go into Round Rock. Sit our horses in front of the bank until a minute or two after nine o'clock and then go riding out of town shooting our guns in the air." He half smiled. He said, "That was one reason we didn't have but them four cartridges between us when we run afoul of you. 'Course we'd been whooping it up pretty good in a San Antonio whorehouse when somebody seen that paper you showed me, an' right then we realized what a jam we'd got in."

Otis said, "Cap'n, we never had no idee what was goin' on. All we ever done was ride out of town fahrin' our guns in the air."

Warner looked at them and marveled. He said, "And it never occurred to any of y'all to ask why somebody would be willing to pay you fifty dollars a head for that kind of work?"

"Cap'n, if you was as broke as we all was you'd understand."

Les said, "We don't know that Darcey and Jake were that broke." As an afterthought he said, to Warner, "Jake was the one you kilt."

"I know. How come you didn't know if they were as broke as you?"

"Well, mainly 'cause it was them put the proposition up to us. We was in Austin, hangin' 'round different saloons, lookin' to cadge a drank here or there. You unnerstan' we wasn't together. I'd happened on Calvin, but I'd never seen him before that day. Ner Otis neither. Then 'long came Darcey an' Jake. I reckoned they picked out the brokest-lookin' three men they could find that still hadn't sold their sidearms and propositioned us. Least that's the way it happened to me." He looked over into the other cell. "Y'all said it was about the same with you."

"Was me," Otis said. "They come up an' this Darcey bought me a drank, which I was damn glad to git, an' then him and Jake ast me did I want to make an easy fifty bucks? Well, does a hog like watermelon? O' course I wanted to make fifty bucks, hard, easy, er sideways. I ast 'em what I had to do an' they said it was a joke on a friend that some folks in Round Rock had hired him and Jake to play. Wadn't dangerous. All we had to do was get up early in the mornin' and go to Round Rock and shoot in the air and ride on off. Hell, I didn't believe him at first, did you, Les?"

"I did when I seen the color of that money he come out with. An' when he went to buyin' drinks I damn sure believed him."

Calvin said, "Him and Jake had us all together by then. We was all gathered up in this saloon called the sompthin' er other."

"The Longhorn," Les said.

"Yeah, that's it."

Warner stood there looking at them, studying their faces, trying to determine if all of what they were saying was the truth. He said, "How come all of y'all was so broke? Two of you"—he indicated Les and Otis—"are obvious cattle hands. With calving season just getting over you should have had three months' wages in your pockets."

Les said, "I don't told you I'd got hurt. Hurt my back. I'd gone to lookin' for work. I don't know if you ever rode the grub line, Mr. Grayson, but jest try an' git work with the calvin' season over. Jest try and git day work. You'll find it's a hard go. I was damn close to selling my saddle."

Warner looked at Otis Quinn. "What about you?"

Quinn hung his head and looked down at the floor. He said, "Aw, I got a good ol' fashioned screwin'. I was workin' at the Three Bar near Drippin' Springs. You know, right outside of Austin. They fired me."

"For what?"

Quinn was still looking at the floor. He said, "Well, they claimed I kilt a horse. Rode him to death." He looked up defiantly. He said, "But I be damn if I'll take blame fer that horse. They give me a short string. Five horses! Kin you 'magine workin' that country with jest five horses?" He shook his head. He said, "So the damned old horse I was riding took the blind staggers and went to sweatin' an' shiverin' an' died 'fore I could git him to water. Docked me all my wages fer the horse. Hunnert an' twenny dollars I had comin'. Said I had bought the horse. Huh! Best day thet horse ever saw he was worth maybe seventy-five. Tied a can to my tail an' run me off the place."

Warner stared at him. In Warner's eyes there was no excuse for riding a horse to death except to save a human life. True, a five-horse string was a mighty short work string for that rough country. But there were a lot of things Quinn could have done before he rode the horse to death. He could have switched off more often. Of course, that would have meant coming into camp and unsaddling and unbridling the horse he was on and then rigging out the horse he was fixing to ride. Or he could have gone to the straw boss or the foreman and said he had to have a horse or two more or he couldn't answer for the consequences. Or he could have taken the pace a little slower. Otis Quinn didn't look like the kind of man who would worry overmuch about his employer's calves getting branded and worm doctored and the bull calves castrated in record time.

As if he was reading Warner's mind Otis Quinn said, "They was pushin' us! Nobody keered to hear about no overworked horses. They jest wanted the work done! An' then they seen a chancet to skin me outten my wages they up an' done thet! I never set out to kill no horse and that's God's truth."

Warner looked at Calvin. "What about you?"

The young man shrugged. He said, "Ain't much to tell. I been a jack-of-all-work. Commenced when I was fourteen an' I'm twenny now. Done a little cowboyin'. But when all this come up I'd jest got back from West Texas where I'd been freightin' wagons to towns where the railroads didn't run. Was mighty lonesome work. An' didn't pay much. So I come on back here to see what was what." He made a gesture at Les. "Me an' him kind of tried to hit each other up fer a drank at the same time. But that was the fust I'd ever seed of the man. Then Jake an' Darcey showed up an' they arready had Otis with 'em." He shrugged. "They put it up to us an' I was damn shore willin'. Fer fifty dollars? Hell! I hadn't seen fifty dollars in a coon's age."

Les said, "Which we pretty nearly spent up the first night in that whorehouse in San Antonio. That was Jake an' Darcey's idee."

"Yeah," Otis said, "an' they kept tryin' to slip off from us too."

"How you mean?"

Les said, "Jest that. They'd go outside an' one of us would foller 'em out an' ast them whar they was headed and they'd say nowhere and come on back in."

The sheriff said, "Austin is between Round Rock and San Antone."

"Yessir. We cut clean on 'round Austin. Darcey said it was fer the best."

"What best?"

Les shook his head. "Never said. Jest said they was the best whorehouse in the world in San Antone an' we ought to make it 'fore we spent any of our money. Him and Jake kind of acted like we ought to put some miles between Round Rock and ourselves but we never thought nothin' of it other than they might have been a city law agin firin' your weapons downtown."

"Then what?"

Les said, with some heat, "Next mornin' we woke up pretty near broke an' I seen that newspaper you had. I tol' you I could read. Well, the blood run cold in my veins. I rousted out the rest of 'em and we got up and started cross-country, gettin' out of thar. Headin' south."

The sheriff said, "How come you waited all this time to tell your story? Might've been a good deal more believable about a week ago."

Les glanced over at Otis and Otis dropped his head and shook it. Calvin said, "We was scairt of Darcey fer one thang. He swore he'd have a look at our insides if we blabbed."

Les said, "It warn't so much that fer me. I was plain ashamed to think I'd been sich a damn fool. Why would anybody give a feller fifty dollars to go ride out of town firin' his gun? Hell, Mr. Grayson, I went to the sixth grade in school an' I ought to have had more sense than that. I was the ramrod on a short cattle drive when the regular pusher got hurt. I've worked men, I've taken responsibility. Hell, I ought to have known better."

The sheriff said, "You reckon Jake and Darcey was in on the real holdup? You know the bank reward poster didn't give no descriptions to amount to beans."

Les shook his head. He said, "I don't know." He looked over at Calvin and Otis. They both shook their heads.

Les said, pointing at Warner, "I will tell you one thang. You seen that stone bruise on that pinto? An' you seen I knowed how to fix it. Right?"

"Yes."

"Well, when that pony first got that little bruise I told Jake I could take care of it and the horse would carry him on quite a spell. The bruise didn't amount to nothin' at first an' if he'd've let me pad it you'd've never seen it nor us. But he didn't want to do that."

"Why you reckon not?"

"Cause he wanted to git shut of that horse, he wanted that horse hurt so we'd have to steal another. He didn't want no more part of that pinto, not once the job was done. An' if I'd've had a lick of sense I'd've cottoned on to the idea that that was a hell of a horse to pull a bank robbery on. A pinto? Hell! Ain't nobody thet dumb except on purpose."

Warner looked over at Harvey Pruitt. "What do you think?"

The sheriff straightened up from where he'd been slouching against the door sill. "I think there was a bank robbery all right. I jest ain't so sure now who done it."

Warner said, "Y'all got anything else you want to add?"

They all looked at one another and then shook their heads. Calvin said, wistfully, "I shore wouldn't mind gettin' a look at the outside. Smellin' a little air don't smell like it's been used three or four times afore it gits to me."

The sheriff said, "Outside's still the same, Calvin. Ain't changed a bit. So you might's well make yourself comfortable in here."

Warner and the sheriff walked out. While the sheriff locked the door Warner put on his hat and stood thinking. He said, "I reckon I better get on over and talk to Darcey. If he and Jake were in on the real bank robbery I might find out something."

The sheriff said, "He's a hard case." He shook his head. "I don't reckon you'll find out any more than you did the other day. Onliest difference is he ain't gonna be able to cut you."

Warner gestured toward the cell door. "If what they are saying is the truth it would explain a lot."

"How?"

"Well, that the checkered shirt and the leather leggings the bystanders outside of the bank saw didn't go with the robbers inside."

"That still don't explain the pinto."

Warner thought a moment and then sighed. "No," he said, "it don't. Damn it, this is the most snarled-up mess I was ever in that I wished I was out of. Why did them son of a bitches have to pick me to try and rob? Why not some little old lady with a matched span of buggy horses?"

It was only two blocks down to the doctor's office and infirmary. The doctor had his office in a failed mercantile store with plate-glass windows facing the street. The infirmary was in the back, walled off from the office with new, unpainted wood. Warner could see the doctor sitting at his desk against the back wall of the office, writing on a piece of paper. He looked up as Warner came in. He said, "Good afternoon, Mr. Grayson. How's the side?"

"Still a little sore." He found a chair and sat down gratefully. He could tell he still hadn't gotten his full strength back, but he didn't think it would be much longer. "When you thinking about taking out those stitches?"

The doctor got up and came over to Warner. He said, "Let's have a look."

Warner stood up and pulled his shirt out, exposing the wound.

The doctor unwound the dressing that went completely around Warner's midrift and took off the pad that covered the wound. He said, "That's coming along nicely. I'll change the dressing and figure to take out those stitches in, say, oh, a couple of days. I could damn near do it today."

"That's all right," Warner said hastily. "I ain't in no hurry." The wound was still sore and the idea of having the stitches pulled back through the aggravated flesh made him wince. He said, "Actually, it wasn't me that I come about."

The doctor was getting a fresh bandage out of his desk. He came back over to Warner and put a gauze pad in place and then began rewinding the dressing to hold it. He said, "If you come about that man you shot you're a little late. He died this morning."

"Damn!" Warner said. "I can't buy a break. Damn my luck!"

The doctor said, "Well, I wouldn't say he was running in the best of fortunes himself. You didn't shoot him in the luckiest of places."

Warner grimaced. "I didn't have a hell of a lot of selection, Doc. Him running and me with a hand gun. I'm sorry he died on account of it was me that killed him. But I'm also sorry he died because I needed to talk to him. I figured that in his weakened condition I might be able to get some information out of him."

The doctor tied off the dressing and indicated that Warner could put his shirt back in. He said, "I doubt you'd've got much out of him. That infection I was scared of took hold within twelve hours after you shot him. He was out of his head with fever the last day and night. Didn't know where he was or what was happening. Of course, I had him so dosed up with laudanum he was pretty woolly-headed anyway. I didn't even try to take the bullet out."

Warner shook his head sadly. He said, "The only two men

that I had my hands on that maybe knew the truth about that bank robbery are now dead. Why did this damn fool have to cut me and then run? Given time he would have told me what I needed to know."

The doctor yawned. He said, "If it's any help he kept talking about somebody named Crabtree."

"Crabtree? What'd he say?"

The doctor shook his head. "I don't know. He mumbled a lot of stuff I couldn't make out, but I'm pretty sure about the Crabtree part because he said it so often and I think it was a person because part of the time he'd say 'Mr. Crabtree.'"

Warner was anxious. "Is that all? Search your mind, Doc. Any little thing might help. Anything to do with a bank holdup?"

The doctor shook his head again. He said, "He might have said something about that, but I wouldn't have been listening for it. Remember, I wasn't interested in a bank holdup, I was trying to save a man's life."

"Yeah," Warner said, discouraged. It had been an unexpected blow to have found Darcey dead. He'd counted on finding him weak and willing to cooperate. Instead he'd gone mute forever. "Well, if you think of anything I'd appreciate you letting me know. Just leave word at the sheriff's office."

The doctor was at his desk. He said, "I will, but I wouldn't get my hopes up if I was you."

Warner put his hand in his pocket where he carried his cash. He said, "What do I owe you?"

The doctor said, "I'm not quite finished with you. There's the matter of the stitches to come out."

Warner gestured vaguely toward the back. "Well, you're done with him."

"You paying for him, too? I thought he'd be a county expense."

"No, he was my prisoner. Besides, I'm the one as shot him."

The doctor shrugged. He said, "He ain't going to come to much because there wasn't much I could do. The undertaker has done already collected him. But whatever the amount, we'll settle up when I'm through with you."

Warner put his money back in his pocket. He said, "Well, I'm much obliged, Doc. Next time I'll be sure and send my business straight on over to the undertaker's."

The doctor laughed. He said, "I shouldn't have said what I said before. But I didn't know much about guns. I'm since told that was a hell of a shot you made. I suppose I was thinking of a rifle."

"Handgun and a rifle don't shoot the same."

The sheriff was at his desk and Warner was sitting in his chair tipped back against the wall. Almost an hour had passed since he'd returned from the doctor's and, except for Warner's announcement about Darcey, very few words had passed between them. Lonnie had come in once or twice, but Warner had barely noticed. He'd spent the most of the time thinking. He'd decided that if he had any sense, he ought to cut his losses and get on back to work. Turn the three prisoners loose, wire Laura to get her beast of burden back to Corpus, and turn himself in that direction.

But instead he said, "Harvey, you any good with a gun?"

The sheriff roused himself. He said, "Middlin'."

"Handgun?"

The sheriff shook his head. He said, "In my line of work around here I am generally dealin' with three or four drunken cowboys and I need to get their attention. Handgun won't do that." He jerked his thumb over his shoulder at a rack that contained rifles and shotguns. He said, "I generally go in for one of them scatter guns. I got a twelve-gauge little beauty with no more than a twenty-inch barrel that will cut down fair-sized trees. It will generally get anybody's attention. And I'm a decent shot with a rifle, though the occasion don't come up that often. Why?"

"Can you take some time off?"

The sheriff pulled a face. "You might have taken note that this ain't the most lively place in the world. Yeah, I got some time off comin'. A lot of it, fact of the matter."

"Four or five days? Right away?"

The sheriff looked over at him. "What you got in mind?"

"Making a visit to Round Rock. I'll pay you ten dollars a day to go along."

"I don't want no day money. You done made me a

generous offer on that reward. If you going after that and you git it, why, fine and dandy. I ain't gonna turn my back on three hundred dollars. But you do know my badge ain't worth nothin' in whatever county Round Rock's in, don'cha?"

"Yeah, I know that. I want you along because you're a steady man and I figure you can handle yourself if things get tight." He got up. "You know a good carpenter around here?"

The change of subject took the sheriff off guard. "A what?"

"Carpenter. Man that can drive nails and saw wood."

The sheriff shrugged. "I reckon J. C. Cook is a fair hand. He's done ever'thang from buildin' porches to whole houses."

Warner started toward the door. He said, "Then have him here first thing in the morning. I'm going by the depot and then I'm going to spend the night out at Tom Birdsong's. I'll be back early."

The sheriff said, "Say, jest a—"

But Warner was already gone, closing the door behind him.

7

He had gotten off a telegram to Laura telling her to stay put, that he would be there in two or three days. He'd ended it by saying

BY ALL MEANS CONTINUE TO MAKE AN ALLY OUT OF THE MAYOR STOP ANY MAN FOOL ENOUGH TO BE IN YOUR COMPANY LONGER THAN NECESSARY IS A BRAVE MAN INDEED STOP

After that he had gone around to the other side of the depot and found the stationmaster, a tubby little man named Homer Long. When he had finished telling Mr. Long what he wanted, the stationmaster had stared at him for a few minutes. He'd said, "Mr. Grayson, lemme get this straight. You want me to wire for the next train through here to drop off a cattle car and spot it on our siding?"

"Yes."

"Well, sir, ain't goin' to be no trains stoppin' here as a regular thang until tomorrow. They's a train through here at nine tonight, but it don't stop. I ask it to stop and drop you off a boxcar—"

"Stock car. I don't want no enclosed boxcar."

"All right, stock car. Don't make no difference. It will still

98

cost you *fifty* dollar fer that train to stop and twenny-five more to drop off a car. That's seventy-five dollar."

"That's fine." He reached in his pocket and pulled out his roll. "I'll give you a hundred dollars in advance."

"Jest let me finish," Homer Long said. He took a breath. "An' then, after that amount of money that same car is gonna cost you ten dollar a day jest to set thar on account we ain't askin' fer it fer our regular trade."

"All right."

Homer Long was blinking in disbelief. He said, "An' that don't even *count* what it will cost you to have that car hooked on to a train and hauled wherever you be takin' it. And I reckon that will be at least ten cents a mile. This ain't at all the kind of way we do our business. Man got some cattle to ship, why, he notifies me a week in advance and we're ready for him on the day the train stops. Train stops an' we load his cattle an' off they go. Simple as that. But this here thang *you* be wantin' to do, why that is jest plain irregular, an' it is goin' to cost a pretty penny."

Warner handed him five twenty-dollar bills. He said, "Then I reckon you better get busy sending off your wire, Mr. Long. I'd hate for that car not to get here tonight."

He left the stationmaster staring after him as he mounted the Andalusian and rode for Tom Birdsong's.

That evening he asked Tom if he had a good man on his payroll that he could spare for a few days.

Tom said, "Good how?"

"Steady, dependable, cool in a tight place."

Tom narrowed his eyes at Warner. "You mean good and steady with a gun."

"Well, yeah, I reckon I do. I'm going into Round Rock in a couple of days, maybe day after tomorrow morning, and I'm going to take my prisoners with me."

"Your bank robbers?"

Warner looked uncomfortable. "It's a little hard to explain. They may or may not be the men who robbed the bank. But I think there are some folks who are going to be a little nervous about having them back in town. Anyways, if you've got such a man I'll pay him a flat fifty dollars for his time, plus I'll reimburse you for what you're out on his wages."

Tom cocked his head. He said, "I've got a good hand, Willis Drake. He appears to know more about firearms than an old cowboy ought to. I've never inquired into his background or his past business. He might be a little long in the tooth for you. I'd reckon he's pushing forty. Might be past it. But he can still put in a day's work with any hand I've got on the place. I don't know him all that well because he ain't the kind of man that encourages a lot of talk. But he's worked for me 'bout four years an' I've never had no complaints."

Warner said, "The sheriff is going with me."

"Harvey?" Tom Birdsong gave a little laugh. "What's that ol' dog want to go to messin' around for in somethin' that might be a little dangerous?"

"He's a better man than I first thought he was," Warner said.

"Well, what about Willis? You want me to call him in? I can spare him, but it's up to him if he wants to give you the time. How much time you talking about anyway?"

"Can't be more than five days. That's all the time I intend to give it. I expect it to be less."

"All right," Tom Birdsong said. He clapped his hands for one of the housewomen and, when she came in, gave her orders to have Willis Drake sent in.

While they waited Tom said, "So you're going to the mountain."

Warner said, "Well, I sent the son of a bitch two telegrams and it wouldn't come to me so I don't see where I got no selection."

Willis Drake came in a few minutes later and Warner liked him on sight. He was a short, bowlegged man with a weathered face and thinning hair. He had his hat in his hand, but he was just carrying it casually. He hadn't taken it off because he'd come into the presence of the boss. There was a capable, calm look about him that took Warner's eye. Tom Birdsong made the introductions and Warner got up to shake the man's hand. Still standing, and without going into much detail, he laid out the job for Drake. He finished by saying, "Most of the time you are going to be sitting in a stock car with a shotgun across your knees guarding three prisoners. Some folks may try to get at those prisoners or they may not. I don't know. But the only time you'll be obliged to shoot is if somebody is shooting at you or about to shoot at you."

Willis studied over the proposition for a moment and then nodded his head. He said, "Arright. I'll work fer you. Onliest thing I ast is if you kin let me have ten dollar. I owe one of the hands here ten dollar an' I'd like to git him paid off case somethin' was to happen to me. Wouldn't want to see the man out his money."

Warner took out his roll and handed Willis the money. He said, "Be ready to leave with me day after tomorrow morning."

After Drake was gone Tom Birdsong didn't say anything for a moment, just fiddled with the spoon on the saucer of his coffee cup. Finally, he said, "Warner, you dead certain you know what you're doing?"

It took him by surprise. He said, slowly, "I think I do. Seems the only thing to do."

Tom lifted his chin. "How much money you out of pocket now?"

Warner shrugged. "I don't know. I could count up, but I'd reckon it to be going on for two hundred dollars."

"With how much more promised? To the sheriff and Drake there and what you'll owe the railroad and God only knows what other expenses you will run into?"

Warner frowned. He said, "Hell, Tom, I don't see what that has got to do with it. This piddling amount of money I'm laying out is nothing besides that twenty-five-hundred-dollar pot I'm playing for. I——"

Tom Birdsong put up his hand. He said, "Hold it right there. That's what I'm talking about. One minute you are angry because you think that bank is not on the up and up and the next you are going, come hell or high water, to collect the reward. Now which is it? Are you on an errand of justice or are you after the money?"

Warner frowned again. He said, "Well, I don't see where you can split the two matters. They appear to be one and the same to me. I don't get you."

Tom fiddled with his spoon for another half a minute. He said, "All right, we'll let that simmer for the time being. But there's another thought comes to my mind. You are going into a strange town and you are going to take on a bank. At least that's what you think. Only it will be one hell of a lot more than just that bank you'll be facing. Don't you reckon that bank will have the local law in with them? Especially if they are doing something crooked? The town marshal, the sheriff, and his deputies? Have you given any thought to that?"

"Well, of course I've given some thought to it. Hell, Tom." Warner looked injured. "I didn't just crawl out of a gopher hole."

"Well, what are you going to do about it?"

Warner looked agitated. "How the hell do I know until I get there? Hell! I don't know what I'm up against."

"That's my point. You *don't* know what you're up against and yet you are going to go boring right straight ahead. Where'd you learn to think like that? How did you get so goddamned cocksure of yourself?"

Warner stared at the old man for a moment. He said, "Well, in point of fact I never took myself for being cocksure. But you know who learned me and who raised me and who give me my way of looking at a matter."

Tom Birdsong's eyes narrowed. He said, "If you're talking about your grandfather you've got holt of the wrong end of the stick. If there was one thing that Carver Grayson wasn't it was cocksure. He was—"

Warner raised his chin slightly. He said, "You ain't gonna tell me he didn't go straight ahead when he thought he was right."

Tom Birdsong stared at Warner for a moment. He said, "I don't want to bring your granddaddy down in your eyes none, but, yes, there were times when Carver thought he was right and did not forge ahead."

"I don't believe it."

"Believe what you want. Your grandfather was a human man. We lived in a rough country in rough times. I know you think times are rough now, but they was double rough then and the men that settled this country were double rough. You think Carver was hard as nails. He was, but ain't never been a nail wouldn't bend if you hit it with a hammer hard enough. Carver was as brave a man as I've ever known, but he wasn't a damn fool. And he wasn't a show-off. He didn't go rushing in just to prove he could. He thought matters out, he made him a plan to succeed. There was never any boast or brag to Carver. He was a man who knew when to gee and when to haw, something I don't think you've learned yet. Do you really never doubt yourself? Or is that just what you've got yourself fooled into believing?"

Warner stared at Tom, blinking. He didn't say anything.

Tom Birdsong continued. "If you've tried to pattern yourself on Carver Grayson you have been going at it all wrong. First of all, you weren't old enough to have known him long enough to see who he really was. He was a man with his doubts, his fears, his worries. As I've said, he was the best man I've ever known, but he was only a man. And he knew it."

Warner said, almost hesitantly, "He doubted himself? From time to time?"

"Hell yes. What man doesn't?"

"And he was afeared? From time to time?"

"Of course he was. You show me a man that's never been afraid and I'll show you a lunatic. And Carver backed off from time to time. When it was common sense. Look here, boy . . . ain't no man going to win all his battles. Try and win more than you lose. And don't lose a big one that can be avoided."

Warner looked away, a torrent of thoughts and memories running through his mind. He was silent a few long moments, thinking of the mold he thought he was expected to fit and despairing of ever fitting. He said, huskily, "I reckon I've overloaded my ass a few times trying to live up to what I thought the old man would have done."

Tom Birdsong said, "Of course you have. You seen him bigger than nature. He was big enough as it was. I can't reckon how a teenage boy would have seen him. But I think it would grieve him you going around with the wrong idea and taking more of a load on your shoulders than you need to over some idea of what he would have expected of you. The man left big boots, ain't no question of that. But, hell, I was sired by a curly wolf and suckled by a she bear and I can't fill his boots." He laughed and clapped Warner on the shoulder. "All he ever wanted you to do was what you thought the right thing was. 'Be able to sleep with yourself at night,' that's what he used to tell me. So now you can unload the wagon about halfway."

Warner smiled, ruefully. He said, "It's a hell of a chore acting like you ain't scairt of nothing, when you're about to spook."

"I'm glad to hear you admit that. Ain't nothing wrong with being afeared. Now. Does that mean you'll give further thought to this business in Round Rock? Maybe give some thought to getting on back to your own business?"

Warner shook his head slowly. He said, "Well, yes and no. I reckon I still got to see this Round Rock matter through. It plagues me as a concern that needs looking into."

Tom Birdsong stared at him blankly. "Then what have I been doing all this talking for?"

Warner said, "Well, it hasn't been wasted. I feel considerably relieved about the size of the boots I've got to fill. And it is also going to make me considerably more cautious in the way I approach the situation." A small smile came into his eyes. "I had planned to go rushing right in and declare myself the grandson of Carver Grayson and the grandfriend of Tom Birdsong, but I'll lay off that now."

Tom gave him a fixed look. He said, "I feel ever so good about that."

Warner said, "But, seriously, you have given me thought about the law. They are a factor I hadn't given as much thought to as I should. I will now."

Tom stood up and reached for a bottle of whiskey. "Well just don't get cocksure."

Warner said, "No, sir. Especially not like some little banty roosters I've heard would go on the prod against the Devil himself."

That night, lying in bed, he thought about all of what Tom had said and he couldn't help feeling a sense of relief, a sense that some sort of weight had been lifted from his shoulders. He reckoned himself to be as brave as the next man, but sometimes it got to be a chore to never let anything show except hard words and an even harder face.

Next morning, he and the carpenter, J. C. Cook, were inside the cattle car that had been spotted off from the main line on a siding. J. C. Cook was a slow-moving man who chewed tobacco and looked matters over for a long time. They were inside the slatted cattle car. Warner was explaining to Cook that he wanted a barred wall built across the middle of the car, starting behind the two side loading doors. Warner said, "I want you to take two-by-fours and build me a wall. Set the two-by-fours close enough so a man can't wiggle through."

"Yessir," Cook said, chewing his tobacco slowly.

Warner said, "Think of it like a cell, only with the bars made out of wood. Run a couple of stringers across to make it stronger. I don't want two or three men to be able to throw their weight against it and force it down."

Mr. Cook said "Yessir," still chewing his tobacco slowly.

"And then you got to make a door in it. Make it where it joins one side of the car. Make it a narrow door so only one man can go through at a time. And, of course, you've got to put hinges and a hasp so it can be padlocked. You got all that?"

Cook studied the matter for a few minutes and then shrugged. He said, "Ah reckon. Don't seem so hard. Jest want a jail door is what you be sayin'. Only out of wood."

"That's right. Need it finished by tonight."

Cook stopped chewing. "Tanight?"

"Yep. There's a train at ten tomorrow morning. This car is going to be hooked on to it."

Mr. Cook started looking worried. He said, "Tha's a considerable 'mount o' work fer jest the one day."

Warner took two twenty-dollar bills out of his pocket. He said, "There's for the materials and the best day's wages you'll ever have made. And don't forget to get me a good padlock. Now, can you do it?"

Cook looked at the money in his hand, his face as animated as it ever got. It was a lot of money for a man used to making two or three dollars a day at the most. His wagon with its team of mules was outside and he knew the lumberyard had the materials he needed. He said, "Ah reckon."

Warner shook his head. "Don't reckon you can do it. I've got to *know*."

Mr. Cook sighed. It made him nervous to be asked to be so definite. But he did have forty dollars in his hand. He said, "Wall, shore. I'll git it done."

Since he didn't plan to help, Warner mounted his horse and started slowly past the train depot. He was expecting a visit from the stationmaster and he was not disappointed. All morning, while he'd been explaining to J. C. Cook what he wanted, he'd noticed Homer Long peering out windows and lurking about the platform of the depot. Now, as he rode past, Mr. Long came popping out the door of the station, clearing his throat. He said, "Uh, Mr. Grayson, Mr. Grayson?"

Warner reined in his horse. "What?"

Mr. Long said, "Uh, Mr. Grayson, uh, what are you adoing to that stock car?"

"Mr. Long, I am having that stock car improved."

"Well, now, now, listen here. That car is property of the Texas and Rio Grande railroad. You can't go to makin' changes in its rollin' stock. I—"

Warner said, cutting him off, "Mr. Long, if I don't return that car to the railroad in exactly the same shape as I took it I will buy the son of a bitch. Do you understand? And I will sign a paper to that effect. But you ain't going to tell me you haven't seen partitions put up in stock cars when a man is shipping different kinds of stock, are you?"

"Well . . ."

"Have you, Mr. Long? Or have you not?"

"Well . . . well, yeah, o' course. But it's gen'lly the railroad what makes the modifications."

"Then let's say that I'm saving them some money."

Long shook his head. He said, "Well, this is the damnedest affair I ever seen an' I been with the railroad fer near on thirty year."

"Homer," Warner said, "take it easy. I ain't going to hurt your cattle car."

He rode into town, stopped by the jail, and got the sheriff to go to an early lunch at the café next door. They got sat down and ordered the blue plate special, which was pork chops and collard greens and mashed potatoes with biscuits and gravy. When their food had come Warner told the sheriff they'd be leaving the next morning. He said, "Better kiss the wife good-bye tonight because we are going to get mighty busy in the morning."

Harvey chewed a moment and then said, "What we gonna be so busy doing in the morning?"

"Well, J.C. is busy building me a rolling jail in a cattle car. We'll need to get that provisioned for us guards and the prisoners. And we'll be taking two horses, so we'll need feed and water for them. The two horses are mine and that pinto the man I killed was riding. You and your helper, a man off Tom Birdsong's ranch, won't need a horse since you'll be inside the car guarding the prisoners except when I relieve one of you."

"What we going to be guardin' them from? Escapin'?"

"Well, that. But I'm hopin' to attract some business from certain folks in Round Rock."

"I see." The sheriff bit into a biscuit and chewed slowly. "You figure there's still folks hangin' around Round Rock that knows or had a hand in that robbery?"

Warner shook his head. "Harvey, I don't *know* nothing. I'm doing a lot of guessing here and I'm guessing that when word gets out that we've got the men was supposed to have robbed the bank it will cause a stir. And sometimes, when you kick up a stir, information comes out that you couldn't have got no other way."

"You must also think that stir is gonna cause some trouble else you wouldn't be wantin' a couple of shotgun hands."

"I won't lie to you. There is that. It could happen."

Harvey drank some coffee. He said, "Well, then it's jest as well I ain't got no wife to kiss good-bye. She run off about ten years ago with a travelin' horse trader."

Warner flushed slightly. He said, instantly, "Harvey, I'm sorry. It was a figure of speech. I didn't know one way or the other about your matrimonial situation." Then, as a thought crossed his mind, he said, awkwardly, "Well, if you get right down to it, I'm kind of a horse trader. I hope you ain't got no ill will toward the whole bunch of us."

Harvey shook his head. "Naw, as a matter of fact I'd like to find the man just to shake his hand. But if I was to go looking fer him I'd start with one of them places they put insane people. I'd figure if he kept Myrtle around long enough she'd've drove him crazy. She had a pretty good start on me."

By nine o'clock the next morning they were all ready to go, waiting only for the ten o'clock train to hook them up. The prisoners were in the cell that J. C. Cook had built and, using a wagon that the sheriff had borrowed, they'd loaded the guard's end of the cattle car with provisions for a week and feed and water for the horses. The horses made the guard's end a little crowded, but they had the biggest part of the car so they couldn't very well put the animals in with the prisoners. The sheriff had arranged for a half a dozen small chairs and stools to be borrowed and everybody, prisoners included, had a seat. As it had turned out, Willis Drake hadn't had a shotgun, so the sheriff had had to loan him one of his twelve-gauges. In addition they all had rifles and revolvers and plenty of ammunition.

They had gotten lucky on their route. Their train would go into San Antonio, drop off their car, and they'd be connected to another train heading to Austin and on through Round Rock on its way to Dallas. All told, the trip shouldn't take more than eight hours counting the two- or three-hour layover in the San Antonio yard.

Warner was standing outside the car, waiting on the northbound freight coming up from the border, when he spied four horsemen heading toward them from town. From inside the car he heard the sheriff say, in a disgusted voice, "Aw, hell!"

Warner looked around. "What's the matter?"

"It's that goddamn Elton Pomroy."

"What's he want?"

"Want? He *wants* anything he can get his hands on. Right now he wants to make trouble."

Warner was smoking a cigarillo. He took one last draw as the horsemen neared and then dropped it and ground it under his heel. He said, "What if I don't want no trouble?"

"Elton don't give a damn what the other feller wants."

"Maybe I can make him give a damn."

"Good luck."

"Who are the other three with him?"

"Well, one of 'em is the town marshal. You'll remember him. The other two is a couple of ne'er-do-wells he's drug out of the saloon an' likely sworn in as town deputy marshals."

"Any of them dangerous?"

The sheriff said, "I person'lly consider anybody carryin' a gun is dangerous."

"But are they any good?"

"With a gun or a bottle? They hell with a bottle. I'd imagine at least two of 'em are already lit up, the two that the mayor drug out of the saloon and swore in. Elton wouldn't touch the stuff 'less there was money in it. Or votes. I don't know about George."

The riders came on until they were about ten yards away and then the mayor put up his hand and they pulled their horses to a halt. He said, raising his hand in the air, "As the duly elected mayor of this town I demand, *demand,* that you turn them thar prisoners over to me an' my duly an' legally swore-in marshals. You leave town with them prisoners and you be in violation of city codes. They ain't in that jailhouse no more that the county rents, so they belong to the town of Hondo, Texas, an you will hand them over to me! And be right quick about it."

Warner looked the four over, from the banty rooster red-faced mayor to his sad-faced, dried-up marshal to the two saloon bums he claimed were duly sworn deputies. As he looked at them he noticed that the saloon tough next to the mayor had a rifle across the pommel of his saddle. The stock of the rifle was pointing at the mayor and the stock was broadside to Warner, making a nice target six or seven inches wide. And the range was not all that much. The party had gradually eased forward until they were only five or six paces away. Warner straightened up. He said, "Mayor, git!"

The mayor raised his right hand and began to talk. As the first words left his mouth Warner drew his revolver in a smooth motion, cocking it as he did. In the same motion he aimed and fired. The slug hit the stock of the rifle a little below the center line and toward the butt. The force of the slug sent the rifle spinning up in the air and sideways, splinters flying from the stock. The rifle whirled up and hit the mayor's horse on the neck. The startled animal let out a loud snort and jumped backward and then turned and bolted back toward town. They all watched, fascinated, even the "marshals," as the horse raced across the prairie with the mayor grabbing at the reins and swaying in the saddle. Then, after about a hundred yards, the horse suddenly pulled up and went to bucking. On the first jump the mayor lost his right stirrup. On the second he pitched headfirst off the horse and landed in the weeds.

The three men turned back to look at Warner.

Warner said, "Git. Now."

The man who'd lost his rifle pointed at it on the ground and said, "Goddamn, you've blowed my—"

Warner cocked his revolver. The sound was very loud. He has it down by his side. He said, "I got to go to the trouble to bring this weapon up I'm going to use it."

The town marshal said, "We be goin', we be goin'."

Warner watched them ride away. When they got to the mayor, the town marshal got down to help him. The two saloon recruits kept riding. Behind him Warner could hear Harvey laughing like he was never going to stop.

"Harvey, you ain't supposed to laugh at that. That's your mayor."

The sheriff said, "That man has got to be the biggest fool in Matagorda County. We ain't even in the city he's the mayor of. Lord, that was funny."

Not much later the northbound train arrived and hooked them into the long line of freight cars. Before they pulled out of the station Les said to Warner, "You ain't takin' us to no hangin', are you, Mr. Grayson?"

Warner said, "If there's a hanging it won't be yours. Not if you've told me the truth."

"We told you our truth, what we know. What Darcey and Jake done we don't know about. But we still might git blamed fer it."

Warner said, "You do what I tell you and say what I tell you to say and you'll be all right. Now settle down. We got a long ride ahead of us."

It was almost six o'clock when a switching engine left their car on a siding a quarter of a mile from the depot and a mile and a half from the town. They'd been delayed by a late-arriving train in San Antonio and then the train had had to wait on other trains making use of the switching facilities. Consequently it was going on for dark by the time they were settled into their resting place in Round Rock. On the way they'd made a good lunch out of ham and cheese and some fried chicken Warner had brought from the café. He'd brought along a big sack of four dozen biscuits and plenty of canned goods, and he figured that and the twenty-pound smoked ham and the cheese ought to see them through for a few days. If it didn't they could always reprovision right there in Round Rock. They'd had water to drink and Warner had passed the whiskey bottle around, even among the prisoners. The only man who hadn't drunk had been Willis, who'd said that he'd drunk up his share a few years back. It was one of the few remarks he'd made the whole trip. Warner had decided that Willis and Harvey made a nice balance. One talked a little too much and the other didn't talk at all. But they were both alert and both gave off an air of seriousness about the shotguns, which they never left far from hand.

It had been a dusty, windy, cramped, uncomfortable ride. When the car was sitting still it was hot; when the train was moving the wind blew through the slats swirling the dust and hay and, as Harvey said, "anythang under the weight of a blacksmith's anvil." They'd brought along a wooden ramp to load and unload the horses and Warner slid back the side door on one side and they all three wrestled the ramp into place. While he tightened the girth on his saddle Warner told the other two that he reckoned the first step was to get into town and find his partner and see what new information she might have for him. He nodded toward the prisoners and said, "If one of 'em has to go out in the bushes just one of y'all take him. I don't really expect no trouble tonight, but y'all ought to figure on watch and watch about until I get back. I'm going to stop at the depot office—loan me your badge, Harvey—and tell them I don't want any yard workers coming around this car. So figure that anyone approaching is hostile."

Harvey said, "I can't see no trouble tonight, Warner. They can't know we be here."

"I can't either. But would you rather be ready or dead?"

Willis said, quietly, "We'll be ready."

Before he left, Warner said to the prisoners, "I know it ain't the Palace Hotel in there, but this is as it has to be. So make the best of it. Bitching about it won't get you nothing but trouble. Behave and you'll get your meals and your tobacco and a little whiskey."

Calvin said, in a small voice, "What be gonna happen to us, Mr. Grayson?"

Warner shrugged. "I don't know. To tell you the truth, Calvin, I'm using you for bait. I'm going to put it out around town that I've got the bank robbers and then I'm going to see what happens."

Otis Quinn came jumping off his chair. He said, "What!? Say, you cain't do that! Thet ain't raight!"

Les said, quietly, "Oh, sit down, Otis. Can't you see he be joshin' you. He ain't gonna do no such thang, be you, Mr. Grayson?"

But Otis was not so easily mollified. He said, "He *ain't* joshin', Les. He means what he's sayin'!"

Warner said, "Contain yourself, Otis. You'll rupture a blood vessel you keep on that way."

Les said, "See?"

Otis sat back down, but he was not content. He said, "I believe the man. I believe he was speakin' the truth."

Warner led the Andalusian down the ramp. The sheriff came down behind him. He said, "Now don't git that badge in no trouble. You hear?"

"I'm just gonna flash it at the stationmaster so he'll understand to warn any curious yard hands away from the boxcar. Tell him we're transporting prisoners. You can tell him if you'd druther."

Harvey shook his head. "*I* was joshin', as Otis said. Fact of the bid'ness, you look more like a sheriff than I do. You keep the badge an' I'll tell folks I'm just a hired gun."

Warner mounted. "Don't be silly, Harvey. Was never a sheriff looked more the part than you. Besides, I could never sit behind the desk them long hours like you do. Ain't got the padding. Look here, I don't know what time I might get back. It's important I get as much a line on matters as I can. I might not be back at all."

"Where's your partner staying?"

"I don't know. But, if I know her, it'll be the best hotel in town. I'll find her. How big you reckon this place is? Looks pretty good-sized from here."

With darkness coming on and the lamps being lit the town seemed to spread out for a considerable distance. Harvey said, "Five thousand? Six? Hell, I don't rightly know, but I hear it's a pretty good-sized place."

"Y'all take care. I'll be back quick's I can."

He carefully picked his way through the tangle of rails in the siding yard and then rode to the depot to have a word with the stationmaster. After that he started for town, armed with the information that the Castle Hotel was the biggest and grandest place in town. There wasn't the slightest doubt in his mind that it was there that the widow Pico could be found. And, as he had thought, when he asked at the desk after Laura Pico he was told that, yes, she was a guest at the hotel. But the clerk added, looking him over, "I don't think right now would be a good time to disturb Mrs. Pico. She has just ordered some supper sent up to her suite. She's dining in."

Warner was well aware that he looked like a man who had spent all day in a boxcar and probably smelled like one. And if he hadn't been aware of it the look on the desk clerk's face would have confirmed it.

He said, "You say she's got a suite of rooms?"

"That is correct."

"That be more than one?"

"That also is correct," the clerk said stiffly.

"What number did you say it was?"

"I did not say."

Warner took out his wallet and found an old feed bill. He handed this to the desk clerk. He said, "Would you see that *Mrs.* Pico gets that right away?"

The clerk didn't answer, just turned to the rack of pigeonholes behind him. Warner saw him put it in number 210. As he headed for the stairway he called back to the clerk, "Have me a steak and all the fixings sent up to Mrs. Pico's suite. And a bottle of good whiskey. And be damn quick about it."

The clerk pointed his arm and snapped his fingers and said, "Here, you can't—"

113

"Oh, yes I can," Warner said, already taking the curving stairs two at a time, and he was planning on having a word or two with the widow Pico about staying in such an obviously expensive and lavish hotel. She'd better damn well be doing it on her own money because the partnership wasn't paying for such accommodations.

He stopped at the head of the marble stairs, standing on the landing that was covered with a blue rug, and looked down at the desk clerk, who was staring up at him. "Which way?" he asked.

The desk clerk said, "Look here! Just who do you think you are? You can't go busting in on a lady like Mrs. Pico!"

"The hell I can't. I'm her damn boss. Now which way? To the right or the left?"

The clerk made a feeble motion. "To the left."

Warner said, "And I want that steak done, you hear me? Don't you send me no raw cow up here. And when I say good whiskey that's exactly what I mean."

The desk clerk called back, "She's got company, you know. Likely she will not take kindly to you barging in when they are having their dinner."

Warner took a step down the stairs in the direction of the clerk. He had worn Harvey's badge to talk to the station-master and then put it in his shirt pocket. Now he took it out and pinned it to his shirt. He said, "Mister, you are starting to aggravate me. How aggravated do you want me to get?"

The clerk took a step backward. He said, "I was trying to warn you, Sheriff. I meant no harm. I take it you are a sheriff though you are not our sheriff. But she is dining with *our* mayor so I thought you might want to know that."

"Well," Warner said, "I see your point. I am no longer aggravated. Now get busy about that steak and whiskey. Or do they already have whiskey?"

"They are drinking wine, I believe."

He didn't bother replying, but walked down the carpeted hall looking for 210, wondering who had invented the word *suite* and why. Wasn't anything sweet about it, it was another way of charging you more for what other places called a set of rooms or just rooms. But look to the widow Pico to have to have a suite. Well, that was damn *sure* the only thing sweet about her.

Except in bed. Little images started to flitter through his mind, but he fought them off. He'd been on the trail and in the company of men too long to go to remembering some of those moments between the sheets with her soft, smooth body. A pair of jeans didn't have a whole hell of a lot of extra room in them. A wallet and a pocket knife strained their capacity. Anything else was an overload that would be obvious even to the most casual eye. Of course, if she wasn't receiving the mayor it might be a different story.

He got to the door of room 210 and knocked. After a moment he heard some rustling around. He knocked again and heard Laura's distinct voice say, "Oh, hell, now who the hell can that be? If it's the damn waiter from the dining room I'm going to teach him his job."

The door was suddenly flung open and Laura stood there. Her butter-colored hair with a faint tinge of strawberry was pulled back and tied in the middle with a bow. She was wearing a light tan linen gown that did nothing to detract from what he knew firsthand and at close range was under there. The neckline of her gown was cut off square so that it suggested the swell of her—as far as he was concerned—perfectly sized breasts. Looking down he took in the gather of the gown at her waistline that showed off her slim waist and the flare of her hips. Peeking out at the hem of her gown he could see the shiny black tips of her patent leather pumps. He knew they had little silver buckles on them, but he couldn't see them.

She said dryly, "Seen enough?"

He said, "I always try and get in a quick look before you open your mouth and spoil the effect."

Then she looked him up and down. "How long since you've considered shaving or having a bath?"

"I'm getting a little tired of standing out in this hall, Laura."

"Oh, did you want to come in?"

He said, "Naw, I knocked on the door to see if it was wooden."

"Well, try and manage your manners. I've got company."

"So I heard."

She stepped aside and he preceded her down a short hall and into a small sitting room, where a dining table had been set up. Sitting there was a diminutive woman with soft, light auburn hair and soft features that blended agreeably together. Where Laura was striking and handsome without being beautiful, this woman was pretty without quite being beautiful. Warner's eyes immediately were taken by the swell of her bosom and the way her hair fell to her shoulders. She was wearing a light blue gingham gown faced with velvet On sight of her Warner stopped short. He said, "How do you do? I'm Mrs. Pico's partner."

Laura had come around him back to her chair at the table. She said, "This is Mrs. Martha Roads."

Warner was going to make a slight bow, but the woman put out her hand and he took the small, soft article by the tips of her fingers and gave it a slight shake. She said, "I'm pleasured to meet you, Mr. Grayson. Mrs. Pico has told me considerable about you." Her voice was throaty, low, and controlled, the words coming out precisely and not run together.

Laura said, "There is another chair in the bedroom, Warner. You'd better get it."

As he fetched the chair he was wondering where the mayor was. He felt sure the lady was the mayor's wife, but he couldn't imagine where the mayor had gotten to.

If he'd had to leave, one would have expected his chair to still be in place. But he figured he'd find out about that later. He sat his chair down at the table so he was facing both women. They had apparently finished dinner and were now having some sort of dessert and coffee. The dishes from their meal were sitting on a sideboard and it appeared, from the remains of the carcass, that they'd had baked chicken. He said to Laura, "I've sent for a steak and a bottle of whiskey, but if you've got any handy it will save me a wait."

"I have some brandy," she said.

"That will have to do."

"If you want any it will have to do." She got up and went to the sideboard and opened a cabinet door and took out a bottle and poured him out a tumbler of cognac. She set it in front of him. She stood by with the bottle.

He gave both the ladies a slight nod and then drank off half the glass. Laura, as if she had known what to expect, filled his tumbler back up, put the cork back in the bottle, and set it on the table.

She sat down and said, "Well, tell us the latest. What have you found out?"

He glanced at Mrs. Roads and then at Laura. He said, "The desk clerk told me the mayor was up here."

"She is."

"Who is?"

"The mayor."

"What mayor?"

Laura indicated Martha Roads. "This is Mayor Martha Roads. Who were you expecting, some portly gentleman wearing suspenders and muttonchop whiskers?"

He turned and started at Martha Roads, not conscious that he was staring, but looking at her as if he'd just noticed her. He said, "You're the mayor? Of this town? Of Round Rock?"

She said, "What's the matter, haven't you ever seen a woman mayor before?"

In her question, well hidden in her soft, precise way of speaking, he caught a hint of steel. She was smiling at him, and there was amusement behind her eyes. He said, awkwardly, "Well . . . well, no, I can't say that I ever have. Heard of a lady mayor before. You sure you ain't the wife of the mayor, a kind of stand-in mayor?"

She said, in her throaty voice, but with the steel even more evident, "My husband is the furthest thing from a mayor you could imagine. He runs a saloon and whorehouse outside the city limits."

Laura suddenly laughed. Warner turned to her, feeling his face coloring. He said, "What the hell strikes you so funny?"

She pointed at him. "I wish you could see your face now. You look like you just swallowed something and you're not quite sure what it is."

He colored more. He said, "Well, damn it, Laura, you might have given me some warning instead of springing it on me like it was some kind of joke. How many lady mayors *you* seen?"

Mayor Roads put out her soft little hand and patted the back of his. She said, "Mr. Grayson, Mrs. Pico didn't mean to embarrass you. It's a long story how I came to be mayor and a rather unusual one. You have every right to be surprised."

He looked at her gratefully. She was, he judged, right in an age group with Laura, whom he knew to be thirty-one or maybe thirty-two. He said to the mayor, "Don't be too sure she didn't set out to embarrass me. Okay, maybe she didn't, but you don't see her passing up the chance, do you?"

Laura said, patting his other hand, and casting a slight frown at the mayor, "Poor baby, I'm sorry."

"You could have mentioned it in the telegram you sent me."

"As much as you gripe about spending money? Why, I wouldn't think of adding any extra words to a telegram."

He gave her a hard look. "Like beast of burden?"

Now she colored.

The mayor said, "What? Did I miss something? What about a beast of burden?"

Laura said, "It's a private joke between Warner and me."

A knock came at the door and Warner got up to let the

waiter in. There was a bottle of good whiskey on the tray. While the waiter was setting his steak with potatoes and green beans on the table, Warner looked at the bill, whistled, gave the waiter a five-dollar bill, and then waved him out the door. He said, "We better collect that reward or this whole trip is going to be a dead loss."

Laura said to Martha Roads, "My partner expects everything to show a profit. I wouldn't call him tight with money, but he expects it to stretch."

Martha Roads said, looking at Warner, "I don't see anything wrong with that."

Warner glowered at Laura. He said, "Some of us have to work for what we get. Unlike some I could take to task from where I'm sitting."

Martha looked amused. "You two sound like an old married couple."

Warner said immediately, "Like hell!"

And Laura said, "Not while there's still breath in my body."

The women finished their desert and coffee and then Laura poured them a brandy. Warner nodded his head sternly at the bottle of whiskey. He was hungry and he finished his steak and the side dishes and then looked a question at Laura. She nodded. She said, "Yes, we discuss our business in front of Martha. She's got a few questions about it herself."

"What about answers?"

The mayor said, "I might have a few of those also. Depends on what you want to know."

Warner said to Laura, "The first thing I want to know is why that goddamn bank didn't reply to my telegrams."

She looked over at the mayor. "It's complicated."

"You told me that in that useless telegram you sent me that didn't say a thing I didn't already know."

Laura said, "Well, it's even more complicated than that. The reason one of the bankers gave as the specific reason for not replying to your telegram was that they'd had about ten of the same ilk. But he wouldn't show them to me. He said they were leaving the matter in the hands of the law enforcement agencies."

"What law enforcement agencies?"

The mayor said, "The sheriff. And that's a laugh."

Warner was getting impatient. He said, "All I want is the goddamn money I got coming on the reward. Now, Laura, who the hell did you see at that bank?"

Laura looked over at the mayor. She said, "Martha, why don't you explain it to him? He's come in here completely convinced that I've made a mess of things and he never should have sent me in the first place. He's not going to believe me when I say it's not a matter of saying, 'I've got your robbers, give me the reward.'"

Martha said, gently, "She's right, Mr. Grayson. The Mercantile is one of two banks here in town. They're about the same and mainly make farm and ranch loans and charge people to take care of their money for them."

"Sounds like they done a poor job of that."

"This bank, the Mercantile, is one of the oldest in this part of Texas. Its president is a man named Bob Thomas. The vice president and treasurer is Harry Wallace. Wilbur Crabtree is the cashier. He's been at the bank a number of years, but Wallace and Thomas came in a couple of years ago and bought controlling interest for what I hear is around forty thousand dollars. The reason I'm pretty familiar with the bank is that my husband is a stockholder and Wilbur Crabtree"—she made a slight face—"is on the city council. One of six members. Besides those three officers there are two tellers, Wilma Bainbridge, who is a spinster in her late thirties, and Wayne Goddard, who is a young man just getting started."

"That's the sum total of the people that was in the bank when it was robbed?"

"If it was robbed. And Wilma Bainbridge wasn't there. She'd been out a couple of days with the grippe."

Warner gave the mayor a look. "Did I hear you right? Did I hear you say 'if' it was robbed?"

"You did."

"You care to talk about that?"

Martha Roads got up. She said, "I think you and Mrs. Pico should have a talk first. She has told me considerable about you." She said the last dryly. "I think it's better that she fills you in slowly. So I'm going to go along now. When you think you have a good picture of the situation we'll have another talk."

Warner said, "It might be that I know a considerable amount that neither of you know and maybe nobody else in this town knows except the scoundrels involved."

The mayor said, as she moved toward the door, "From what Mrs. Pico has told me about you, that wouldn't surprise me in the least. Laura, I can see myself out. Thanks for a good dinner."

But Laura walked her to the door. Warner heard her ask the mayor if she'd tell the desk clerk to have someone come up on her way out. Then they exchanged good-byes and Laura came back in the room. She took a position to the side of the table and put her hands on her hips and appraised Warner for a long moment.

She said, "When did we go into the reward business? I thought we were horse breeders."

He said, "It's a long story. Right now I'm the one who wants some answers. I also want a kiss."

She bent over and put her hands behind his head and kissed him for a long moment, her lips parting and moving against his. Then she straightened up and was all business again. She took a chair across from him and folded her hands on the table and said, "Now, tell me what this is all about. You send me on an errand and expect me to work blind."

"Before that I want to know what this damn town is doing with a woman mayor. Or are you pulling my leg? Who in hell would elect a woman mayor?"

Laura arched an eyebrow at him. "She is not only the mayor, she is the city court judge and the justice of the peace. All three jobs go together. As to how she got elected—well, it's about as strange as some of the affairs you get up to. First off, women can vote in this town."

Warner sat up straighter in his chair. "Get out of here! What are you talking about? Women voting?"

"I know," Laura said dryly. "And next we'll be wanting to eat at the same table with you. Round Rock grew to prominence during the Civil War, and so many men were gone that the women had to run a lot of matters out of

necessity. Then came Reconstruction and so many carpet-
baggers and scalawags came in and tried to take over the
town that the local women were given the vote in order to
hold the town against the invaders. The law never got
repealed. I know that horrifies you, but it happened."

"So the women elected Martha, is that her name?"

She gave him a look. "Don't give me that business about
not remembering her name. You two were doing enough
hand touching I felt like I should leave the room. But, no, it
wasn't only the women. The city council is divided three
and three, bitterly. And each side thought if they got a
mayor in they thought they could push around, it would be
them doing the pushing. Except both sides got fooled. They
thought they'd get a gentle little soul, and Martha looks it,
who'd come to council meetings wearing an apron with flour
on the end of her nose and she'd do whatever she was told.
Unfortunately for them, they picked the wrong woman. She
does more pushing than they do. And if she gives a favor to
one side she expects one back. That woman collects chits
like a poker player does chips." She gave him a cool look. "I
wouldn't be playing hanky-panky with her, Mr. Grayson.
She's a little out of your league."

Warner said, "Sounds to me like somebody in this room
wearing nearly blond hair is making jealous noises."

"Me?" Laura looked at him. "Jealous of her? Don't make
me laugh."

"Laugh is not what I make you do," Warner said. "Sounds
to me more like moaning and screaming."

Laura said, "Oh, shut your nasty mouth and tell me what
the hell is going on."

Warner said, "I will. But first tell me this woman mayor
stuff ain't likely to spread."

Laura took a sip of brandy. "No," she said, "it's strictly
local. And a very unusual circumstance. Now, goddammit,
tell me what all this is about."

Warner told it from first to last, beginning with the
attempt to rob him on the road, taking in every detail he
could think of, and ending with his cattle-car jail sitting on
the rail siding not three miles from where he was. Warner
had expected Laura to be specifically interested in the three
prisoners' consistent denial that they'd had anything to do

with any bank robbery anywhere, but she surprised him by saying, "Show me your side."

He blinked. "Do what?"

"Pull up your shirt. I want to see where that man cut you. I want to see how bad it is."

He grimaced. He said, "Are you out of your damn mind? It's nearly well and it never was much to begin with."

"Nevertheless, I want—"

A knock came at the door. Laura leaned toward the hall and said, "Come in."

Warner turned to see who it was and his side immediately reminded him that it wasn't completely well. He very nearly let it show on his face. It was the desk clerk from downstairs. The clerk said, "Yes, ma'am, Mrs. Pico. You sent for someone?"

She said, "Henry, is it too late to light the boilers so we might have some hot water for a bath? My brother and business partner has a wound that needs to soak."

The desk clerk said, "There may still be some hot water in the roof cistern, Mrs. Pico, but I'll light the boiler again, just in case. Will that be all, Mrs. Pico, or is there anything else I can do?"

"That will be all, Henry. Thank you."

When he heard the door close Warner said, in a falsetto voice, "Es they anythin' else I kin do fer you, Mizz Pico? Git in yur britches? Kiss your feet?"

"You're not funny, Warner. Henry is a nice little man." She stood up. She said, "Now, come along and let's get you undressed. This hotel has got the biggest bathtub I've ever seen. You need a good soak and a good soaping. You are filthy."

He said, "What's the good of taking a bath? I ain't got but these clothes to put back on and they may never get clean again."

She said, "You're not sleeping with me until you've had a bath. I'll go out in the morning and get you some new jeans and a shirt and socks."

He was tired and the idea of a bath was very appealing. He scratched his neck. He said, "I got whiskers. Which you always complain about. And no razor."

She said, "I have a razor."

He looked at her in some amazement. "Were you expecting me? Or just any man who might need a shave?"

She said, "I believe when we first met, you let on to me in your best-man-around-town manner that you were not so inexperienced when it came to women."

He was struggling with one of his boots, trying to act like it didn't hurt his side as he pulled it off. He said, "Sometimes I think I regret every word I've ever said to you. They always come back. Worse than an egg-sucking dog. Can't get rid of them."

Laura said, "Well, if you are such a hand around the ladies you might have known that the more elegant ones shave their legs. Of course, the kind you're used to probably need to shave more than just their lower legs."

He reached out and made a grab at her, but she was too quick for him, backing away laughing. She said, "Oh, I'm sorry if that one hit home. Maybe you'd be more comfortable if I wore woolen underwear and smelled like I'd been tending pigs."

"Laugh," he said. "Go ahead and laugh. And see who gets to stay on her side of the bed all night long."

She said, "Ha, ha. I'd love to see that. I could make you sit up and beg if I was mean enough."

"You're mean enough," he said, "for nearly anything. But I know you, girl. So don't try and work me. It ain't going to do you no good."

He'd finally gotten his other boot off and was standing up, taking off his gun belt and unbuttoning his jeans. She came over and said, "Here, let me help you. You are all thumbs."

He said, "I can take my own clothes off. You go in there and get some water running in the bathtub. Better be hot, too. Of course I know *Henry* wouldn't let *Mrs. Pico* down. He's done got himself smitten, poor fool."

She saw his wound the minute he went into the bathroom. She immediately put both hands to her mouth and said, "Oh, my, Warner. Look at what you've done to yourself!"

He said, "*I* didn't do it to myself, you know."

"Maybe not, but you got careless enough to let someone else do it to you."

He grimaced. "I can't argue with that."

She was sitting on the side of the tub, feeling the water

running out of the two taps. She said, "It's not real hot, but it ought to be warm enough." She looked at his wound again and shook her head. "When are the stitches supposed to come out?"

"Couple or three more days, I guess. At least that's what the doctor in Hondo said." He looked down at it. Most of the swelling and all the redness were gone. He said, "Hell, that don't look bad at all. In fact, it looks nearly well. Maybe I'll hunt me up a doctor tomorrow and get these stitches yanked out."

While he got into the bathtub she took off her gown and hosiery and shoes and sat down on the side of the tub in her camisole. While he washed and soaped she said, "So you feel that the three men you've got in your rolling jail, as you call it, didn't really have anything to do with the bank robbery."

"That's what I feel. Damn it, Laura, they just ain't the type. If you talked to them you'd understand what I mean. They wouldn't know *how* to rob a bank. They are out-of-work cowhands."

"What about the two you killed?"

He said, grimly, "I ain't all that sure about them. I don't know how, because the other three say those two were together, but they might have had a hand in it."

She took the soap from him and began to wash his back, being careful to wash close to the wound but not touch it. She said, "Sounds like you killed the wrong two."

He looked around at her. "Yeah, like I had a selection. Listen, damn it, I don't care who robbed that bank. I just—"

"—want your reward. Well, it might not be as easy to get as you expected."

"Now tell me why that mayor is suspicious about the robbery."

She said, "It first struck her, like it did you, that the people in the bank were damn vague about descriptions of the robbers. Everybody on the street saw them, but the bankers seemed to have gone blind. Then when the reward poster came out she went to the sheriff and wanted to know why the descriptions were so vague, and he said he just took what information he was given, and she asked about the bystanders on the street, and he said what the hell did they know. Then he claimed that he was doing everything that could be done to apprehend the robbers. That was after she noticed that the bankers didn't seem to be all that concerned. So she went to the sheriff and he claimed to have notified the Texas Rangers and the U.S. Marshals Service and the sheriff of every surrounding county. Only she went down to the telegraph office and used her authority as a judge and demanded to see the telegraph logs and no such telegrams had been sent. So she went back to the sheriff and confronted him with that."

Warner said, "I imagine she was getting real popular with the sheriff about that time."

Laura smiled. She said, "Actually, I don't think Martha is very popular with any of the male officials around here. She hasn't exactly lived up to their expectations."

"What did the sheriff say when she caught him in the lie?"

"Got huffy about her checking up on him, told her he worked for the county and not the city of Round Rock, and it wasn't any of her goddamn business how he ran his office. Then he told her he'd sent the notices out by mail and why didn't she go and try and check that."

"By mail?" Warner laughed without humor and said, "Might as well have entrusted them to a small boy. Well, that makes it pretty clear that the bank and maybe the sheriff are not very interested in catching any bank robbers. And I don't believe they got any ten telegrams just like mine."

She took a towel off the wall and told him to stand up. While she was drying him off she said, "But do we really want to get involved in this? What have we got to gain?"

"Twenty-five hundred dollars, that's what."

"Or your pride? Which is it?"

He stepped out of the bathtub and put his arms around her, his face close to hers. He said, "You go get in bed while I wash my teeth and then I'll tell you about my pride."

9

It was about an hour later when he suddenly sat up in bed and swung his legs around. He said, "Aw, hell. What am I thinking about?"

She sat up, the sheet falling away from her breasts. She said, "Where are you going? You're not going back out to that cattle car tonight, are you? I thought you had it well guarded. Besides, nobody knows it's there or who's in it."

He was pulling on his jeans. He said, "It's not that. I left my goddamn horse tied in front of the hotel."

She said, "What!? You left Paseta tied on the street all this time?"

He stood up and looked around at her. He said, "I said I left my *horse* on the street. I don't know anybody named Paseta."

She said, "Don't put those dirty clothes back on. I'll get dressed and go down and have him put in the hotel livery stable."

He said, "I'm just going in my jeans."

"You can't go through the lobby of a hotel like this in your bare feet with no shirt! My heavens, Warner! *Warner! WARNER!*"

He was already out the door.

When he came back up to the room she appeared to be asleep. As quietly as he could he shucked off his jeans and

127

eased into bed beside her. He lay very still, letting the tiredness take him, preparing for sleep. Just as he began to doze off he felt her hand come stealing over his chest and move downward on his belly. He turned over to face her, bringing his mouth close to hers. In a whisper he said, "You know that *this* is the only reason I put up with you."

She went down next morning and bought him some clothes as soon as the dry goods stores had opened at seven. Before that she'd gone down and brought them back up a pot of coffee and he'd sat there in a towel, drinking coffee with a little whiskey in it and smoking a cigarillo while he thought. She'd said, "Does it ever occur to you that I might want to talk in the morning?"

"No," he'd said.

She'd said, "You have all the class of a one-room school."

He'd said, "What's that supposed to mean?"

"I have made my point."

She was able to buy clothes for him because she knew his sizes. She'd often bought him clothes in Corpus Christi when she was coming out to the ranch, and she'd usually gotten it right. But this time she'd bought him whipcord breeches when he'd wanted plain old denim jeans. The shirt had even been a little fancy for his taste, a light linen that would never stand up to a day's work. He said, "Goddammit, Laura, I'm not going to church or to a wedding. Couldn't you have just bought me the kind of clothes that I wear instead of them whipcord riding britches and this fancy shirt? I'm a working horseman, not some dude."

She said, "They're dressier. You're going in to see those bankers, I presume, and I think you ought to look substantial."

"Looking substantial ain't got nothing to do with the clothes on your back. Looking substantial is *knowing* you got money in the bank." He paused. "Well, maybe not this bank."

She said, "I like the way those slim-cut whipcords look on you. I like their taper."

"I like your taper, too," he said. "But that don't mean I want every other son of a bitch looking at it."

After he was dressed they went downstairs and had breakfast in the hotel dining room. He took notice of the quality of the tableware and that even the tablecloth was starched. He said, "How much is it costing to stay in this high-priced cathouse?"

She was eating scrambled eggs, a dish he thought ruined the whole point of an egg. He'd once told her, "The good Lord made the yoke separate from the white. If he'd intended they should be mixed together He'd've done it in the first place. I know that your mission in life is to bring me to heel, but when you go to messing around with the way nature intended an egg to be eaten you are showing your ignorance."

She said, "I'm surprised you've gone this long without asking. Well, it's none of your business. I'm paying for it with my own money, not partnership money. But if you're going to sleep in that suite, you're going to pay your share."

"That's fine with me because I intend on being out to the railyards most of the time. All I'm going to do now is see if I can't bait me a trap."

She stopped eating and put her fork down. She said, "That's what I thought you were doing. You know, don't you, that if you're right, and the mayor's right, that there wasn't a robbery, just five men hired to ride out of town making it look like there was one, that you are asking for trouble? Thirty thousand dollars is a lot of money and if those bankers can hire men to fake a robbery they can also hire men to make sure you don't expose them."

"That's what I'm counting on." He was eating steak and eggs and biscuits with gravy. "But I figure the man I really got to watch is the sheriff. He is either in on it or he is letting it happen. Unless he is deaf and dumb and wrapped in a quilt he's got to know that the way he's been going about it ain't the fastest way to catch bank robbers was ever invented. Oh, yes, Laura, he's got to have a hand in it some way. I don't know how, but he's some little part of it. And if he is, and he's any good, he's my biggest threat."

"When are you going to see him?"

"Just as soon as I establish my legal position at the bank, that I am claiming the reward and that I am there to find out why it ain't been paid."

She gave him a grim look. She said, "Warner, don't get cocky. God knows, I have reason to know how good you are, how capable. But that man has a badge to go with his guns. You can't fight a sheriff the same way you did those Mexican bandits."

He made an offhand motion with half a biscuit. "A thief is a thief. If he's a thief he'll know he is. And I'll let him know I know he is. And then he won't feel so much like a sheriff. He'll feel like a thief."

She shook her head quickly and gave a slight shudder. She said, "I don't know why I don't learn to keep my mouth shut. You never listen to a word I say. You're going to do what you are going to do no matter what. But is it worth it, Warner? It's only twenty-five hundred goddamn dollars. Is that worth risking your life for? You ought to be back at the ranch right now instead of—of . . . She searched for the word. "Instead of chasing some copper-plated golden goose. It's not that damn much money."

He gave her an even look. He said, "I won't be cheated, Laura. It ain't really about the money anymore, though I will have that. I don't like to be played for a fool."

"They're not playing *you* for a fool! Hell, they don't even know you!"

"Eat your mangled eggs. It's nearly nine o'clock. I want to be the first trouble at the bank today."

"Oh, shit!" she said. She slammed down her fork and glared at him.

He said, "Such language for a lady. Now who's got all the class of a schoolhouse?"

"A *one*-room schoolhouse, you hardheaded bastard. You can't even get that right."

He left Laura with the understanding that she would be at either the hotel or the mayor's office and that he would seek her out as soon as he'd scouted the land and tell her what he thought. "But I got to go out to the railyard first. I need to see how matters are there and how the grub is holding up."

The last thing she said was, "At least keep your hole card hidden until you get a look at their hand."

They sometimes played two-handed poker when she came out to the ranch and it was a bitter pill for him that she was a better poker player than he was. If anything had numbers on it she could figure it out while he was still counting up. He'd never seen anyone, man or woman, with her head for figures.

He got his horse out of the livery and then rode straight toward the railyard, looking for the cattle car. Some other freight trains had come in during the night and left cars on the siding, so he had a little difficulty in locating his car. It now had cars on the same track in front of and behind it. He hoped to hell that some railroad employee didn't make a mistake and hitch on his car and haul his prisoners and guards off.

It was about twenty of nine when he rode up, singing out well in advance that it was him. He had no desire to catch a load of buckshot, especially from men he was paying.

The situation was much the same as he'd left it, though the prisoners were getting restless in their small space. Harvey was sitting in the door of the car, his legs dangling over the side. He had his shotgun across his lap. He took a look at Warner and said, "You preachin' this mornin'?"

Warner gave him a look. "Leave the clothes out of it. I didn't buy them. Where's Willis?"

Harvey jerked a thumb over his shoulder. Curled up on the other side of that pinto taking forty winks."

"No problems last night?"

"Naw." Then the sheriff laughed. "Though I scared the hell out of some drunk come stumbling along. He was gonna pull the side door back and find him a place to sleep an' I lit that coal oil lamp all of a sudden an' he let out a scream you coulda heard a mile off."

Warner had not dismounted. The prisoners were crowded up to the slats of the car, obviously wanting to talk to him. He edged his horse down until he was facing them. He said, "How are y'all making out?"

Les said, "Little close in here, Mr. Grayson."

"You ought to be getting plenty of fresh air."

"Oh, we gettin' that," Otis Quinn said. "But a man would like to be able to take more'n three steps in a direction 'thout runnin' up against somethin' solid."

Warner looked over at the sheriff. He said, "What would you think about letting them git out and stretch their legs?"

The sheriff spat tobacco juice and shifted the shotgun in

his lap. "Wouldn't thank nothin' about it a' tall long as they stayed in shotgun range."

"Well, why don't you let them out a little after I'm gone?" He looked at all three. "You try and run and the sheriff will cut you off at the legs. I saw Darcey and I promise you you'd rather he killed you outright."

They set up a chorus of vowing and swearing, which Warner paid not the slightest attention to. When they had subsided telling him just how trustworthy they were he said, "I want to get something straight." He was talking to Les.

"Yessir?"

Warner said, "Y'all was all together, there at the bank, all the time? Y'all were never split up?"

Les looked puzzled. He said, "Well, no, not so's you'd notice. I mean, we wadn't cheek by jowl, but we was close."

Otis Quinn said, "Except when Jake and Darcey rode around the corner to take a look up and down the street."

Warner was suddenly alert. "What are you talking about? Rode around what corner? When?"

Les said, "See, the bank's on a corner. 'Course we didn't know nothin' 'bout no bank then because we didn't know we was gonna git accused of robbin' no bank. But it's right there on the corner, part of it on the little side street we was waitin' on."

"What were you waiting on?"

Les shrugged. "Word from Darcey or Jake that it was time to go."

"So y'all was just up there on the side street by the bank."

Otis Quinn said, "And then Jake and Darcey told us to stay put and they rode up to the corner and turned right on the main street."

"What time was that?"

Les shrugged. "Beats the hell outten me. Jake was the only one with a watch. I didn't see no clocks. Anybody see any clocks?"

Otis said, "I heared a bell chime, but I don't know if it was just goin'-ons at the church or givin' the time. Never thought nothin' of it. But as soon as the chimes commenced, Jake and Darcey told us to wait and rode off."

"How long were they gone?"

The three of them looked at each other. Les said, apologetically, "Mr. Grayson, I had me a hangover you could have used fer a club. Didn't a hell of a lot make sense that mornin'. Jake an' Darcey bought us dranks the night afore until the whiskey was runnin' out our ears."

"Well, think! Was it five minutes? Ten minutes?"

They looked at each other again. Otis said, uncertainly, "I'd put it more like five minutes. Wadn't all that long, but not that short either. I mean, I 'member thinkin', when they didn't come back right away, 'How the hell long does it take to look up a street and make shore the sheriff ain't thar?' "

"Five minutes." Warner nodded. It would have been plenty of time. It could actually have been done in two or three. He said, "And then Jake and Darcey came back and y'all pulled out your revolvers and rode up the street firing into the air."

Les nodded. He said, "Yessir. That's when I noticed the 'stablishment on the corner was a bank. Jes' noticed it because it had the big gilt letterin' in its big front winder sayin' it was the such-an'-such bank. But then we kicked the horses on up and whipped right on out of town. Darcey had told us it was important for the joke we was playin' to git away fast." He suddenly looked down at the tops of his boots. He said, "I'm hanged if I know how I come to be so ignorant as to fall fer a prank like that."

Warner said, "Don't feel too bad, Les. This could all be over here pretty quick if things go right."

Otis said, "Yeah, but all that means to us is you'll be puttin' us in a different jail er prison."

Warner shook his head. He said, "If I get this bank robbery business straightened out I figure to cut you loose." He looked at Otis. "Even if you was pointing a gun at me."

Otis said, indignantly, "Well, I's the one got shot."

Warner was about to turn his horse when Les said, "Had we ought to figger they's gonna be folks out here tryin' to kill us?"

"That's what I'm hoping," Warner said. But, seeing the look on Les's face he added, "But I wouldn't worry. It won't be you that gets shot. I promise you that."

Les said, "Is that the kind of promise a man can keep?"

"I don't make promises I don't keep." He was about to move to where the sheriff sat for one last word when a thought struck him. He said to the three of them, "Say, doesn't Willis, Mr. Drake, look a little like Darcey? Short and muscled-up and bald?"

They all three looked toward the end of the car where Drake was sleeping. Les said, shrugging, "Yeah, a little. Iffen you don't look right close."

Otis said, "Darcy rode kind of hunched over in his saddle. Does Mr. Drake do that?"

Warner smiled slightly. He said, "He will at the right time."

He took a moment to tell Harvey some of his plans and to say that he'd be back sometime in the early afternoon to relieve him and Willis Drake. He said, "Then you and him can go into town and get yourself a real meal and get a bath or a shave or whatever you want."

Harvey said, as he started to leave, "You be damn careful with that sheriff. If he's in with them folks he might take a mighty dim view of you pokin' around. I don't want to have to come break you out of no Williamson County jail."

Warner did not go to the bank. He had changed his mind about trying to be the first customer in the door. Instead, he got to town and began hunting for the mayor's office. There were still some details he needed to know, and he thought she might have the answers. At least he felt, though he didn't know for sure, like they were on the same side.

As he dismounted in front of city hall he was feeling very discouraged. The whole matter had gotten so complicated he felt like he was fighting a fog bank; he didn't seem to be able to get his hands on anything solid. It was like grabbing a column of smoke. Once he'd caught the men who'd tried to hold him up on the road and found out they fit the bank robbers he thought it was a simple matter of identification and then the payoff. But now he was out considerable money and time and he was no closer to a solution than he'd been when he'd read about the robbery in the San Antonio paper. In some ways he felt he was even further from it than when he'd started, though he didn't know how that was possible.

He finally found the mayor's office at the very back of the city hall. The door was standing open so he stepped in, taking off his hat. She was behind her desk, looking very pretty and dainty in a blue gown with a clutch of lace at the throat. Before he said anything he looked around the office. It was very small, not much larger than a big closet. It had her small desk and two wooden chairs besides the one she was sitting in and they, plus a small bookcase, nearly filled up the place.

Warner said, "Well, Mayor, it's a good job you ain't no bigger than you are or there wouldn't be room for you in this here auditorium. Y'all hold dances in here?"

She smiled. "One couple at a time. And then the fiddler has to stand out in the hall. Sit down and tell me what's going on."

He took a seat in one of the wooden chairs fronting her desk and crossed his legs and put his hat on his knee. He said, "I'm here kind of trying to get the lay of the land. This bank-robbing business is about as far from my trade as you can get, 'less it's understanding women."

She smiled and said, "And how is Mrs. Pico this morning?"

"Same as ever. Butter wouldn't melt in her mouth."

She picked up a hand fan and made a few passes past her face. "Little warm this morning. So, what can I tell you about bank robbing?"

He put his hand to his jaw and felt the slight stubble. He said, "Well, if I was keeping money in a bank and I heard it got robbed for thirty thousand dollars, I'd get pretty upset and would go running down there wanting to know how safe my money was."

She said, "Well, folks did. But this Bob Thomas and his partner Harry Wallace let it be known right quick that there was plenty of money to cover all the depositors. They personally guaranteed it. I don't know if you know it or not, but banks can buy insurance against such things as holdups and embezzlement and loss of currency by fire or other reasons. It's expensive and a lot of banks don't take it because of the cost. But Bob Thomas and Harry Wallace did, and not too long after they bought out control of the bank. And they took out a big ad in the newspaper and advertised that fact and that caused a lot of folks who'd been trading over at the other bank to take out their money and put it in the Mercantile Bank."

Warner was surprised. He said, "So that bank never lost a penny. No wonder they wasn't just blazing to catch the robbers."

But the mayor shook her head. She said, "No, that's not the way it works. You can only get insurance up to fifty cents on the dollar. And, of course, once you have one stickup and the insurance company gets stuck for a large sum they'll raise the rates so high you can't afford them anymore."

"So folks didn't go rushing down to get their money out?"

"They did. But Thomas and Wallace were ready for them. They had a pile of greenbacks stacked up on a table behind the tellers' cages and they showed it to folks and said, 'Look here. We got plenty of money.'"

"So it never got to a panic."

She nodded. "They are very shrewd men, Thomas and Wallace."

He said, "But I don't understand—it says the bank was capitalized for a hundred thousand dollars. You take thirty thousand out of that and that's a mighty big withdrawal."

She smiled. She said, "That hundred thousand means the amount the bank was started on. It doesn't have anything to do with how much is in the bank on any given day. They are constantly making loans and paying out checks and taking in deposits. A bank can't make any money keeping its cash in its vault. It's got to be loaning it out on interest. Of course, they do charge people for its safekeeping."

"Then where the hell did they get all those greenbacks to put on display?"

She smiled slightly. "I've wondered that myself."

"Well, has there ever been any other trouble with this bank?"

Shaking her head, she said, "No, it's been steady right along. I think I told you my husband was a stockholder, five thousand dollars' worth. The bank has always paid a dividend. In fact, the last one, under Thomas and Wallace, was the highest one yet."

"What does your husband think?"

She smiled. "My husband is under siege himself right now. Muddy owns a whorehouse and gambling casino just outside the limits of the town. The city council has been trying to get me to move the limits out past his business so they can shut him down. I have carefully explained to the good members of the council that the reason we have a city limit is so we'll know where our limits are."

Warner slouched back in his chair. He smiled. "Your husband owns a cathouse?"

"And a gambling casino and a saloon."

"You don't mind?"

She shrugged. "I just feel like he's filling a need the same as the Mercantile or the dry goods store." After a pause she said, "Besides, they don't really care if he's operating or not. Most of the council are some of his best customers. It's mainly a way to get at me. I've been in office two years and they've done everything they can to run me off except set fire to my dress."

"I guess that came after they found you couldn't be led around by the nose."

"Actually, it was vanity on the part of the two factions. Each one was sure they could control me. When they both found out they couldn't they joined forces to try and get me out of office." She half smiled. "Only issue they've agreed on in ten years."

He looked around. "But I see they still give you the best room in the house."

She laughed. "This is the third time they've moved me. Every time I lock horns with one of the faction leaders they move me to a smaller office. I don't know what's left, the broom closet or the outhouse. I got this one for catching Wilbur Crabtree trying to change the tax evaluation on some town property he owns to save some taxes. I had him up before me on that one as city judge. Fined the hell out of him. Next day I was moved in here."

Warner said, "Of those three officers, who would you figure to be the easiest to crack, the scaredest if he'd been a part of something wrong?"

She thought a moment. "Don't let Wilbur Crabtree's turkey-necked look fool you. He's a tough old bastard. I'd say Bob Thomas."

"But he's the head man, the president."

"Because Harry Wallace wants it so. Thomas is all smiles

and handshakes. Wallace doesn't say much, but I wouldn't want to cross him. I think he might do more than move my office."

Warner stood up and put on his hat. He said, "Did I hear you call your husband *Muddy?*"

The mayor laughed. "With a last name like Roads you've got to get that kind of nickname. Muddy, Dusty, Bumpy. His real name is Arthur. I call him Art when I can think of it. Go out and meet him. He's got some mighty pretty girls working for him. Oh, I forgot about Mrs. Pico."

Warner let his eyelids lower slowly. He said, "Mayor, I think maybe you got a little mischeivous streak in you. I reckon them ol' boys made a bad mistake when they picked you for the India rubber ball they figgered to bounce around."

She smiled demurely. "I don't know what you're talking about, Mr. Grayson."

Warner let out a laugh. "I reckon you ladies, all of you, could give backwoods bushwhackers lessons in playing dirty. Say, does this town have a newspaper?"

"It does. A weekly. The *Round Rock Gazette.*"

"When does it come out?"

"Well, as it happens it comes out tomorrow morning. Why?"

Warner tipped his hat. He said, "Because I'm going to give it a little trade. Now I reckon I better be off to the bank to see what the gentlemen have to say about not replying to my telegram."

Try as he would he could not see Bob Thomas. In the end it was Harry Wallace who received him in an open cubicle behind the tellers' cages. The bank was fairly small, with a little lobby area and then the line of tellers' cages manned by the spinster Bainbridge and young Wayne Goddard and the turkey-necked, lean, and lanky Wilbur Crabtree. Warner paid close attention to Crabtree because his name was the one the doctor said that Darcey had muttered several times before he died. He judged him to be a man in his mid-forties. He had long, bony fingers and a thin face with stray strands of hair on his bony head. He was wearing a vest with sleeve garters and a green eyeshade. Wayne Goddard, on the other hand, was young and bulky and dressed in a full sack suit with a foulard tie. Miss Bainbridge, as near as Warner could figure out, was frightened to death that some part of her skin might be seen. Her dress hem reached the floor, her collar effectively covered her neck, and her sleeves came all the way to her hands. Even her hands were partly covered in lace, half-gloves that left only the tips of her fingers exposed, a necessity, Warner imagined, for the handling of money.

Harry Wallace was a different kind of animal all around. The suit and vest and tie he was wearing didn't disguise the fact that he would have looked more at home in a back-alley brawl than sitting behind a desk. He had a thick neck and big, thick hands. His shoulders strained at the material of his suit coat and his eyes looked tiny because of his ham-sized face. He said to Warner, "Now what's all this about sending us two telegrams claiming to have caught the men who robbed this bank?"

Warner said, cheerfully, "Well, unless you've got a bad memory that was exactly what I said before you had to get up and go confer with whoever is behind that door marked *President.*" He nodded his head at an office that was set along the right-hand wall of the bank and stretched halfway across. The rest of the back wall was taken up by an empty desk that Warner figured belonged to Crabtree when he wasn't at the teller's window, and by the cubicle he was sitting in with Wallace. The tellers' windows were to his back as he sat facing Wallace. "Is that where Mr. Thomas hangs out? The man I asked to see?"

"I done told you Mr. Thomas is busy. His business is seeing people who want to borrow money from this bank or put money in it or other transactions that make money for this bank and its stockholders." He didn't say it, but his implication meant clearly, Not some crackpot like you.

Warner said, "Speaking of your stockholders and your depositors, I'd figure they are a sight more interested in catching these robbers than you and Mr. Thomas appear to be."

Wallace stared at him heavily. He said, "What give you the idea that we ain't interested in catching those responsible for robbing this bank?"

Warner said, "Well, one reason might be that you don't seem the slightest bit interested in what I might be able to add to your investigation. You advertise for five men who robbed your bank and put out a reward poster. I wire you and say I got these five men captured and am holding them in a jail in Hondo. And I don't hear a goddamn word from you. Then I wire you again reiterating what I said in the first telegram and I *still* don't hear word one from you. That might be the first indication that you didn't give a shit. What would you think?"

Wallace leaned back and looked at Warner. He had heavy-lidded eyes. He wasn't, Warner thought to himself, a pleasant-looking man. Wallace said, "How many of them damn crank telegrams you reckon we got? If we'd've spent our time answering them damn-fool telegrams like yours we'd have had no time for anything else. As it was we had a bank to run and our customers to calm down."

"That sounds good," Warner said. "But why did you put out a reward paper in the first place if you didn't hope to get a lead on your robbers?"

Wallace's voice came out unpleasantly. He said, "Mr., uh—"

"Grayson."

"Mr. Grayson, did you ever consider minding your own business and lettin' us mind ours?"

"Mr. Wallace, this happens to be my business." He leaned slightly toward Wallace. "I got considerable time and money invested in your reward offer and I intend to collect it because I've got the prisoners."

Wallace just sat there like a huge frog with his eyes half closed. "Just what makes you so goddamn shore that you got the men that robbed the bank that you're sitting in, taking up my time?"

"Well, it damn sure ain't from reading the descriptions you had on your reward poster. That would have fit any five men in the world." He reached into his back pocket and pulled out the San Antonio paper. He said, "But they fit the description in this San Antonio newspaper given by eyewitnesses that were standing near the bank and saw them ride away." He slapped the folded paper, open to the story on the robbery, on Wallace's desk.

Wallace's eyes barely flickered at it. He said, "That ain't official. I seen that. It come from our local paper. All it describes is five men riding out of town." He turned his head and spit in a spittoon by the side of his desk. His cheeks were so heavy that it was the first time Warner had realized he was chewing tobacco. He said, "It ain't got a goddamn thing to do with our bank."

"You got insurance against bank robbery, don't you? I hear you got insurance pays you fifty cents on the dollar if you have a robbery or a fire or some other calamity. That right?"

Wallace leaned forward and put his heavy hands on his desktop. He said, "That ain't none of your goddamn business."

Warner leaned forward also so that their faces were not more than two feet apart. He said, "I think it is. I heard your policy says you got to make an honest attempt at the apprehension of the bandits and the recovery of the money. Being unwilling to hear all of what I've got to say don't sound like no honest attempt. I'd like the name of that insurance company. I'd like to put a bug in their ear. You want to tell me the name of your insurance company and where I can send them a wire?"

Wallace didn't say anything for a moment. Finally he moved his lips slowly. He said, "You ain't offered no information. You claimed a reward."

"I wired asking you to send eyewitnesses and a local law officer to Hondo."

Wallace yawned. "We got a dozen telegrams like that. Or is your memory bad?"

Warner said, "Show them to me. Show me these dozen telegrams. You told my business partner that same line of malarkey nearly a week ago. All right, let me see them."

Wallace raised his hand and made a dismissive gesture. He said, "We don't clutter the place up with that sort of trash."

"In other words you never got 'em."

"I didn't say we never got 'em, I said we didn't keep them."

Warner said, "Well, it won't take me long down at the telegraph office to see how many such telegrams you got." He said it hoping that Wallace wouldn't know that it took a law officer or a court order to open a telegram log.

Wallace smiled as much as he was capable of doing. He said, "Well, you just run right on along and see how quick that telegrapher is to show you our incoming wires."

Warner was sorely tempted to tell him he could do that very thing through Mayor Martha Roads, but he had the uneasy feeling that he had better not tip off his connection to the mayor yet. He had the feeling he was looking at a man who might be capable of anything, and he didn't want to be the one to sic Harry Wallace on Martha Roads.

Instead, he said, "I don't think you got any insurance, Mr. Wallace. I think that's something you and your partner, Bob Thomas, made up to keep your depositors and stockholders calmed down. I don't think you got a scrap of insurance."

Without moving anything but his mouth, Wallace said, "Mr. Grayson, you are trying my patience. I think it's time you got up and got the hell out of here."

Warner didn't make a move. He said, "Oh, yes. I'll leave. But I think you ought to know, Mr. Wallace, that I got those bank robbers right near here. Maybe I'll bring them to town and let them actually rob your bank."

He saw the shot hit home. It was nothing more than a couple of rapid blinks of Wallace's heavy-lidded eyes, but Warner knew that he had scored.

Wallace's tongue came out and licked at his lips. His voice came out like gravel. "What do you mean 'actually' rob the bank. What are you trying to say?"

Warner stood up and put on his hat. He said, "Does the name Clinton Darcey mean anything to you, Wallace? How about ol' Jake? Unfortunately, he died before he could tell us everything, but that ain't the case with the rest."

Now Wallace was blinking his eyes rapidly. He said, "Maybe you'd better sit down for a minute. I'll go and have another talk with Mr. Thomas."

"Naw," Warner said, "I've got business to tend to." He pointed his finger, making it look like the barrel of a pistol. He said, "But you be sure, Mr. Wallace, that I will have my twenty-five hundred dollars. Either from you or the insurance company. Of course, if I get it from the insurance company that might mean you'll go to jail."

Wallace swallowed. He said, "I'm askin' you to sit back down."

Warner shook his head. He said, "Naw, it's getting on for noon and I got to go see that my prisoners get fed. They're money in the bank to me." He took a few seconds to look around. "Of course, not this bank. I wouldn't deposit a corpse in here."

Wallace said, licking his lips, "You've actually got those men here? In this town?"

Warner gave him a pitying look. He said, "I didn't say I had them *in* this town. I ain't all that stupid. But they are handy. You understand, of course, that ol' Jake couldn't make it, but, with Darcey and the rest, he ain't no great loss. I'll be going along now."

Wallace lumbered to his feet. "I said I'd like to talk some more."

Warner shook his head. "Naw, you ain't quite in the mood to do the kind of talking I want you to. But you'll get there. I'll drop back by."

"When?"

"Pretty quick."

He turned and walked away, circling the wall of tellers' cages and heading for the front door. At the door he turned in time to see Harry Wallace disappearing into Bob Thomas's office. He smiled slightly. As he opened the door and stepped out onto the boardwalk he said, "Well, now, I wonder what them old boys had to talk about all of a sudden?"

He knew he was walking a very thin line, but he didn't know any other way to go about the matter. He was playing a pair of deuces like they were four aces. When you did that, Wilson Young had once told him, you had to first believe yourself that those two deuces were four aces if you were going to get anybody else to believe it.

But they still looked like deuces to his eyes.

The newspaper shop was two blocks down the street, in the direction of the Castle Hotel. It was a little after eleven so it gave him plenty of time to do his business at the newspaper and then get back to the hotel in time for lunch with Laura.

He went into the *Round Rock Gazette*'s office and stepped up to the counter that ran most of the way across the shop. It had a familiar smell to it. All newspaper offices and printing shops smelled the same. He reckoned it was the ink, though he couldn't think of any reason for ink to smell.

In a second a young man came from the dark back of the shop where he could hear the steady sounds of machinery. He guessed they were already setting up for the next day's edition. It made him suddenly realize he might be too late to get an ad in. His heart sank. A good deal of his planning was built around this newspaper notice.

The young man was wearing a black rubber bow tie. He said, "Yessir?"

Warner said, "I hope I can still get a notice in the paper tomorrow."

The young man looked doubtful. He said, "I don't know, mister. We in the midst of makin' up the paper right now. How big a notice?"

"Big," Warner said. "Set in big, black letters. Won't be that many words."

The young man turned around and yelled back into the dim recesses behind him. "Pop! Hey, Pop! We got room fer a notice fer tomorrow?"

Over the sound of the printing press a voice came back, "Depends on the size."

Warner said, "I don't know nothing about sizes. Not when it comes to newspaper ads."

The young man took a paper that was lying on the counter. With a pencil he pointed at one of the rows of newsprint. He said, "This here's a column. You go down a inch that's what we call a column inch. Ad that size will cost you a dollar and a half. Cow and a calf." He grinned. "Someday I'm gonna be a cowboy and get out o' this printin' business."

Warner said, "Oh, I want something considerably bigger." He took the pencil from the young man and showed the size he wanted.

The young man said, "Hell, mister, that's a eighth of a page. That'll cost you twelve dollar and fifty cents."

"That's fine."

The young man yelled back again. "Pop! We got us a real uptowner here. Wants a eighth of a page. Kin we fit that in?"

A voice came back out of the dark. "Have I got to answer thet one fer you?"

The young man laughed. He said, "I reckon you got you an ad." He reached under the counter and came out with a blank sheet of paper. He said, "Jest put down there what you want to say and we'll run 'er."

Warner hesitated with the pencil poised over the piece of foolscap. He said, "Would you happen to remember the exact date the bank was robbed?"

"Shore do!" the young man said. "Biggest story I ever wrote. I'm the main reporter around here, you know."

"What was the date?"

"April fourth. A Satiday mornin'. Ain't likely to ever fergit it. Nearly ever' paper in the area taken it from us by wire, even the big paper in San Antonio."

Warner took the San Antonio paper out of his back pocket and showed the story to the young man. He said, "Is that basically the story you wrote?"

The young man gave it a glance and then said, proudly, "Damn near word for word. 'Course they changed it a little here 'n' there. You know them big papers. They got to act high-falutin. Wouldn't do to take a little country paper's story straight up without changin' somethin' or other."

"But basically it is the same? I mean, there were eyewitnesses on the street who saw the robbers riding out of town."

"Talked to 'em myself. About a dozen. Some seen this little thang, others seen that little thang. Some kind of dressed it up a little, but a good reporter can spot them kind right off."

"What did you find in the bank?"

The young man shrugged. "Not a hell of a lot. They all claimed to have been struck deef and dumb. Mr. Goddard, he's one of the tellers, was the first to see 'em. But they had him down on the floor and bound and gagged and blindfolded so fast he swears he never got a good look at them. Said they had bandannas over their faces. He jest remembers the guns and that one of them was kind of short and stocky. Muscled up, you know. The other'n wasn't."

"They didn't tie any of the others?"

"Mr. Crabtree said they blindfolded him and gagged him and tied his hands, but he didn't look mussed up like Mr. Goddard. Mr. Thomas and Mr. Wallace said they was used to sack the money up fer the robbers. They said they couldn't give no descriptions. Said they was scared to death the whole time for their lives."

"Uh-huh," Warner said.

The young man said, "Why, did you lose some money in the robbery?"

"That," Warner said, "remains to be determined."

He left the kid giving him a perplexed look while he bent over the paper and laboriously wrote out his advertisement. It said:

REWARD NOTICE

ANY PERSONS HAVING KNOWLEDGE OF THE ROBBERS WHO HELD UP THE MERCANTILE BANK ON APRIL FOURTH JUST BEFORE OR AFTER NINE O'CLOCK IN THE MORNING, ESPECIALLY PEOPLE ON THE STREET OR SIDEWALK WHO OBSERVED THE GETAWAY OF THE BANDITS, ARE ASKED TO PRESENT THEMSELVES TO WARNER GRAYSON AT FIVE PM ON THE DATE OF THIS PAPER.

THESE PERSONS ARE ASKED TO MEET MR. GRAYSON AT THE FREIGHT END OF THE RAILROAD DEPOT AT THE AFORESAID TIME AND PLACE.

THOSE HAVING SIGNIFICANT DESCRIPTIONS OF THE ROBBERS WILL BE PAID TEN DOLLARS ($10) A HEAD.

A FURTHER REWARD WILL BE PAID FOR PERSONAL IDENTIFICATION OF THESE ROBBERS WHOM MR. GRAYSON HAS IN HIS CUSTODY.

He handed it over to the young man. The reporter did a quick scan and then looked up, startled, at Warner. He said, "Are you a law officer?"

Warner said, "I reckon so."

While Warner counted out the twelve-fifty the young man read his notice again. He said, "Mister, this ain't none of my business, but you are really askin' fer it here."

Warner looked up. "What do you mean?"

"I mean half the town is gonna come out there an' claim to have seen them robbers ridin' out so as to take ten dollar from you. I talked to the folks what seen them. Wasn't more than eight or nine, maybe ten, maybe a dozen seen anything of consequence. But you'll have fifty folks out there. This here notice is a invitation to a free watermelon supper."

Warner pitched five dollars on the countertop. He said, "All right. Why don't you take that and show up out there yourself? We'll work up some kind of signal and you can steer me off the ones trying to hand me a line of bull. You save me some money, I'll add to that fiver."

The young man's face lit up. He said, "Mister, you got yourself a deal! An', by golly, I'll set this notice up myself. Make damn shore it gits a good spot."

"What's your name, son?"

"Ned, Ned White."

Warner turned for the door. "Well, Ned, I'll see you tomorrow at the freight end of the depot."

"Yessir. I'll be thar. Early!"

Warner went out of the shop and turned toward the hotel for lunch with Laura. He'd put a lot of gears in motion that morning and he was going to get more going that afternoon. He wondered how she would view it.

He knew he wouldn't have long to wait. The widow Pico was not one to keep a body in suspense about her opinions.

10

When he'd finished telling her what he'd done and what he was going to do, Laura sat looking at him for a good long moment. They were having lunch in the hotel dining room, and the crystal was still shiny, and the tablecloths were still starched, and he still didn't know what the place was costing. He'd had pork chops and black-eyed peas and mashed potatoes and Laura had had some kind of baked chicken with thin gravy over it. They'd both had iced tea and he recollected that about all the good he'd ever got out of her was that she'd taught him to put lemon or lime and sugar in his tea. Of course that was outside of bed. In bed she was the best-quality stock he'd ever ridden; out of bed she was more trouble than a bad-tempered mule.

She finally said, "Are you trying to get yourself killed?"

He pulled a face. "Does that always have to be your reaction? That is so damn womanish!"

"What the hell you expect? I'm a woman."

He gave her a look but didn't say what he was thinking. He said, "Laura, I've got to push. I've got to shove them off-center to see what happens."

She said, "Damn it, you're showing them your hole card."

He put his fork down. "I most certainly am not, mainly because I don't have a damn hole card to show."

"You know that," she said, "and I know it. But they don't.

148

And, meanwhile, you are walking around town and stirring up a hornet's nest you may not be able to swat."

"I'm not alone. I've got two good guns out at the railyard."

"Yes, and they'll do you a hell of a lot of good when you get jumped here in town."

She frustrated him almost beyond speech. He said, "Laura, it's *all* I got. Don't you understand that? Jake's dead, Darcey's dead. I shot both of them. I know it and I've told them Jake is dead, but they don't know that Darcey is dead. Listen, Wallace completely changed his tune when I brought up Clinton Darcey. Before, it was 'Why the hell don't you get on out of here and quit wasting my time?' And then, after I brought up Darcey and mentioned he'd told me some mighty interesting things, Wallace damn near shoved me down in my chair. But I left because I was out of bait."

"You are playing a dangerous game."

He sat back in his chair and stared at her. He said, "Then you tell me some other way to play it and I will gladly comply."

She leaned toward him and he could smell her perfume. She was wearing an off-white day dress with a V neck that showed her soft, creamy skin. She said, "Give it up. Let it go! Let's pack up and go back to our real business."

He gave her a look. "Hell no! Are you crazy? I got too damn much invested in this matter to just fling it away."

Her voice got hard. "So do those boys at the bank. And they are not about to let some horse handler come along and tear down their little thirty-thousand-dollar playhouse."

"It ain't thirty thousand, I think it's more. And did you just refer to me as a horse *handler?*"

"Where do you get the more?"

He shrugged. "It ain't important. I want you to understand that I'm deliberately trying to make them tip their hand, to come out from behind the log. I want them to try and attack me. On my terms, of course. It's the only way I've got of proving anything. Right now I'm operating on guesses."

"Give it up, Warner."

"No. They owe me twenty-five hundred dollars. And I intend to collect it."

149

"Aw, hell!" she said. She threw her napkin on the tabletop and looked around the room. It was after one o'clock and most of the other diners had cleared out. She said, "If it's the damn money, hell, I'll give it to you."

He stared at her until she, unwillingly, turned her head and stared back into his eyes. He said, "One of these days you are going to make one of them kind of remarks you make when you have throwed a wagon brake on your brain and you are going to rue the day. I don't know what I'll do to you, exactly, but I can guarantee you that you won't like it worth a damn."

She flared back. She said, "Well, what do you expect? You make me so damn mad sometimes I'd like to scratch your eyes out. Or pull your hair. No. Kick you. That's exactly what I'd like to do right now, kick you. You son of a bitch. Go ahead and get yourself killed and see if I give a damn."

He took a sip of iced tea and said, "For somebody who'd like folks to think you are as cool as this glass of tea here you do a mighty good job of getting hot under the collar." He set his glass down. "But forget that. And forget wanting to kick me. I'd twist your leg off at the hip for your troubles, you tried something like that. This afternoon I want you to go down and see the mayor and invite her and her husband to dinner. I guess we can eat here unless they prefer some other place. But I got to get her up to date and I want to meet her husband. I got a feeling he might be a pretty handy man to know."

She said, coolly, "I thought it was the mayor you wanted to get to know."

"Aw, godammit!" he said disgustedly. "You don't even believe that yourself so I don't know why you bother to make such remarks. A season or two with a woman like you sure don't make a man anxious to have another one. Now do what I tell you and quit acting like a beast of burden."

She smiled slightly. "You liked that, didn't you?"

He got out of his chair. "That Baptist deacon telegrapher in Hondo liked it a hell of a lot less when I explained it to him. You sign the check or pay for it. I'm on my way to see the sheriff."

The smile left her face. "By yourself."

He sighed. "Laura, I'm simply going in there to ask him

150

what he's doing about the bank robbery and if he's made any progress so far. I'm going to ask him some questions. That is the right of any citizen."

She said, "Don't kid me, Warner. I know better than to believe that boyish innocent look on your face, because I can see beyond it. You're going in there to stir up that sheriff worse than you stirred up the bankers. Aren't you?"

He said, "The man has got a badge and a gun and deputies and jail cells. Do I look that foolish?"

Her eyes narrowed. "That's the funny thing about you, Warner. You don't look the least bit foolish, but you do the most uncommonly foolish things. Well, at least one thing—I'll get my other Andalusian back, Paseta, that you practically stole from me."

He shook his head, turned around, and walked out of the dining room. He knew she was staring after him, but he was damned if he was going to look back. He sometimes didn't know if he loved the woman or would just love to tie her to the end of a fast-moving freight train and watch her rope run out of slack.

He went out of the hotel and turned left, leaving his horse hitched in front. He'd already spotted the sheriff's office and knew it wasn't but a couple of blocks from the hotel.

Round Rock, for the most part, was a pretty little town. It was laid out along a main street, but there were a goodly number of side streets that held some shops and stores with well-kept dwellings spaced in between. He couldn't give the town much future, not as fast as Austin was growing. Round Rock was a market town, but soon enough Austin would be pulling in more of those market goods and the customers.

But that was of no concern to him. So long as the town lasted a few more days and there remained twenty-five hundred dollars in the whole pot he'd be satisfied.

He came to the sheriff's office and opened the door and went in. A little bell over the door jingled, like the ones in trade goods store. He found it an odd feature for a sheriff's office.

The office itself was bigger than he'd expected. There were two desks on each side of the room, unoccupied, and a number of chairs and benches along each wall. Toward the back there was a low railing set out some ten feet from the back wall. At first he thought the place was unoccupied, but, as he took a few steps forward, he saw a man in the right corner of the office, behind the railing, hunched over a rolltop desk.

Warner kept walking until he came to the railing. The man still hadn't looked up. Warner cleared his throat. The man said, without looking up, "Be with you in a minute."

While he waited Warner got out a cigarillo and lit it. He shook out the match and dropped it into a cuspidor. The back wall held several racks of shotguns and rifles. He had an idea that the desks outside the little fence belonged to deputies who were out on other business. A sheriff and two deputies would be about the right amount of law for a county like Williamson that had only two decent-sized towns, Round Rock and Georgetown.

Finally the sheriff finished and dropped his pencil. He spun around in his swivel chair and propped his boots up on the railing. "Yessir," he said. "What can I do fer you?"

Warner could see by his badge that he was the sheriff. He couldn't tell, since he was sitting down, but Warner judged him to be a big man. He guessed his age at a little over forty. He had big hands and a florid, flat face made to look flatter by a big nose. He wasn't wearing a hat and Warner could see the balding spot where most men his age started to lose their hair.

Warner said, "I'm here to inquire after a few facts concerning that bank robbery you had on the morning of April fourth."

The sheriff's face suddenly seem to draw together. He dropped his boots off the railing and sat up straight. He said, "What business of yours would that be?"

Warner said, "Well, I have good reason to believe I have the robbers in question, but I ain't getting no cooperation out of the bank. I've been to see a Mr. Wallace and—"

The sheriff stood up and Warner could see that, indeed, he was big. He was as tall as Warner but much heavier, though the extra weight was mostly fat and not muscle. The sheriff said, "Lookit, feller, I ain't got no way of knowin' who you be er carin' less. But if you be so ignorent you don't know that the place to come you got information 'bout a robbery is right chere. Right chere in this shur'ff's office. Not whar the damn robbery tuck place."

Warner stared at him a moment. He said, "I didn't hear you call me ignorant, did I?"

The sheriff glared at him. "You did if you be. An' goin' to the bank about a bank robbery ain't the way the matter is handled. You come here."

Warner said, evenly, starting to get very cold inside, "I went to the bank because they advertised a reward. You didn't. Now, if you're in the reward-paying business then say so and I'll take up my business with you."

The sheriff got even redder in the face. He said, "Sounds like you got a little streak o' smart-ass in you. What the hell's your name?"

"My name is Grayson," Warner said. "But that ain't none of your business either. I sent that bank two telegrams from Hondo, Texas, saying I was certain I had their five bank robbers in custody and—"

"In custody? You be a law officer?"

Warner said, carefully, "Not in your county. But I was mighty surprised when I didn't hear from that bank either the first or the second time. If I'd lost that much money they claimed they did I reckon I'd be checking up on every word that come my way. Makes me mighty curious to find they ain't interested. So I come down here in the best interests of honesty and justice to see what the sheriff of this *town* is doing about it and I get called ignorant for my troubles. Makes me all the more interested."

The sheriff moved a step to his right so that he was standing right in front of Warner. He said, "Whar you got them suspects? An' what makes you thank they might be the robbers?"

"I think they're the robbers because they fit the description printed in your local paper. I *know* they're the robbers because one of them told me they were. Little heavyset man. Name of Darcey. Of course, you wouldn't know because you haven't got time. You haven't even *wired* the Texas Rangers or the U.S. Marshals or any other law agency that's got the authority to cross county lines. I believe you *wrote* them."

The sheriff's anger was becoming very evident on his face.

Through almost clenched teeth he said, "Whar you got them suspects? They still in Hondo?"

Calmly, Warner said, "No, I brought them with me."

The sheriff raised his right hand. He said, "If they be in my county they belong to me. You be hidin' 'em out you be breakin' the law."

"I'm not hiding them, Sheriff, I'm just not going to tell you where they are. I got a bad feeling that they'd get accidently killed if they fell into your care."

The sheriff stuck out a sausage-sized finger and jabbed Warner in the chest. He said, punctuating his words with jabs, "I want them fuckin' suspects in my jail or—"

Warner suddenly whipped up his left hand and caught the sheriff's wrist. He let the man feel his strength, pushing him bodily back with just his grip on the wrist. He stared into the sheriff's eyes for a long second. He said, "The sign on the window says 'Dick Hawser, Sheriff.' You jab me in the chest again with that goddamn finger of yours and we're gonna find out in an instant who can put a hole in who first. And I don't think you'll be the sheriff much longer than that instant. Or however long it takes you to hit the floor." Then he suddenly shoved the sheriff's arm away from him, causing the sheriff to stumble backward for a step.

Little white spots of rage were appearing in the mottled red of the sheriff's face. He said, "Boy, are you athreatenin' me?"

Warner leaned forward. He said, quietly, "Listen, you dumb fucking windbag. I don't threaten. You want to find out you jab me with that finger again."

The sheriff's chest was heaving. He said, "Boy, you must have got tired of livin'. You better tell me whar them suspects is."

Warner took a step backward. He said, "What I'm gonna do is wire the U.S. Marshal in Austin and ask that a deputy be sent down here to investigate the whole matter, you included."

"Whar the fuck you gonna git the authority to wire the marshal's office?"

"Authority?" Warner took two more steps backward toward the door. He said, "Hell, I'm a stockholder in the bank. I own twenty-five hundred worth of it. I'm protecting my money."

The sheriff stuck out a long arm and pointed a finger at Warner. "You better be fer gettin' somebody to pertect yer ass. Cause I mean to have me a piece of it, you little shit eater."

Warner smiled. He'd reached the door. He felt behind him and turned the knob. "We'll see who does the shit eating, Dick. I'm surprised Harry Wallace didn't run down and warn you about me. By the way, be a notice out in the paper in the morning. Might be a way for you to make ten dollars. I imagine it is going to interest more than a few folks around here. But you're welcome to show up. That is, if you're willing to tell the truth."

The sheriff was still pointing his finger at Warner. He said, "I want them goddamn suspects. You better listen to me, boy."

Warner pushed the door open. He said, "Sheriff, those men are in custody on private property. You come and try and take them you better damn sure have a warrant." Then he smiled slightly. "But I don't think you are going to have much luck in that department. I want to make it clear that you come at me, where I am, you will be out of your authority and I'll take the necessary steps. You understand me?"

The sheriff started to move toward the little gate in the railing. Then he stopped. His voice was shaking with rage. "You sumbitch, you wait'll I git you in my jail. Then we'll see you come down a peg er two. And, mark you, I will have your cornbread ass in my jail."

Warner said dryly, "I doubt it."

Then he turned and went out the door and started up the boardwalk to retrieve his horse from outside the hotel. He imagined that Harvey and Willis Drake were getting mighty anxious to get into town and have a decent meal and maybe a shave and a bath.

Riding out to the railyard he had to smile. Laura had said he'd no doubt stir up the sheriff worse than he had the bankers. Well, he had done that. At least the bankers hadn't threatened to throw him in jail.

And that was another thing that infuriated him about the damn woman. She insisted on being right often enough to give her foundation for further opinions.

Well, he'd meant to stir the sheriff up. He had to stir up a lot of people if he was going to smoke out the truth. It was a damn cinch it wasn't going to come out by itself, not with the money at stake in keeping it supressed. He thought how it felt to know the whole story and yet not be able to prove a particle of it. It was very frustrating and he was not a man given to frustration. He liked matters that could be handled directly and quickly and this bank business had more twists and turns than a cow trail in the brush country.

At the cattle car he found an impatient Harvey Pruitt and perhaps an equally impatient Willis Drake, though Willis wasn't showing it. Willis had signed on for wages by the day and he was the kind of man that considered a day's work to be twenty-four hours if that was what the man who was paying his wages decided on.

Warner swung down from his horse and apologized for being late. He said, "But I had a bunch to do. The rest of the bad news is that you got to be back here by at least five-thirty because I've got to be back in town by six and it's going on for two o'clock now. But hang on for a second, Harv, I got to talk to you both for a minute before you go. Willis, would you get that pinto saddled and ready to go?"

While Willis was getting the colorful horse rigged out Warner said to both of them, "Now, you got to be careful and not call any attention to yourselves. Harv, here's your tin star back. But I don't want you wearing it around town. Put it in your pocket. Are y'all taking clean clothes in with you?"

Willis nodded silently, standing with the reins of the pinto in his hand. But the sheriff said, "Lord, yes. I feel like these duds I got on have growed to me. I am bad looking forward to a decent bath and a shave and a good meal set on a table instead of my lap."

Warner said, "Willis, I got something I want you to do. It's gonna sound strange, but I want you to do it exactly as I tell you. Savvy?"

Willis nodded and Warner was struck even more by his resemblance to Darcey, at least in build. Plus he was wearing an old slouch hat that shaded his face. Pulled down a little further it would do a good job of disguising his features. But it was the combination of the pinto and Willis looking something like Darcey that he was counting on. The fact that it had been Jake who'd been riding the pinto during the robbery didn't make any difference. It was the pinto the people on the street would remember.

And maybe the officers of the bank.

Warner said, "Y'all ride double just to the edge of the town. I can't let you take my horse, Harv, because I might need him here. But y'all ride double to the edge of town and then you get down, Harvey, and go on about your business. Willis, I want you to do an impersonation for me."

Willis looked at Warner for a few seconds. He said, "Mr. Grayson, I don't reckon I know what that is. I know it ain't got nothin' to do with cattle or horses an' thet be all I know."

Warner smiled. He said, "I want people to take you for someone else. When you let Harvey off I want you to pull your hat down in the front so it covers as much of your face as possible and then I want you to slouch up one side of main street to the end and then come back. When you get to the front of the Mercantile Bank I want you to stop your horse and then sit there for a moment. Then I want you to ride on back out of town and tie the horse someplace safe, someplace you and the sheriff have agreed on beforehand. Then you walk back into town and do your business and y'all come on back and get the horse and be here no later than five-thirty. Now, you reckon you can do that?"

Willis said, "You want folks to think I was one of them bank robbers, ain't that it? I take it this pinto pony was used in the robbery."

"Willis, you have hit the nail on the head. I'm proud of you."

"What'm I suppose to do somebody comes up an' asts me what I'm about?"

"Nobody is going to approach you on the horse. If they do, tell them your name and that you are passing through."

"What about the law?"

Warner smiled. "I guarantee you the law is not going to stop you."

Willis nodded. "I reckon I can handle her."

Harvey said, "I ain't overly fond of walkin'."

Warner stuck a finger in Pruitt's ample stomach. "I can see that."

He watched them ride off, the sheriff sitting awkwardly on the rump of the pinto. It was a good thing, he thought, that they weren't going horseback more than a mile, doubled up, else the pinto would probably crater.

After he'd made sure Willis and the sheriff were going to make it out of sight he walked up the ramp and sat down in one of the chairs in the cattle car in what they'd taken to calling the guard's compartment. Les and Calvin and Otis Quinn all crowded up to the wooden bars. Otis Quinn said, "You shore look mighty spiffy, Mr. Grayson. Them be new clothes?"

"Yeah," Warner said. "A woman bought them for me so they ain't of my choosing."

Les said, hunger in his voice, "I had a woman to buy me clothes, I wouldn't cere what she brung back, farmer's overalls."

Warner looked at them. They were a mess. They all had a three- or four-day growth and they'd been wearing the same clothes since they'd tried to rob him. But worse was the look in their eyes. It was that of men with no hope. They were as beat down as men could be. To their minds, he reckoned, there was nothing they could do or say that would help them out of their plight.

Warner was about to tell them something he'd been thinking on for the last twenty-four hours. He said, "I got some news for y'all."

But Otis Quinn said, "Mr. Grayson, kin I tell you somethin'? I been wantin' to git it cleared up from the very first, but I never thought I had a chancet of you believin' me."

"What, Otis?"

The lanky young man said, hesitantly, "Wall, it's 'bout me being one of the two was holdin' a gun when we come at you on that thar road."

"What about it?"

Otis rolled his eyes around and stubbed his toe against one of the two-by-fours. He said, "This is gonna sound like a made-up story to he'p myself, but it's the God's truth. Jest

158

'fore you come around that curve in the road Darcey taken my gun outten my holster. I had it thar on account I knowed it was empty. Anyhow, he tuck my pistol an' shoved his in my hand. Said somethin' about him bein' no account of a shot an' he'd heard that I was a good one. Well, truth be tol', I ain't. Never was much of a shot. But while I was thinkin' to tell him that, you come 'round the curve and Jake said, 'Let's go,' an' thar I was." He shrugged. He said, "I know it ain't gonna he'p, I jest wanted you to know I never had no intention of pullin' no trigger. I made some smart-mouth remarks back then an' I know you ain't fergot 'em, but I kinda do that when I'm scairt or nervous."

Les said, quietly, "He's tellin' you the truth, Mr. Grayson."

Warner reached over and picked up the bottle of whiskey and took a swig. He said, "I don't doubt it. Otis, I never really, once I got to know you, thought you intended me any harm. I think you'd've taken a horse if I'd left him carelessly in the way, but I don't think you robbed a bank and I don't think you meant to shoot me. I'm glad that I missed when I shot at you."

He leaned forward out of his chair and handed the bottle through the wooden bars. While they passed the bottle amongst themselves he said, "Fact is, that kind of leads right in to what I've got to say. I—" He stopped to lean forward again to take the bottle back from Calvin who had drank last. He said, "I've been doing some thinking and I figure this is about all over with. I'm not going to press any charges against ya'll." He gave that a moment to sink in while they looked from one to the other. Then he said, "And I know you didn't rob that bank or knowingly have anything to do with robbing it. All I think you're guilty of is poor judgment."

Les said, "When you say you ain't gonna press charges agin us about the road waylay, does that mean you ain't gonna put us in prison for it?"

"That's right," Warner said.

They looked at each other. He could almost see the hope growing in their faces.

He said, "Problem is, I need you for two or maybe three more days. Now I can keep you locked up for these few days, or I can let you out of that cage and let you wander around loose. Of course you'd have to stay close. You couldn't go into town."

Les said, anxiously, "I wisht I knowed what you was sayin' exactly, Mr. Grayson."

Warner said, "It's simple. I'll open the lock of that cage door and you can come out." He pointed at a tank about fifty yards distant that was used for putting water in the boilers of railroad engines. "You can walk over there to that water tank and pull down the spout and have yourself a shower bath, as I've heard 'em called. I mean you ain't going to be prisoners anymore. But I'm going to get your promise that you will stay right here, that you will not try and go into town, that you will not grab a shotgun and turn on me or Willis or the sheriff. You'd be free men except for hanging close around here until I get one or two more chores done here in this town."

Les said, "It's about findin' out who actual robbed that bank, ain't it, Mr. Grayson?"

Warner said, "Oh, I already know who robbed the bank. It's just a question of proving it. And for that I need the three of you."

Otis Quinn said, "As bait?"

Warner shook his head. "Naw, not really. You wouldn't ever be in any danger. What I mainly need to do is kind of put you on display."

"In the cage?"

"Of course in the cage. I'm supposed to have the bank robbers captured. How the hell would it look if I had them wandering around loose right near the town they'd robbed the bank in?"

Les said, cutting his eyes sideways toward Otis, "What would happen if just one of us run off? What would happen to the two that kept their word?"

"Nothing." He didn't look straight at Otis Quinn, but neither did he look away from him. "Nothing would happen to the two that stayed, but I'd spend the rest of my life running down the one that broke his word to me and made a fool out of me. I don't like to be played for a fool. I believe that makes me madder than anything." He took another drink out of the bottle and then set it on his knee and looked them over. He said, "Here's my deal. You stick with me for three more days and nights and not cause no trouble or mess up my plans and I'll haul you back to Hondo and give you a little money to get started on. You'll also get your horses and your gear back and you can sell Darcey and Jake's horses and split the proceeds amongst yourselves and then you can go your own way. But I'll want your word. You break that word and you know what I'll do. So, if you ain't sure you can keep your word it would be a good idea for you to stay locked up until we get back to Hondo. I'm still going to turn you loose there anyway."

Calvin said, in his boyish way, "You could take our boots, Mr. Grayson. Man cain't walk fer in his stockin' feet."

Les and Otis gave him a look. Les said, "Mr. Grayson, if you are expecting men with guns to come for us would you let us have guns?"

Warner said, "I don't even know if the sheriff brought your guns. But, yes, if it come down to giving you a chance to protect yourself, I reckon I would arm you somehow."

Otis said, "Ain't nothin' fer me to think about. I'd kiss a pig's ass to git out of this tight place."

"That's what's worrying me," Warner said grimly. He looked at Les. "What about you?"

Les said, thinking it over carefully, choosing his words, "I wouldn't run off or break my word 'less I felt I was in mortal danger. I'll give my word to your conditions other'n that."

Warner nodded. "That's good enough for me. Calvin?"

The young man's eyes got big. "You really willin' to take my word?"

"If you're willin' to keep it."

"Yes, sir! I reckon you'd have to drive me off with a bull whip. Yessir, I give my word."

"Otis?"

Otis looked surprised. "I done give it."

"Say it. You give your word not to leave this immediate area without my permission."

"I give my word not to leave this imm—immedjit area 'thout your say-so."

Without a word Warner took the key from a hidden place,

unlocked the padlock, and took it off the hasp. He sat back down, leaving it for the prisoners to push the door open.

Les was the first to move. He put his hand against the narrow door and pushed it carefully, as if he were afraid it might explode under his hand. He got it all the way open and still did not go through. He looked at Warner. Warner shrugged. He said, "I ain't gonna shoot you, Les."

Les said, "Mr. Grayson, after a while a man gits to whar he ain't got a lot of trust in folks. You'd had as many kicks in the teeth as I's had you'd be a little skittish your own self."

Warner said, "What makes you so damn sure I haven't?" "You?"

"Me. Now y'all can come and go as you wish. I'm stepping outside for a smoke. There's two shotguns propped up here against the wall. They are both loaded."

Then he got up and deliberately walked down the ramp and went to stand next to his Andalusian, taking the opportunity to pick the horse's feet up, one by one, and examine them. After a moment he felt someone standing by him. He looked up. It was Les. He said, "Mr. Grayson, we are much obliged. Ain't none of us goin' to let you down."

Warner straightened up and put out his hand and they shook. Then he said, "Was I you I'd get over there and get under the spout of that water tank and take me a good rinsing down, clothes and all. We ain't got no soap, but I can loan y'all my razor. After that y'all can sit out in the sun and dry off."

Les looked off at the tank, some fifty yards distant. "We can go that far?"

"Shore," Warner said. "That's in the area. One thing—I don't want y'all gettin' drunk. We've got whiskey here and you're welcome to it, but a man gets drunk sometimes does things he wouldn't do sober."

"I understand," Les said. He started to walk away, but Warner called after him. He turned. "Yessir?"

"Les, I think you know I run a breeding ranch. Blooded horses. When this is over I'm gonna offer you a job. I know you know cattle and horses, but my kind of ranching is a little specialized so I'd have to start you out as a man of all work, a roustabout."

Les opened his mouth as if he were going to say something

and then closed it and nodded and walked away. Warner lit a cigarillo.

Willis and the sheriff got back a few minutes before five-thirty, about the time Warner was starting to get nervous. They got down off the pinto, staring across toward the water tank where the three former prisoners were sitting on a rail drying out in the sun. The sheriff said, "What in the hell!"

Warner, as quickly as he could because he was pressed for time, explained what he'd done. Willis nodded and grunted, but Harvey stared at the three men and scratched behind his ear. He said, "Well, I don't know . . . I don't reckon I ever heard of a thang like this afore. I reckon I'll unload them shotguns and sleep with one eye open."

Warner explained, patiently, "Harvey, they ain't really criminals. Just a little misguided. Look at Willis here, he ain't worried."

"He ain't worried because he figures you make the choices and that's good enough for him. But, hell, *I'm* a sheriff!"

Warner smiled slightly. He said, "Did you bring their guns?"

"I brung all their possessions. Didn't know where we'd be goin'."

"Well, give them a change of clothes." He tightened the girth on the Andalusian and swung aboard. "And their guns."

"Aw, hell!" Harvey said.

Warner said, "Y'all look a sight better cleaned up. Willis, how did it go in town on the pinto?"

Willis said, "Lots of folks stopped and stared at me."

"Anybody say anything?"

"Not till I went into a café fer a meal. Lady ast me what I wanted."

"What about at the bank? Was the door open?"

"It was gettin' opened and shut. Oncet a man come to it and looked out at me an' then shut it right quick. I took the horse on out of town then like you told me to."

"So there was no trouble?"

The sheriff said, "Not in town." He pointed to the three newly freed men. "I wisht I could say the same fer here."

163

Warner said, "Harvey, you are an old woman. Those boys are on our side now."

"I'll be damned if I'll give 'em their guns. You can do it. I ain't havin' no hand in such."

"Well, at least give them a change of clothes. You look the better for it." He reined the Andalusian around. "I've got to get. I don't know if I'll stay in town or not. Since you're as worried as you are I'll try and make it back here before Calvin chokes you in your sleep."

Harvey gave him a sour grimace and spat tobacco juice on the ground. Warner put a light spur to the Andalusian as he started for town. He figured Laura was already fuming about his absence.

11

When he finally got to the hotel and up to Laura's suite, she informed him that they had been invited to have dinner at the mayor's house. Laura said it was only a few blocks from the hotel so they could walk, but she insisted that he shave again and take another bath. For her part she was wearing a deceptively simply gown that ended at her ankles and clung to her body. It was obviously intended to let everybody know that she had a good body as well as the money to buy the kind of clothes to show it off. The material, she informed Warner when he asked if it was the sort of thing respectable women were seen in, was Shantung silk, and the gown was worth as much as most men made in six months. Warner thought of several remarks he might have made, but since they were already running late, he kept his tongue and hurried through his preparations.

The Roadses lived in a big two-story house on a large corner lot set one block back from the main street. It was a white frame house with a big porch that ran around two sides of the front. From the gingerbread and other carved gewgaws on the porch railing and balustrades Warner figured the place was pretty new. When you could go to adding ornaments to the roof that sheltered you it was a sign you were doing well.

Walking up the concrete sidewalk to the front door, Laura said, "My God, did you ever see so much white in all your life? This thing looks like a white elephant."

Out of the side of his mouth Warner said, "Well, you look like a silk seal. You don't have to worry about spilling nothing in your lap at supper. The material of that dress is so slippery it'll just slide right off."

As they went up the steps of the porch she said, "Can't you ever say anything nice?"

"All right," he said. He reached out and banged on the door with the brass knocker. "You sweat less than any ugly woman I've ever known."

But before Laura could come back at him the door was opened and the mayor was standing there. She had on a blue linen frock faced with lace. As soon as they got inside Warner took a quick look at the two of them and realized, from the way they were dressed and the trouble they'd taken with their hair, that some sort of war was in progress. He just figured to stay out of the line of fire.

He heard the opening salvo as Laura said, "That is Chantilly lace, isn't it? It surprised me so because I just hadn't seen anyone wearing it in *years.*"

Warner saw the mayor smile. "You're certainly right about that. I took it off an old Shantung gown I'd quit wearing. Thought just for tonight I'd wear it."

But by that time they were in the drawing room and Muddy Roads was coming forward. Warner felt a kinship with him at first glance, like one bronc buster feels toward another.

The mayor's husband was a genial-looking man of average size whom Warner reckoned to be in his mid-thirties. He was wearing a plain broadcloth vest crossed by a gold chain that no doubt held his watch in one pocket and a fob of some kind in the other. He had on a white shirt with no tie, the sleeves partly rolled up past his wrists, and pressed cotton-duck trousers. He was wearing flat-heeled boots and did not have on a sidearm. Warner had worn his because of the uncertainty of his popularity in some quarters of the town. Mr. Roads came forward and gave Warner a firm handshake and then bowed to Laura. He said, "Well, I am pleased to finally make the acquaintance of you two. Martha has nearly talked my ear off about what's been going on."

Warner was studying him. He had a neatly trimmed mustache and wide, smiling eyes, but Warner was willing to bet he knew his way around in a fight or a poker game or a business deal. To Warner he looked like a man who would be competent in just about anything that fell to his hand to do.

The ladies went off so that Martha could show Laura the rest of the house, which Laura claimed she was "dying to see."

As they left, Muddy Roads looked after them with a faint smile on his lips. He said, "Either one of them can probably draw more blood in a minute than a drunk Mexican can with a machete given a whole month. That city council shore fooled the hell out of itself when they run her for mayor on the idea she'd be an easy mark." He glanced up at Warner. " 'Course part of it was they was trying to get to me. I was the one caught Wilbur Crabtree trying to change deed registrations on some town lots to beat some taxes and get himself a little more land. Thing he didn't understand was that two of them lots was mine. He thought they belonged to absentee owners who wouldn't notice. But I had them in my company name." He laughed. "Mr. Grayson, you have fell among thieves. This is the crookedest town I ever ran a straight gambling game in. Sometimes I think my casino gives the best odds in town."

Warner liked the man. Muddy poured them a drink of whiskey and Warner took off his gunbelt and hung it over the back of a chair. They sat down and Muddy offered him a cigar. Warner waved it away. "Naw, I got some I smoke. Little black Mexican cigarillos. Strong enough to light themselves."

Muddy said, "So you figure you got a line on our bank robbery? I almost want to laugh when I say that."

"I'll do it like we're doing it with the cigars, save it for after dinner."

"Suits me," Muddy said. He drained his tumbler and then reached for Warner's. He said, "I hear them women coming down the stairs. I figure we got time for another quick one 'fore we go into dinner. By the way, Martha sure admires the style of that lady friend of yours. When they quit scratching and clawin' I figure them to be good friends."

Warner said, taking his drink, "She's my business partner, not my lady friend."

Muddy looked over the rim of his glass at Warner, his eyes smiling. He said, "Oh, excuse me. I guess I mistook you for a lucky man."

Warner had to smile slightly. "Well, maybe I'm a little lucky. Maybe it ain't all business. But I never turn my back on her when she's got an account book in her hands."

Muddy finished his drink. He said, "I know what you mean. And I consider myself a pretty fair hand with figures." He paused. "Both kinds. By the way, come out sometime if you're a mind to. On the house."

Warner put his empty glass down. He said, "Reckon not." He glanced toward the double doors where Martha and Laura were coming in. He said, "Might interfere with business."

Muddy laughed.

After supper they went back into the drawing room and Muddy shut the heavy double wooden doors. Martha and Laura took a glass of wine and Muddy poured himself and Warner large glasses of cognac. Then they all got settled. Martha Roads had served fried chicken and new potatoes and spring peas. They'd finished up with chocolate pudding with whipped cream on top. Warner had done his best to make a pig out of himself with the chocolate pudding.

Now they were all settled and they looked toward Warner. He said, "I guess y'all have figured out how this so-called bank robbery took place?"

Muddy Roads said, "I damn sure haven't. Do you know?"

"Well, I know what the only thing that could have happened is. There ain't no other explanation for it."

Martha said, "Why don't you tell it from the first? Let us get a good grip on it."

They had made nothing but small talk while they were eating because of the servants coming in and out.

Warner said, "Well, I'm not laying this down as the gospel, but if I'm right, certain things are going to happen because

I've been going around stirring up the pot pretty good all day."

Laura said, "For God's sake, get to it, Warner. You don't have to apologize for what you don't know for sure. We're here trying to figure it out."

Warner lit a cigarillo and leaned forward in his chair. He said, "All right, here's the way I figure it happened. Either one of them bank officers, Thomas or Wallace or Crabtree, or all three hired either one man or two—either a man named Jake, and I don't know his last name, and a man named Clinton Darcey, to help them stage a holdup. To do that Jake and Darcey went out and hired three other men, men I've got in custody right now, for fifty dollars a head to come to Round Rock from Austin and, at the appointed time, ride out of town firing their revolvers in the air. They were told it was a joke on a friend."

Laura said, "Warner, nobody is that dumb."

Warner looked over at Muddy Roads. Muddy smiled. He said, "If they weren't, Mrs. Pico, I'd be out of business. Go on, Warner."

"On the morning of the robbery Darcey and Jake stationed the other three men around the corner from the bank and told them to wait there for instructions, that they were going to make sure the main street wasn't all clogged up or something. But they didn't do that. Instead, they went in the bank right before it opened. I don't know who let them in but it was one of the officers. And I don't know if the robbery was planned that day because the spinster lady was out sick. I don't think it would make much difference. But in about the time it takes to tell they grabbed Wayne Goddard and tied him up and gagged him and blindfolded him. That was so he couldn't see what was going on with the other officers. Oh, I imagine they made some scuffling sounds and carried on, but they were doing it on their own because as soon as Darcey and Jake had finished with the *only* witness in that bank that wasn't in on the plot, they were out the door and on their horses and waving up the other three and leading them out of town, firing their guns in the air and yelling and doing everything they could do to attract attention." He looked over at Muddy. "If you was gonna rob a bank would you have one man in leather leggings, one in a red-checkered shirt, and one riding a pinto horse?"

Muddy drew on a big cigar. He said, "When I read that in the paper I kind of wondered about it. If they'd been that dumb and managed to get away with thirty thousand dollars, I was kind of hoping they'd stop by my place. I could have used that kind of money myself. But, look here, how you know them other three wasn't a part of the scheme?"

Warner said, "I reckon I better take you all back and tell this from the first. Some of y'all know this and some of y'all know that, but you need the whole picture."

He began with the attempted robbery of his horses on the road to Hondo, the shooting of Jake, to taking his horses into San Antonio and seeing the newspaper article to being convinced he'd made a quick twenty-five hundred dollars, to wiring the bank, to getting no answer, to wiring the bank again, and then finally coming to suspicion and dispatching Laura to see what was going on.

He said, "These men, with the exception of Darcey, didn't seem like bank robbers. The best of them, a cowboy named Les Russel, was ashamed. He'd been suckered because he'd read that same paper and realized they'd been involved in a bank robbery and he hadn't even known it! At that time Darcey was threatening them all to keep their mouths shut. Of course I later had to kill him, so I lost my last bird in the hand that knew what took place in the bank. But then the others came forward with their stories of being out of work and broke and Darcey and Jake getting them good and drunk and offering them fifty bucks for this little prank."

Muddy said, "How you know the two that went into that bank didn't make off with the money?"

Warner leaned forward again. He said, "Because they were never out of sight of the other three and thirty thousand dollars, even all greenbacks, makes a considerable pile. Les said that Darcey and Jake tried to get away from them, but they were sticking to the two because they were scared of what they'd gotten into. Supposedly, when they run across me, they were headed for the border. But they didn't have any money on them. When I got them in jail in Hondo and the sheriff stripped them down and turned out their pockets they had seventy-six dollars between them. Les said they'd been urged to all go to a whorehouse in San Antonio to celebrate. He thinks that's when Darcey and Jake planned to lose them and go somewhere to get their split of the robbery. But by then they'd known a robbery had occurred in Round Rock at the time they were there and there was no way Jake and Darcey were going to get away."

Martha said, looking at her husband, "So you think Wallace and Thomas and Crabtree staged a robbery and kept the cash themselves?"

Warner said, "It's the only thing that makes any sense. Look at how interested the sheriff was. You went to see him yourself. What'd he say? That he'd *mailed* out notices to the Texas Rangers and the sheriffs in neighboring counties."

Muddy laughed. "Dick Hawser. If you wanted to elect a man who understood crooks you couldn't find a better man. He's the biggest one in six counties. Been trying to shake me down at my operation outside of town ever since I opened. Says it's illegal. I tell him to see my lawyer." He smiled around his cigar. "Used to be a fort out there until a few years after the Civil War. It was still Federal land when I bought it and it still is. It's called a government reservation and ain't no sheriff or city marshal can touch me. They keep trying to get Martha to move the city limits out. Wouldn't matter. Only reason she won't do it is just to be mean." He laughed. "When you going to break down and tell them fools what they're up against?"

"When I go out of office," Martha said, looking pleased with herself.

Muddy said, "But go on, Warner. I know about the reward posters. Hell, that could fit anybody."

Warner said, "But it's what got me interested."

Laura said, dryly, "Warner cares about money."

He gave her a furious look. "When I put considerable time and effort into a project and a man or men or company promises me payment on delivery of goods or services or both, I intend to have my money. If you want to call that caring about money you go right ahead."

Muddy said, smiling, "Then I guess, Mrs. Pico, that you'd have to say the same about me because I feel the same way as Warner."

Laura tossed her head. She said, "Get on with it, Warner."

Warner leaned back and drew on his cigarillo. "That's about it. I went in to see Wallace this morning and a sudden change come over him when I mentioned the names of Jake and Darcey. Before, he'd wanted me the hell out. Then, all of a sudden, he wanted to talk. I left. I can't prove anything, so what I mainly been doing is stirring them up, hoping to push them into a mistake. I stirred the sheriff up a little bit also by telling him I had the men I claimed were the bank robbers right here close. He actually threatened me. Said I had to turn them over. I told him he needed a warrant and he'd be at his own peril if he came near me and my prisoners without one." He looked over at the mayor. "He come to you to do any business today?"

"Oh, yes," she said. "He wanted a county-wide John Doe warrant for up to seven men."

Laura said, "What does that mean?"

"Means a free hand. Don't name anybody, that's why they call it a John Doe warrant. It's authorization to go anywhere through any door and do whatever in the hell he wants." Warner looked at the mayor again. "He get it?"

She smiled slightly. She said, "I gave him some forms to fill out. He's a very rude man. He threw them back at me and stomped out of my office."

Warner smiled slightly. "Well, I reckon I can expect a visit from the sheriff pretty quick. Maybe the first dark night." He told them about the advertisement he'd placed in the newspaper. "I'm going to give him a little help in finding me."

Laura said, "Oh, hell, Warner, why don't you shoot yourself and be done with it?"

He said, gently, "Laura, I got to take the sheriff out of the play. That's all there is to it. And I got to stir those bankers up some more. I'm planning on taking five or six of the witnesses back to my rolling jail and displaying the prisoners for them. I figure that will get word around town mighty quick."

There was silence for a moment. Then Muddy said,

"Warner, you quite sure you want to handle this matter this way? Dick Hawser ain't the most moral man you ever dealt with. If he comes, and if he's sent by those bankers, he's going to be intent on making sure nobody will be doing any talking."

Warner looked over at him. "That's what I'm counting on. When I was in his office I insulted the son of a bitch every way that I could. I dared him in his own office. I figure he's so mad at me right now he could bite nails."

Laura said flatly, "This is just dandy."

Warner looked at the mayor. He said, "If he comes at me in the night without a reason or a warrant I am within my rights to defend myself, am I not?"

She shrugged, though she didn't look happy. "So far as this judge is concerned you are. If you want to take the risk."

Muddy said, "You know he won't come by himself, don't you?"

"I won't be by myself, either."

Muddy sighed. He said, "Well, I reckon I better plan to take a bite to eat to you tomorrow night out at the railyard. I got a man works for me is a pretty good hand. I'll bring him along."

Instantly Warner said, "No."

"No? Why in hell not?"

"Because it is going to be dark and targets are going to be difficult to recognize and I'm going to place myself and the two men with me at strategic points. I have it all thought out. I'd be afraid a friend might get hit by fire intended for the enemy."

Muddy shrugged. "You might have a point there. But I hope you realize that the sheriff has four deputies, and if he comes for you and your prisoners he'll probably bring them all."

Warner stared at him blankly. "Four! Hell, I thought he had two! I only saw two other desks in his office."

Martha said, "He's got the county regulator in his pocket and he can get away with murder." She looked directly at Warner. "And I mean that literally. A lot of folks complain about the salaries of those extra deputies, but there's nothing they can do about it except elect another county regulator and that's two years away."

Warner looked away and shook his head. "Four. I hadn't counted on that. Look here, one thing I want to get straight. Muddy, you're a stockholder in the bank. The bank put out a reward poster for five bank robbers. Was that poster put out by Thomas and Wallace and Crabtree? I mean, are they the ones promising the reward?"

Muddy Roads shook his head slowly. "I wouldn't think so. It was the bank that was robbed. It was the bank that is out the money. If the crooks are caught and the money recovered—"

"That reward poster don't say anything about recovering the money, though I think I can do that. It just says five hundred dollars a head, dead or alive."

Muddy looked over at his wife. "What do you think?"

She said, "Well, I'm no lawyer, Mud, but it seems pretty straightforward to me. The bank has made a general contract with anyone that fulfills it. Bring in the robbers, dead or alive. I guess the only question is proving they're the robbers."

"How many town marshals you got, Mayor?"

"Two."

"They report directly to you?"

"Of course."

"They any good?"

She looked over at her husband. "Honey? Answer the man. I don't know, Warner. I'm no judge of that sort of thing."

Muddy said, "Well, they're more like night watchmen. But Hawser has got them buffaloed. He'll let them handle a drunk in a saloon, but other than that ain't much they do. He runs them off of anything else. Like this bank robbery. He made them scat right quick."

"What is the man doing with four deputies anyway? I know this ain't a wild town. Is Georgetown?"

Muddy said, "Well, two of the deputies are his cousins and one is a brother-in-law if that will give you any idea. No, this ain't a wild county. Though, from time to time, we've had some cattle theft and one thing and another. I think he's got four deputies because it makes him feel like a big shot. But, you understand, he keeps two of them in Georgetown, which is the county seat. He's got an office over there also.

But if he comes for you tomorrow night you can bet he'll have all of 'em. Ain't but a thirty-minute train ride from Georgetown and it won't take but one telegram."

Warner went back to Martha. He said, "But your town marshals have got authority? I mean, are they authorized to uphold the peace and make arrests?"

"Oh, yes. By rights Hawser is supposed to stay strictly out of their way in the city limits, but he doesn't do it. I've warned him to leave them alone, but I might as well be trying to outhowl the wind."

Muddy Roads was frowning. He said, "I'd damn sure like to know what went with that money. They don't seem short on cash. Piled it up for the public to see so they wouldn't get panicky."

Martha said, "Well, that was that insurance money. What *I'd* like to know is when they took that insurance policy out. How long before the robbery. I call that just handy as hell."

Muddy said, "I guess we'll know at the next stockholder's audit. But that ain't for a month."

Warner said, smiling, "Maybe we'll find out sooner. Does the bank make a lot of loans?"

"They have here lately. An uncommon amount. Which is why I was so surprised about the cash. But maybe they saw the loans coming and took out the insurance in advance just in case."

"Who were the loans to? Local people?"

Muddy shook his head. "I have no idea. A stockholder gets his dividend and gets to vote the officers back in, especially when they control the majority of the stock. Other than that he don't know nothing except what they tell him at the quarterly audit."

"I'd imagine that insurance policy cost a pretty penny."

"Now they did tell us about that. It's an odd way they do it, but it makes sense. You pay five thousand for a fifteen-thousand-dollar policy. At the end of a year if you haven't lost any money or made any kind of claim against your policy they give you a thousand dollars back. Same thing a year later. Then a year after that they give you five hundred dollars back and another five hundred a year after that. That comes to three thousand. After that they give you two fifty a year until you've gotten back four thousand dollars. Then the policy ends. The insurance company takes a thousand for their risk and I guess the interest they've made off the money of yours that they've held. Ain't a bad deal all around.

"But I don't know when he took out the policy. I know at a past stockholders' meeting we approved the purchase, but that was just a courtesy. Being the majority holders they could have done it without our okay."

"How much you figure that bank is worth? I know it was capitalized for a hundred thousand, but there have been a lot of deposits and withdrawals and loans made during that time."

Muddy Roads looked up toward the ceiling. "Well," he said, "counting money out in loans—and they ain't necessarily all good loans you understand—I'd reckon upwards of two hundred thousand."

Warner glanced over at Laura. He said, "That sound about right?"

She shrugged. "Depends on how much they've got out in loans and whether they are short-term or long- and how good they are."

Warner said, "Tell me about Thomas and Wallace and Crabtree."

Martha said, "We don't know much about Thomas and Wallace. They only came here about two years ago. Thomas is a glad-hander. Always dressed to the nines. Shakes hands with everybody. Muddy says he buys more drinks than anybody he's ever seen. But he doesn't go out to Muddy's place. He says he's married, says his wife is in Fort Worth and is coming any day." She smiled slightly. "But he's been saying that for two years. Supposed to be nursing a sick mother.

"Wallace?" She shrugged and looked at her husband.

Muddy laughed. He had a good, mellow laugh. He shook his head. "I don't know any more about the man than the first day I met him. Strictly a loner. Lives at the Castle Hotel. I don't know what he does with his time, but you never see him around town."

Warner said, "And Crabtree is a small-time chiseler, always trying to move deeds around and take a slice off his taxes."

Martha said, "That's the man. And he's one of my council members, too. You ought to know how much that thrills me. He's got a shrew of a wife and about nine kids. When him and his wife get into one they wake the whole town up. She looks just like he does, like a boiled chicken."

"Huh," Warner said. He got up and helped himself to a little more cognac. When he sat back down he said, "Muddy, are you a gambling man?"

Muddy looked up, startled. "A gambler? Hell no. I own a casino. Gambling is for suckers. I like the odds on my side. Why?"

Warner said, looking at his brandy, "Oh, I was going to offer you a little wager, but forget it."

"What kind of wager?"

Warner smiled at him. He said, "I was going to bet you a hundred-dollar bill that your bank hasn't got any insurance policy with any insurance company that covers bank robbery."

Muddy Roads cocked his head and gave Warner a quizzical look. He said, "It sounds to me like you're opening with a pat hand."

"Nope," Warner said. He shook his head. "I haven't seen anything you haven't seen or heard anything you haven't. In fact, I probably know a good deal less than you do about the bank. You're a stockholder."

"But you're willing to bet me in the blind about something you claim to have no information about?"

"That's not what I said. I said I haven't seen or heard anything you haven't. I'm not saying I don't have some information. I'm saying I haven't got any more than you do."

Muddy looked over at his wife and smiled. He said, "Goddammit, now he has got my curiosity up."

Martha said, "Remember how much good that done the cat."

"I don't care," Muddy said. He looked at Warner. "I call. What's the deal?"

Warner drew on his cigarillo and stubbed it out in an ashtray before he answered. "I don't know it's a fact, but you're a businessman, Muddy. If you'd had to pay out a sum like fifteen thousand dollars on a supposed bank robbery, wouldn't you send somebody to investigate or to have a look around? Wouldn't you send an official of your company to contact important stockholders like yourself or"—he jerked his head at Martha—"important people like the mayor, who is also the city judge as well as the justice of the peace?"

Muddy was looking at the floor, not saying anything.

Warner said, "Any such person contact you?" He looked back and forth from Muddy to the mayor. They both shook their heads.

Martha said, "Maybe there hasn't been enough time."

Muddy answered her. He said, "Martha, the whole point of a policy like that is to get some more money in the bank fast so that the depositors don't get scairt and draw out all their money." He sighed and looked up at Warner, a wry smile on his face. "If any insurance officials were coming down they would have already been here. And for a pot of money that big they would damn sure have done some looking around."

Martha laughed. "So the shepherd finally got shorn."

Muddy said, "I ain't got a hunnert-dollar bill on me right now but I will have it in your hands tomorrow."

Warner waved it away. "Forget it. I was having a little fun. For all I know an investigator has come. But the way I got this robbery figured it didn't make sense for them to take out insurance."

"A bet's a bet," Muddy said. "You beat the house, the house pays. At least in my casino. I'd hate for this to get around."

Warner said, "I'm not gonna say a word."

Muddy looked at his wife. "It wasn't you I was thinkin' of."

They stayed a little longer and Warner told them about sending Willis in on the pinto horse. He said, "Willis ain't much of a hand for talking, but it sounded like he'd drawn some attention. He said a man looked out of the bank and then slammed the door like he was seeing a ghost."

Martha said, "I heard about that! That's all people talked about all afternoon. About half the town thinks the bank is going to be robbed again. I might have known your fine hand was behind that."

They left after one more drink. Martha seemed very concerned about Laura walking back to the hotel in what she called "those darling little ballroom slippers." But Laura dryly assured her they had brought her over so she was sure they would take her back. She said, "I know you don't see such styles around your lovely little town, but they are quite in vogue."

Martha said, "Oh, now I understand why your dress was cut so short. It's so the shoes can be seen. What an excellent idea. What will they think of next?"

Warner got Laura away as fast as he could. He'd finally convinced Muddy that the bet couldn't be settled until the next audit, and Muddy had said, "But hell, you'll be gone. That's a month away."

Warner had said, "Well, you never can tell."

Now, walking back to the hotel, Laura said, "Warner, do you really have any idea how you are going to catch those bankers?"

"Smoke 'em out."

She said, "You keep saying that, but I don't understand how you are going to do it."

With a trace of irritation, mainly because he was worried himself and he didn't like her giving voice to his worries, he said, "Goddammit, Laura, I've got to get the sheriff out of the way first so that Martha and her marshals will be the main law. The sheriff could interfere with my big play."

She said, "Warner, you are driving me crazy. I don't care about you personally, but I'm in partnership with you. If something happens the partnership is ruined and I will lose a lot of money. You may not be good for anything else, but you do know horses. I am ordering you to reconsider facing off with that sheriff or having any more trouble with him."

He laughed. "Oh, Laura. My darling little bitch."

She stopped in the middle of the street and stamped her foot. "Damn it, I'm serious!"

"You better look out, you are liable to ruin them 'darling little ballroom slippers' stamping your foot like that."

She stopped and glared back in the direction they'd come. "That woman! She doesn't know any more about style than you do. I'm surprised she didn't show up tonight in a little gingham Mother Hubbard with flour on her cheeks."

Warner said, "Oh, now we're not being nice. I'm surprised at you, Laura June."

They got to the hotel with Warner still laughing. He said, "Did you get those dirty clothes of mine cleaned?"

"Of course. They came back this afternoon."

He said, "Well, I'm going to come up and change out of these fine duds you bought me. Laura, I think I'd better be out at the railyard tonight. The sheriff is not supposed to find out where we are until tomorrow, but I don't want to take the chance. I'll go up with you and change."

They entered the hotel and Warner veered off and started for the desk. He said, "You go on up. I want to have my horse brought around from the livery. I'll be a minute."

He stood for a second, watching admiringly as Laura ascended the curving staircase. She did cut a figure in the emerald green shiny silk dress. But his mind was too full of the matters that had been discussed that evening. Warner had learned that a cash balance was totaled up as the last item of business at the end of every banking day. The cash was counted by the three officers and then Crabtree entered it into his ledger. It had been the final determination of how much the bank had lost. According to that cash balance the day after the robbery the thieves had gotten away with $30,320. A few days later the cash balance had reflected the influx of the $15,000 in cash from the insurance company. Muddy, of course, had no idea how it had arrived. Neither did anyone else, nor did they have any reason to question it. They were glad the officers had been foresighted enough to have taken out the policy. But after that day the insurance money had gotten absorbed into the business of the bank and had disappeared into loans and the balance had settled down to what it was the day after the robbery, a figure that Muddy believed fluctuated between thirty-five and forty thousand dollars.

But it was too soon to be thinking about that step in his plan. The business with the sheriff had to be brought to a successful conclusion or he was finished and would have no alternative except to do what Laura wanted—pack up and leave town.

Warner, still thinking, walked over to the desk and asked the clerk to send around for his horse and have him out front. He started to turn away to go upstairs and change clothes when a sudden thought struck him. He turned back to the clerk and asked what the suite of rooms Laura was occupying cost per day.

The clerk said, "Well, uh, sir, that would be business between the hotel and Mrs. Pico."

Warner said, "Goddammit, I'm her boss and I'm the one paying the bill. Now how much is it?"

The clerk frowned. "I thought you were her brother."

"Brother, boss, what difference does it make? Now how the hell much is it for them rooms?"

The clerk cleared his throat. He said, "Well, of course that is our deluxe suite, the finest in the hotel."

Warner drew near the desk and leaned into the clerk's face. "How damn much?"

The clerk said, in a very quiet voice, "Eighteen dollars a day."

Warner stared at him in disbelief. "Eight—eighteen dollars a day *for a place to lay your head for a few hours?! Eighteen dollars a day!*" He took a step backward. He said, "If you boys are going into the robbery business why don't you get some guns and do it right?"

The clerk said, stiffly, "We've had no complaints."

"I bet you haven't," Warner said, marveling. "I bet this is the first time you've ever rented it and I bet the widow Pico didn't even ask after the price."

"I wouldn't know, sir. It was rented during the day and I'm the night clerk."

"How long has she been here?"

The clerk looked at the register. He said, "I believe it is six nights, sir. But we are not charging you the double rate for the night you stayed here."

"Six days!" Warner stared up at the ceiling. "That's a hundred and eight dollars. Make it a week and that's a hundred and twenty-six dollars. That's near five hundred dollars a month! My God, man, the governor of this state don't draw them kind of wages!"

The clerk was beginning to look nervous. He said, "Well, I'm sure we can make some sort of weekly adjustment. Give her a weekly rate."

Warner stared at him. "You can just bet you're going to do

that. And I better like it or I'll leave with every piece of furniture in that so-called suite. At these prices I ain't renting the damn place, I'm buying it!"

Then he gave the clerk one final glare and turned for the stairs, intent on getting dressed and out to the railyard as quick as he could. It was already after ten o'clock and would be close to eleven by the time he arrived. He turned into the curve of the staircase and took the wide steps two at a time.

12

He whistled loudly and then waited for an answering signal before riding into the camp they'd made around the cattle car. Willis was sitting on guard with a shotgun. While Warner unsaddled and sprinkled out a little grain for his horse, he asked how the prisoners had been doing.

Willis said, slowly, "Wall, seein' they ain't pris'ners no more they done fair to middlin'. I had to take the whiskey jug away from thet Otis Quinn a little earlier this evenin', but they done all right. They ain't such bad fellers. Some of 'em is a little spooky right now, waitin' to see what's gonna happen."

Warner let the Andalusian out on a picket line. He said, "How 'bout you, Willis? You a little spooky about what's going to happen?"

Willis shook his head and spat tobacco juice. "To git spooked you got to go to thankin'. I ain't paid to do no thankin'."

Warner laughed. "You are a prize, Willis. I am going to be sorry to turn you back to Mr. Birdsong."

The nearest thing to a smile that Warner had ever seen on Willis's face flitted across. He said, "Wall, Mr. Birdsong don't pay your kind o' wages, natcherly, but all in all the work is a mite more less reckless."

Warner said, "Who's got the next watch? I mean, I know

Harvey has got the next watch, but what time do y'all change?"

"Midnight. Thereabouts."

Willis was sitting on a chair outside the cattle car. The door was almost pulled shut. He could see the three ex-prisoners sleeping in their old quarters and Harvey Pruitt sleeping in the other end. He put out his hand for the shotgun. He said, "You go on to bed. I'll take it for a couple of hours and then call the sheriff and he can wake you when your next shift is on. I want us all to get as much sleep as possible. Tomorrow is gonna be one hell of a day if my luck holds good."

He went down early to the loading dock at the freight end of the railroad depot. He'd squared the freight clerk with a five-dollar bill, though there'd been no reason to do so since he was doing freight business with the railroad and had the right to use the dock. But even though he was a man who didn't like to be careless with money he was also a man who believed in making every effort to have matters run as smoothly as possible.

He hadn't designated the freight dock as the meeting place in his advertisement for any particular reason other than that it was handy. He had not wanted to take the whole crowd directly to his cattle car, only those few he would select with the aid of Ned White. And, of course, he'd wanted a spot that was generally known and easy to find, but still close enough to his cattle car where he could take his witnesses with little trouble. The cattle car was about a quarter of a mile away, but it was at the very far side of the railyard and hidden by random single and coupled cars that lay waiting to be hooked onto freight trains that had not yet arrived.

At about four-thirty he lit a cigarillo and leaned up against the dock, expecting Ned White along at any minute. Instead it was the mayor, driving her buggy, who came pulling up to where he was standing. He pushed off the dock and took a couple of steps over and put his boot up on the running board of her little surrey. He said, "Well, ma'am, this is a surprise. Have you come to identify my bank robbers for me?"

She looked at him and shook her head. Martha Roads always surprised him at how she could give such an appearance of strength but still seem so feminine. He'd known women of strong nature and strong opinions, but there'd always been something masculine about them. There was no such taint in the mayor. She said, "Warner Grayson, have you the slightest idea of what you are doing?"

He nodded over his cigarillo. "Pretty much," he said. "Pretty much. Or I should say that I know what *I'm* doing, I just don't know what the other fellow is liable to do."

She said, "You told us about that advertisement last night, but I had to see it for myself to realize how far you'd gone. And you say you are going to display your prisoners?"

He smiled. "To a selected few. And they will be disarmed in advance."

She fiddled with the reins as her carriage horse stomped a rear hoof. She said, "If Dick Hawser is in league with the bankers as you think he is then you are going to have hell on fire out here. If you believe they connived in the robbery they cannot let these prisoners live. Or you in the bargain."

He smiled. "Mayor, I think you have hit on the purpose of this little exercise here."

She half smiled with him. For the first time he noticed that her chin dimpled on one side. She said, "You are either cocksure of yourself or you have some plans made that I don't know about or you are plain crazy. Don't you know that the sheriff will send one or two of his deputies out here? They'll be watching your every move. They'll know where you are keeping those prisoners."

"That's the plan," he said, nodding. "I don't figure the deputies will oblige me by wearing their badges, so I've hired Ned White from the paper to spot them for me. I want to be sure I take at least one of them back there in the railyard to look my birds over."

She said, "Hell, I thought *I* was married to a wildman. He's plain sane next to you. You're going to have half the town out here, you know."

"Why don't you stick around? Maybe you can make a speech for your reelection."

She gave him a look and gathered the reins in her hands.

"No, thank you very much." She slapped the horse and said, "Git up, Betsy."

He called after her, "Mayor, I got a feeling you are going to be called upon for a little judicial work before the night is out."

She stopped her buggy and looked back at him. "You think something is going to happen that fast?"

"If the situation was reversed I wouldn't feel like wasting any time. I'm a thorn in their side. The more time passes the more chance there is for me to discover matters they would prefer to keep hidden. Do y'all have a buckboard at your house?"

"A buckboard?"

"Yeah."

"Not that I know of. I suppose I could arrange to have one brought in. Muddy's got one at his place out of town. I'll send word for him to bring it in when he comes home. What time do you expect all this to happen?"

"Unfortunately," he said, "that ain't my choice."

"Well . . . good luck."

She started up again and then stopped. Her head came out again. She said, "Are you coming in tonight to have supper with Mrs. Pico?"

He shook his head. "No, I've got to stay out here. And she's mad as hell at me about it. I went in right after lunch for a few minutes and she nearly took my head off."

"You want me to invite her for supper?"

"I'd appreciate anything you could do. Maybe if you had a spare bedroom you could talk her into staying all night with you. I think she's worried about me. She always gets mad at me when she's like that. Makes her mad that I'd cause her the trouble of worrying about me, lady like her. Says I'm not worth it."

Martha laughed. She said, "I'll see what I can do. I think I understand about you and Mrs. Pico."

Warner did not have long to be alone. Ned White came along about five minutes later, looking very young and very eager and very efficient. They worked out a system of signals for Ned to indicate who the real witnesses were and who were just trying to make ten dollars. Warner said, "I don't want but four. I've got an idea that there will be at least one deputy sheriff here, and I don't think he will be wearing his badge. Do you know all of them?"

"Oh, sure. Yessir."

"Well, if you spot one you get over next to him and tug on your ear or take off your hat or do something around your head. Don't leave me in doubt. I want the deputy sheriff to be the fifth person I take back to view the prisoners."

Ned looked a little puzzled. "You aimin' to take one of Sheriff Hawser's deputies back to wherever you are hiding your bank robbers?"

"That's right. And I want you to come along, too. You can write a story about it."

Ned said, enthusiastically, "Well, I'd appreciate that."

"Now, we're straight on the signals. You stand where I can see you and as I talk to the people one by one you nod if they were one of the original witnesses you interviewed or if they are bogus."

"And do something around your head for the deputies."

"That's about it."

They both leaned against the dock to await the people who had been lured by the prospect of telling gossip and getting paid for it. In the distance, through the gate in the fence that surrounded the freight yard, Warner saw his first customers heading his way. He thought back, going over every detail, making sure that he hadn't forgotten something, any item, no matter how small.

After he'd come back from a lunch that was more of a one-sided quarrel with Laura than a chance to get a meal, he'd gathered his group at the cattle car and set in to school them on their parts when he brought his witnesses back. Willis had been surprised to learn that he was going to join the "prisoners" in the cell part of the cattle car, but when Warner had explained he'd be playing the part, or at least, hopefully, looking the part of Darcey, he'd just nodded. For the others it was a matter of going back to doing something they were very familiar with. Warner had made it clear that he wanted Otis Quinn, who would change back into his red-checked shirt, and Les, in his leather leggings, to be very visible up front in the cage. He wanted Calvin to be seen easily, but he instructed Willis to kind of lie back and keep his hat pulled low. He said, "Willis, yours is the most important part, because Darcey, who you are impersonating, was one of the links with the bank. It's important that it get reported in the right circles that you are doing well and talking your head off."

The sheriff had been the most disappointed when he found that he had no part to play. He had envisioned himself standing on guard and looking stalwart with a shotgun cradled in his arm. When Warner had told him he was to saddle the pinto and ride off out of sight and stay out of sight for the duration of the viewing he was considerably upset. He said, "Well what the hell kind of rolling jail is that going to look like without a guard? Pretty poor stuff if you ask me."

But when Warner had explained, very carefully, that he wanted Sheriff Dick Hawser and his men to think they'd have only one guard, Warner, to contend with, the sheriff had seen his point. He'd said, "So when he makes his raid he ain't gonna know about me and he ain't gonna know about Willis. He's gonna think it be you and four prisoners."

"There you go, Harv," Warner had said. "Now you are getting the idea."

All in all Warner guessed that about forty people showed up. Over half of them were women, which would make sense—them being on the streets shopping while their men were at work. There was the general run of saloon bums and several respectable-looking tradesmen. There were also two hard-looking young men whom Warner would have bet either had their badges in their pockets or had left them back at the sheriff's office.

With Ned's inconspicuous help he slowly pared the crowd down, trying not to hurt anyone's feelings or get the crowd roused. It was easy to tell the ones who'd read the descriptions in the paper and the ones who'd given the descriptions. After the first few he hardly had to glance at Ned to tell the real article from the hopeful. To keep from having trouble with a few of the saloon bums he'd started a practice of giving them a dollar bill for their time. Unfortunately that practice had spread to some of the women and he ended up giving away twenty dollars more than he'd planned. In the end he'd settled on the least dangerous-looking of the deputies and a haberdashery shop owner who'd been out on the street in front of his place of business when the bunch had ridden by shooting in the air. He picked two ladies who looked like they could gossip away with the best, and, most luckily of all, a barber who'd been looking out his shop window at the time. You couldn't, he thought, beat a barber for getting the word spread around.

When it was over he asked the five people he'd chosen if they'd wait and then informed the rest of the crowd, to groans and fits of outrage at the trouble they'd been put to for no good reason, that he required no further help and had no more money to give out.

While they waited for the last of the curious to give up finally and leave, Ned asked him how he'd gotten on to being able to tell the ones he, Ned, had interviewed, and the ones who'd only heard about the robbers. Warner said, "The ones that actually saw the incident spoke straight out with what they knew. The others went to adding too many little details that they couldn't and most likely wouldn't have noticed about five men racing by on horses and shooting guns in the air. One man even told me he got a look at the color of most of their eyes."

Ned laughed. He said, "Most of them, from what I saw when I got there, were just coming out of hiding. I don't know of anybody with any sense that stands around gawking when guns are being fired."

The hard-looking man Warner guessed to be a deputy came up and said, "What's this all about? What happens next?"

The man was wearing a clean, ironed, light brown shirt. Warner could clearly see the pricks in the fabric where his badge had been. He got out his roll and began handing out ten-dollar bills to the five people. The deputy took his a little reluctantly and looked surprised. Warner said, "Well, now that I've got five people I'm dead certain had a good view of the robbers as they left town I thought I'd take you back and let you get a look at them in person."

There was a little stir among the four. The deputy looked interested. The barber said, "You mean you got 'em here? Alive?"

Warner nodded. "Less than a quarter of a mile from where we're standing. I hope you gentlemen will give me a hand with the ladies on account of we'll have to be stepping over some tracks. Mr. White? You are coming with us, are you not? As a representative of the press?"

Ned looked sufficiently solemn. "Oh, of course. It's a big story."

But the barber was looking nervous. He put out his hand and grabbed Warner's arm. He said, "You ain't talkin' 'bout us viewing 'em in the flesh, is you?"

Warner frowned. "Of course. You'll have to do it in court."

The barber looked even more worried. He said, "Say, your notice didn't say nothin' about gettin' right up next to no outlaws. Are they dangerous?"

Warner laughed. He said, "They're behind bars, Mr. Barton. They can't get at you."

With Warner leading the way and Ned bringing up the rear the little party made its way through the snarl of sidings and switches and strings and pieces of freight trains and around individual cars that were spotted here and there. Warner looked back often to catch the deputy carefully noting their direction and route of march. He figured Dick Hawser would have the information within the hour. Which, of course, was exactly what the whole elaborate exercise was about.

Just as they got within seventy-five yards of the camp there were three boxcars off to their right and then a space of about fifty yards to the end of an individual car sitting by itself. As they got nearer to the camp, crossing over sidings, there were other cars scattered here and there in twos and threes and even greater numbers, all making a kind of winding path to the camp. Finally, walking between a sixty- or seventy-yard break between the ends of two incomplete trains, they were within fifty yards of the cattle car. He stopped the group for a moment while they, and especially the deputy, took it all in. Warner wanted to give the deputy plenty of time to memorize the layout and the terrain because he wanted the report he took back to Hawser to cause the sheriff to attack from the direction he, Warner, had already chosen.

In the stock car the men in the cage had been sitting down. Now, as they sighted the group, they slowly got up and crowded toward the bars. Warner was glad to see that the sheriff was not visible and that Willis was hanging back behind the other three.

Warner said, "Let's move closer."

The rest went willingly enough except for the barber, who fell back until he was walking almost behind Ned.

Warner led them to within ten yards of the car. An elderly lady named Mrs. Crutcher immediately pointed at Otis Quinn and said, "Thar's one! I'll never forget him!"

The haberdasher said, "Look at the mean faces on 'em. Look as if they'd as soon slit your throat as look at you."

As instructed, Otis yelled, "What'r you gawkin' at, you ol' hen? Step up here where I kin git my hands on you an' I'll wring your scrawny neck!"

Les yelled, "Lookit that 'un in the back. He's ascairt! Hidin' behind that pretty lady."

Warner glanced back and, sure enough, the barber was behind the lady he thought was named something like Eaver. He said to the others, "How many of y'all recognize these men as the ones you saw the morning of the bank robbery?"

There was a chorus of assents with everyone being sure of Les and Otis and not quite as sure of Calvin or Willis. Mrs. Crutcher, however, said, "That'un tryin' to skulk down in the back was ridin' a paint horse. I'd swear to it on my tombstone. An' as mean-lookin' a feller as I ever seed."

The deputy had not said a word. Warner looked at him directly. He said, "What about you? Didn't you say your name was Charlie something or other?"

The deputy said, "Yeah, I recognize 'em. So what? Ain't they supposed to be in jail?"

That caused the barber to look hard at the deputy. He said, "Don't I know you from somewhere? Don'chou work fer Shur'ff Hawser?"

The deputy shook his head. "You got me mixed up with someone else."

Warner said, "Well, if everybody is satisfied I reckon you are free to go. I hope you can make your way back on your own. I need to stay here. 'Bout time to feed the prisoners. Mr. White, if you'll hang on a moment I've got some information for your newspaper."

They stood together, watching silently, as the five people made their way out of the yard. When they were out of earshot Warner said, "How come none of them people recognized that deputy? Did I make a mistake?"

Ned shook his head. "No. He's new and he's stationed over at Georgetown. No reason for anyone to know him. I reckon he was brought over special just for this."

Warner nodded, satisfied. He gave Ned another ten-dollar bill for his help and thanked him and sent him on his way. He stood watching, waiting for Ned to get clear of the area before he opened the cage. As he waited he thought of all the money he was spending. Today's little play, for instance, had cost eighty-five dollars, not counting the cost of the advertisement in the newspaper. He thought he'd damn well better collect that reward just to break even on the whole operation.

When he was satisfied no one was watching he went up the ramp and opened the cage door. Otis said, "We do all right, boss?"

"Not bad," he said. "I know you nearly scared a barber to death." He smiled. "In fact, looking at y'all like those people were you do look like a pretty bloodthirsty outfit."

Calvin said, "I cain't wait to git outten these ol' dirty clothes an' put my clean ones back on."

Warner shook his head emphatically. "No, you can't do that until dark. As a matter of fact, I don't want you coming out of that cage until the sheriff gets back and makes a circuit on that pinto. There was a deputy sheriff in that crowd that was trying not to act like he was one. I want to make sure he didn't lay behind to have a look when we're supposed to be alone."

There was some grumbling, though none from Willis or Les. He handed them half a bottle of whiskey. He said, "I'm going to have a look around myself. Willis, I'm counting on you two not to let Otis and Calvin get out of hand. Stay in this cage. It's not that long until dark."

As he came out of the cattle car the sheriff rode up and asked how it had gone. "Pretty good, I think," Warner said. "But we ain't gonna know until tonight. Right now I want you to take a scout toward the front of the yard. You take the right side and I'll cinch up my horse and take the left. Look in every nook and cranny. Look under cars and between cars and even on top of cars when you can. Harv, we can't take no chances with this."

The yard, because it paralleled the tracks, ran almost due north and south. Their car was at the extreme eastern side on a rusty siding track, placed there, once it was understood it would be there for some time, to keep it out of the way of the rolling stock that was constantly being turned over and changed. As a consequence they were no more than ten yards from the high-wire fence that encircled the railyard. On the other side of the fence there was nothing but rolling plain with a few bushes and stunted trees to break its openness. Warner looked at it, knowing that anyone who attacked from there would be either truly dumb or suicidal.

He mounted his horse and made a long, sweeping reconnaissance of the cars and the situation to the south. There was a long line of freight cars on the next track west of them, a distance of about twenty yards, but because it was a long line of cars, anyone coming around that way would have a long way to travel before he could hope to attack the cattle car they occupied.

Working further west there were several cars on the next line of tracks, the end car being south of a line from their car to the front gate on the far west side.

He rode almost up to the loading dock, looking carefully for any watchers. Other than a few laborers working on the dock he didn't see a soul. He rode back to the cattle car and sat his horse, waiting for Harvey Pruitt to return.

When the sheriff rode up he shook his head. "Didn't see a thing."

Warner said, "We better water and grain these horses and then get them out of the line of fire."

While they waited for the horses to drink, Harvey got a quarter of a sack of oats and slung it over the saddle of the pinto. "Where you figure?"

Warner nodded toward the north. "We'll take them up that way about a hundred yards, maybe a little less, and then tie them to the fence."

The men inside the cage were stirring around restlessly, at

least Otis Quinn and Calvin were. Willis and Les were sitting quietly, waiting. Warner called, "All right, y'all can come out and get dressed in your clean clothes. But leave your revolvers alone! I don't mean you, Willis. I want to check every one of them."

Harvey said, "Won't be long until it's dark." He looked up in the southwest sky, where a pale moon was becoming visible against the light blue backdrop. "Ought to be plenty light. That'll be pretty near a full moon."

"A shooting moon," Warner said.

"Hunter's moon."

"Yeah," Warner said, grimly, "but our game can shoot back."

"If they come. You reckon they'll come?"

"Hell, Harvey, don't ask me to speculate on something I'm already worried about. You trying to make me jinx my luck?"

"Sorry. You got a plan yit?"

They pulled the horses away from the watering trough and started north up the fence line. "Soon as we get these horses settled we are going to have a meeting about it. Did everybody try and get some sleep today?"

"I know I did. And so did Willis. But that goddamn Otis Quinn was never still. I swear, for a growed man he shore acts like a kid."

When they came back Warner gathered them all in front of the open door of the cattle car. They sat around on a rail and on the ground and on chairs that one or two of the more ambitious had brought out of the cattle car, and made a supper out of the last of their food. Harvey said, "If matters don't pick up around here in the grocery line I'm liable to have to demand more money."

"My fault," Warner said. "I should have brought out more supplies while I was in town this noon, but I'm walking sideways I got so much on my mind. We'll have to make do with this, and once this night is over, I'll see we all get a big breakfast."

They still had some ham and cheese and dried beef and bread, though the bread was reaching a stage where you wondered if it was worth the effort to chew it. And there were still plenty of canned goods. Every man got a can of peaches or apricots or even tomatoes if he didn't care for the sweet syrup on the fruit.

Warner didn't say anything about his intentions until they'd all finished eating, had a drink or two of whiskey, and then, those that smoked, lit up a cigarillo or a cigar.

He had already looked over the revolvers of Les and Calvin and Otis. It still strained the sheriff that Warner was letting them have guns, but Warner had kept reminding him that the men weren't prisoners, that he was having trouble thinking that way because he'd had them in custody. He'd said, "Hell, as far as that goes, it's them that Hawser will be coming here to get. Either to kill outright or take to that jail and put them in a situation where they can't open their mouths."

Even though they had talked about it before, Harvey had still insisted he couldn't understand why Warner was so sure the sheriff had to come for the so-called prisoners. What made him so sure that the sheriff was in with the bankers and, so far as that went, why was he so damn sure that the bankers had robbed themselves?

Warner had said, "The sheriff has got to be in with them, Harv, in some way or another, for their scheme to work. You have a bank robbery, your local law enforcement is supposed to make a mighty effort to catch the crooks. Well, Dick Hawser ain't done enough to stir a cup of coffee. Why not? He don't have to know that the bankers robbed themselves, all he needs to know is that they don't want him doing much. And since they are the power and money in town and he is an elected official he is going to do what they say. Now, why the prisoners? Well, I have scared the shit out of the bankers by talking about Darcey and Jake. And the bankers don't know how much talking they've done, either amongst themselves or to other people. And now I've let Willis be seen in town on that paint horse, as the old lady called him, and word is all over that I've got them out here in a cattle car. The bankers can't let them do any talking to real law enforcement officers or to their stockholders or in court. And now, after this afternoon, word is all over town where the prisoners are. Hawser has to come for them.

Maybe not tonight, but soon. And he can't do it legal because my friend the mayor and justice of the peace won't give him a warrant."

"I still don't see why you so dead-set certain was the bankers robbed theyselves."

"Because it can't be anyone else. Les and Calvin and Otis all swear that Jake and Darcey wasn't carrying a thing when they came back. They didn't have saddlebags and they didn't have a sack in their hands. They didn't even have a grub bag. And it's warm, so nobody was wearing a coat or a duster. They did not come out of that bank with it because they didn't have time to go and hide it before they came back around that corner. We are talking about a lot of money here, Harv. You got any idea how big a pile thirty thousand dollars makes? Even if it's in, say, tens and twenties?"

"Then whar's the money?"

Warner had shrugged. "I don't know. I got an idea, but I don't know."

"Couldn't them bankers have jest carried it off after work in they satchels or something?"

"That's all that makes sense, but it's risky."

"But you feel certain Hawser is comin'?"

Warner looked at the sheriff. Harvey subsided into silence.

Now it was growing dark and Warner began laying out the plan. He said, "First thing you want to remember is that they have got to fire first. Do not pull a trigger until they fire. Shooting a sheriff and his deputies is serious business. We got to be sure that right is on our side. Second, we got one fact in our favor—they think I am here alone. All that crowd saw today was four prisoners in a cage and me. They don't know that you really ain't prisoners but armed men. And they don't know about the sheriff, our sheriff, and they don't know about Willis. That's all in our favor. The big thing they got in their favor is surprise. They know when they are coming and we don't. If I was them I would stretch this night out as long as I could. It's hard to remain alert for thirty minutes, much less three or four or five or six hours. But it has got to be done." He looked around the circle of faces. "Like it or not, you are all in this with me, some willingly, some not so willingly. When it's over you may want to take me to task, but that will have to be later because right now we've got to depend on each other. They are not coming to kill me, they will be coming to kill every mother's son of you. Any of you"—he looked at Les and Calvin and Otis—"who have never been good with a gun before had better suddenly get good. Don't try and shoot at long range. Let your target get so close you can't miss. It will be hard, but it will be a hell of a lot harder if you fire and miss and give away your position. Then you'll wish you had waited. Les . . . I'm going to put you on the left wing." He pointed south, toward the end of about ten freight cars that were on a siding two tracks west of them. "You go down there and you get under the last car, get down and behind the rail. I don't know if they are going to come in a bunch or if they are going to split up, and I don't know which direction they'll attack from. Les, and this goes for you, too, Otis, if they come in a bunch from your direction you slip out and get back here to this car, which is where I'll be, and warn me."

He turned to Otis. He said, "I got the same instructions for you except I want you to guard our right flank. You can see that run of freight cars going off to the north there to the end. I want you to go that way about a hundred yards, maybe a little more, and do like I told Les. Now, if one comes solo, you are on your own. If you can get a chance to hit him over the head, then do so. If you think you can whip him with your fists, do that. If you ain't got no selection"— he shook his head—"then you got to shoot him."

Otis, who always wanted to joke, looked uncomfortable. He said, "Jes' like that? Up an' shoot a body you don't even know? I ain't never shot nobody before. I ain't shore I kin do it."

Warner said, "Was a time, and it ain't been that long ago, that I would have said the same thing. But I did it. And I'm still here alive."

Les said, "Otis, if you don't he is more'n likely gonna kill you an' then he'll have a straight run into our camp."

Otis said, uncertainly, "Wall, I reckon." He pulled his revolver out of its holster and looked at it for a second and then shoved it back.

Warner stared at him a second more and then turned to

Willis and the sheriff. He said, "I'm figuring on you two being my main firepower with your shotguns, that is, if they do what I hope." He pointed due west, toward the gate. "If they come right at us they will have to come through that break between those two lines of freight cars."

The break was about fifty yards wide and fifty or sixty yards from where they were sitting. It was formed on the south end by three freight cars sitting on a siding halfway through the railyard, and on the north side by the end of a string of cars fifteen or sixteen long. From the opening between the cars to the west it made a clear area some sixty to seventy yards wide and about the same in length. Warner drew the whole scene out in the dust with his finger. He said, "Harv, I want you to get on top of one of those end cars with your shotgun, and Willis, I want you to do likewise at the other end. Me and Calvin are going to be back here under the cattle car. Les and Otis will be protecting our flanks from a surprise in that direction. If they do what I'm hoping, they will ride into this cleared area here and if there is to be a fight that's where we want it to happen." He looked around at the faces. He said, "Willis, I don't know about you except that I've observed you as an exceptionally steady hand. I don't know if you've ever had to fire on another man or not and I ain't going to ask you. But when I asked Tom Birdsong for a dependable man with a gun he knew what I meant so I ain't going to worry about you. But so far, for certain, the only two I know here that are experienced with guns are me and Harvey. I can guarantee you this. If you lose your nerve, if you hesitate, if you cut and run, you will get killed and you will probably get the rest of us killed."

The sheriff said, "And that is the long and the short of it. After that is said they ain't another damn thing to say. The men that may be coming here tonight don't mean you no good. You judge your actions by that thought."

Warner stood up. He asked, "How many canteens we got?"

Calvin said, "Four."

"Well, those will go with the men who will be out in position, Harvey and Les and Otis and Willis. Me and Calvin, if we get thirsty, will drink out of the horse trough. Get yourself whatever you can find to carry along with you

to eat because I got to figure this is going to be one hell of a
long night. I don't reckon I need to tell anybody they can't
smoke. And don't nobody take a jug of whiskey." He gave
Otis a look.

Otis said, "Be all right to have a quick pull 'fore we go?"

"Yeah, but just don't make it too big. I want you brave,
not drunk."

He walked over to the end of the cattle car and reached
through the slats to get his rifle. As he did he felt a slight
twinge in his side. He put his hand to the wound. Mostly he
didn't think about it even though sometimes, when he made
the wrong move, it would remind him of its presence. The
stitches were probably more than ready to come out. The
doctor in Hondo had warned him, before he'd left, to be
careful and not let too much time pass before having them
removed. He said, "You let your flesh close up tight on them
and you'll think you've had fun before in your life when
some doctor goes to working them out. I've known cases
they had to be *cut* out. That's catgut and it can cause an
infection all on its own after you're over your original
wound."

And, indeed, his side, even through the material of his
shirt, did feel a little warm. He shrugged. Right then it
didn't make a hell of a lot of difference. If they got caught
off-guard it wouldn't matter if the stitches ever got taken out
or not. It made him think of Laura, who'd brought the
subject up at noon. He'd said he didn't have the time, and
that had set her off on a new track. He didn't believe he'd
ever known a woman who could give a man more hell on
more different subjects and all at the same time. It was a real
talent and one to be admired.

Thinking about her made him smile. When he was away
from her his thoughts of her were mostly fond and loving.
He missed her when they were apart. It was only when they
were together that he found himself wishing he was missing
her.

They had only one other rifle, one brought by Willis.
Willis would be using one of the sheriff's shotguns and he
had his own handgun. Warner borrowed the rifle for Calvin.
He doubted he could hit much with it, but he knew the
young man would be useless with just a handgun. Handguns

were all that was needed for Les and Otis, since they were more lookouts than fighters.

He said, "Now get it in your mind where everybody is and don't nobody be firing carelessly. Ain't no use in us shooting one another."

They stood around looking at each other. The sheriff said, "Everybody looked to their ammunition? Made shore they got plenty? Willis, you got enough shells?"

"Got two boxes."

"Better take another'n."

It was good dark, but the moon was up full and the area was full of shadowy shapes thrown by the weak light. It would be handy of them, Warner thought, if they'd come while the moon was still up, but he doubted they'd be that considerate.

"Now remember," he said, "me and Calvin are going to be on the back side of the cattle car, the fence side. So don't go to getting us confused with the wrong folks. You better get to your places. Willis, you and Harv don't go to sleep on top of those boxcars and roll off and break your necks. Don't nobody get impatient. It's going to be a long night. Les, if you or Otis have to come in for any reason, and it had better be a damn good one, don't just come strolling in. Give a low whistle or chunk a rock or something." He looked around. "All right. Let's go."

13

He figured it was a little past eight o'clock when he and Calvin crawled under the stock car and began to try and arrange themselves between the rails. It was no good trying to lie straight behind one rail so as to be able to look out into what Warner had begun to think of as the target area. He was six feet tall and Calvin wasn't much less, and lying on their bellies with their heads behind the front rail put the far rail right under their knees at their shins. The only way was to curl up and it had to be a pretty tight ball at that. Warner curled on his right side, which gave him a partial view toward the front and a good vista down toward where Les was guarding their southern flank. He could feel Calvin's back so he knew that Calvin had curled on his left side and was looking mostly off in the direction of Otis's post.

It was very uncomfortable. After digging half a dozen rocks out from under the wrong places he said, "Calvin, we ain't going to make it like this. Go up in the car and get a couple of blankets."

"Them rocks been proddin' you, too, Mr. Grayson?"

"Hurry up, Calvin. Be sure and wave at Willis and the sheriff. You don't want a load of buckshot."

He let Calvin wiggle out first and then he came out. They'd both need to be out to get the blankets spread in place. They were going to have to be comfortable because he had not the slightest doubt that it would be a long wait.

He'd elected to take up a position under the cattle car because he knew that it would be the spot Hawser would head for. He, of course, did not want to be *in* the car during a gunfight. The boards the car was made of were heavy when it came to holding cattle or horses, but they wouldn't turn a large caliber slug. Under the car was the best protected firing spot he could think of.

Even if it was cramped and rocky.

Calvin came back with the blankets and they carefully folded them and smoothed them and laid them in place between the tracks. The blankets might make the ground a little softer, but it wouldn't make the quarters any less cramped or the wait any shorter.

They crawled back in, taking the same positions as before. After they got settled Warner asked Calvin if he had a shell in the chamber of his rifle.

"Sir?"

"Have you levered a shell into the chamber of your rifle? Is it ready to fire?"

"Wall, I don't rightly know, Mr. Grayson. I just tuck it like you handed it to me."

He sighed. "Goddammit, Calvin, how old are you?"

"I be twenny year old. This past March."

"How in hell did you manage to get that old as dumb as you are?" He laid his rifle on the rail and rolled over and took the rifle out of Calvin's hands. He jacked the lever. No cartridge flew out. The chamber had been empty, but it wasn't now. He carefully let down the hammer with his thumb and handed it back to the young man. He said, "It will fire now, Calvin. You pull the hammer back with your thumb and then you—not now! Let it back down. Slowly. All right. You pull the hammer back, cock it. And it's ready to fire. You do know how to pull the trigger, don't you?"

"Mr. Grayson, I know right smart about guns. Been handlin' 'em all my life. I know how to work this rifle. Done it a many a time. But you seemed set on showin' me how 'n I didn't want to spoil your pleasure. I learnt to do that with my daddy. It give him pleasure show me how to do thangs. So sometimes I jest acted dumb."

Warner smiled. He said, "I'm sorry, Calvin. This wasn't the time I wanted to find out that the guy next to me in a gunfight didn't know anything about guns. But don't pleasure me anymore by acting dumb, all right?"

Calvin said, hastily, "Jes' don't take the wrong idee t'other way. I ain't oversmart, neither."

"Just keep alert, Calvin. And jab me if you see anything."

He turned his gaze toward the front. By craning his head out a little so he could see beyond the overhang the sides of the car made, he could make out the dim humps of the sheriff and Willis on top and at the ends of their freight cars. He could see that they were careful not to let anything show over the edge to give away their positions. He was satisfied he'd put his people in situations as safe as possible.

He squirmed around and took his hat off and put his hat on the rail and rested his chin on it. It wasn't a particularly comfortable position, but then he didn't figure there was such a thing to be had under the stock car.

He lay there thinking about Sheriff Dick Hawser and trying to figure what he'd do if he was in the man's position. It was a shame, he thought, that he hadn't tried to find out more about the man or to have found some way to have stretched their brief conversation. But, of course, things had come to a head pretty fast on that occasion and he'd more or less lost his option for an extended conversation.

But he did know, as a result of the meeting, that the man was a hothead. He could get into his mind at least that much, even if he didn't know a great deal about him. It was good that Hawser was a hothead. It was good that Hawser thought he was some kind of a big shot. It was good that Hawser thought he ought to have four deputies to run a county that didn't need more than two to keep law and order. And it was good that Hawser liked to do dirty work for rich bankers. The whole package added up to a hotheaded, impatient man. Warner hoped that Hawser's impatience would make him act quickly and that his temper would cause him to come busting in with plans to overwhelm one solitary guard for the four prisoners he either wanted to kill or put in his jail.

He guessed then that Hawser would come not much later than midnight. To Warner he didn't seem to be a man who'd care much one way or the other about the extent of the moonlight. With the odds he'd have on his hand he probably wouldn't think it would make much difference. Warner had learned, mainly from his gunfighter friend Wilson Young, that there were a lot of dead men who'd gotten dead simply by underestimating their enemy. Hawser struck him as the kind who would underestimate as a general rule. He was the power in his county, he had the guns and the badges, and who the hell was this smart mouth who'd come barging into his office? Warner doubted he'd connect his inability to get a warrant with any friendship Warner had with the mayor. The sheriff would think that Martha was being obstinate just for the sake of it. Besides, he probably figured he didn't need a warrant.

Midnight, or before, Warner guessed. Time enough to go to the saloon, have a few drinks, and feel pretty sure Warner was asleep.

He said to Calvin, "You awake, boy?"

Calvin kind of groaned. "Like to know how a body could sleep in this here position. My laigs is wound up like a cheap clock."

"Well, you keep that head moving. Keep looking around. They could come at any time."

"They fire first?"

"Yeah, but that don't mean you got to let one of them stick a gun barrel up your nose before you get the idea."

He had kept Calvin with him because he'd judged the boy the least capable of them all. If Calvin made a mistake Warner wanted to be there to put it right.

Warner settled down for the wait. One of the reasons he was good with horses was that he was patient. You had to be patient with a horse because the only way they could be taught anything was by endless repetition. Horses were dumb. There just wasn't any other word for it. Some of them were a little less dumb than others, like the Andalusian he was riding, but as a group they weren't smart at all. They had a brain about the size of a walnut and that wasn't much brain when you had a big, strong muscle machine that weighed eleven or twelve hundred pounds.

But this waiting required a different kind of patience. It wasn't the patience of doing something over and over; it was waiting for an indeterminate time, waiting, if you looked at the matter realistically, for something that might not happen. Or might not happen the way you'd figured it. His grandfather had told him that the most unpredictable animal, next to a woman, was a man. His grandfather had said, "You can give a man every reason to do something, every advantage, every profit, and then you had better also expect him to turn around and do exactly the opposite. Do the opposite thing when it will not only not profit him but will hurt him. There's only one person alive you can depend on doing exactly what you think he will and that's yourself. And even then it ain't a good idea to bet it as a sure thing."

The time passed. By the moon, which was a very poor gauge unless you knew its path for certain in the place you were, Warner reckoned it to be going on for midnight. He thought of Otis Quinn and Les and hoped that they were staying awake and alert.

He said, low-voiced, "Calvin, I want you to be careful to keep a sharp eye to the north, toward where Otis is."

"Yessir. I'm adoin' that. Mr. Grayson, my laig has gone to sleep."

"Well, kick it around and stretch it out. Have you made sure you can swing your rifle to the right and to the front?"

"Yessir."

The waiting went on and Warner fretted. He was getting thirsty and he wanted a smoke and a drink of whiskey and something to eat. But it was too late to be moving around. Even for water he dared not come out from under the cattle car. Part of the reason for his impatience was because he felt he was near the end of a long trail and he wanted to hurry up and get it over with. He tried to count back how many days it had been since the affair had started with the bunch jumping him on the road. It was impossible, because so much had happened the days just seemed to run together. It seemed like he'd been in Round Rock for a week, but he knew this was only the third night.

He said, in a low voice, "Calvin, stay awake."

"Yessir. I ain't sleepy. I tuck me a good long rest this afternoon. Wonder what time it be?"

"I don't know. Close to midnight I'd guess."

"Whar's that gold timepiece of yore'n?"

"In my pocket, Calvin. But I can't read it in the dark."

Calvin said, "Oh," and then was quiet for a moment. After a moment he said, hesitantly, "Mr. Grayson, that do be law that will be acomin' in here. Is that the fact of the matter?"

Warner said, uncomfortably, "That's one way of looking at it, Calvin."

Calvin persisted. "But we will be ashootin' at the law? Raight?"

Warner did not want to talk about the matter. He was already getting little flutters in his stomach. The waiting was hard, especially hard since he wasn't sure of his enemy and he wasn't certain of any of the men on his side, with the possible exception of Harvey. He said, "Look, Calvin, you got to understand something. It's a sheriff who will be coming here, but he is not really a lawman. He is not a good sheriff like Harvey. He is a bad man. If you took his tin badge off you'd have an outlaw. Do you understand?"

Calvin said, slowly, "I jest want to be shore we doin' the raight thang."

Warner jerked his shoulders in exasperation. He said, "Right thing, wrong thing, hell, Calvin, I only know I'm doing what I think I have to do. Is that good enough for you?"

"Aw, Mr. Grayson, I wadn't meanin'—"

"It's gonna have to be good enough, Calvin, because it's the only answer I can give you. Right, wrong . . . I don't know about that. But I think once I brought us to this town we were heading for a fight. All I'm trying to do is win it. Do you understand that, Calvin?"

The young man was a long moment answering. Then he said, slowly, "I reckon as well as I be able. I was jest wonderin' if you don't never git scairt? Seems like you so certain 'bout thangs."

Warner gave him a quick look in the dark. He said, p"Calvin, right now I am as scared as anyone in this place. Don't get the idea I'm not scared."

Calvin said, "I'm kinna glad to hear that, Mr. Grayson. Makes me feel not so lonesome, somehows er other."

Warner put out an awkward hand and gave the boy a brief

pat on the shoulder. "You'll be all right, Cal. Keep your eyes open wide and watch good and do like I tell you."

"Yessir. But I wisht they'd come on if they's comin'."

"Me too, Calvin, me too."

He looked out into the night. On top of the boxcars he could see Willis and Harvey moving around, shifting positions, trying to get more comfortable.

To himself he said, half aloud, "Come on, Hawser. Damn it, come on."

Calvin said, "You say somethin', Mr. Grayson?"

"No, not really. Just mumbling to myself."

"I use to do thet, but my daddy said folks thet talked to theyselves was goin' loco."

Warner said, "I think I already have gone loco. If that damn sheriff don't come pretty soon I think I'm going to send y'all into the bank tomorrow to actually rob it this time."

"You be joshin', Mr. Grayson."

Warner didn't say anything.

Calvin rolled his body slightly back toward Warner and said, over his shoulder, "Ain'tcha?" There was a note of concern in his voice.

Warner said, "That's what I told the sheriff I was going to do."

He heard Calvin swallow audibly. "Mr. Grayson, I don't know iffen I could do thet. I'd be pretty scairt."

"I'm joshing, Calvin. Get back to watching."

The moon passed across the sky with agonizing slowness and finally disappeared. The shadowy shapes went with it. Now there was only the light from the stars and they didn't provide much. At first it was very black and very difficult to see, but gradually Warner's eyes adjusted and he was able to make out the things he'd been able to see before, but they weren't as distinct. He could see the shapes of Willis and the sheriff, but he couldn't see their shotguns or any other features. They were just blobs.

It was perhaps half an hour later that he heard a distant though distinct sound from the direction of the main gate to the railyard. It sounded very much like iron striking iron, like a horse's shod hoof striking a rail. His every sense became instantly alert. He punched Calvin.

"Huh?"

"Sssshh! Keep your voice down. I heard something coming from the front. But you watch to our right."

He pushed his rifle a little more out in front of him and tried to pierce the dark with his eyes, his ears straining for another out-of-the-ordinary sound.

Nothing came. All he heard was the occasional cry of a night bird, the sound of the wind in the trees, the rustle of a night creature grubbing for food. He lay rigid, listening and trying to see, for what seemed like a very long time. The sound he heard could have come from the loading dock. It could have come from some railroad workman handling a last-minute job that couldn't wait.

He began to relax again, cursing. Hawser was hot-tempered, intemperate, impatient, a bully, a man used to having his way. He should have come, Warner told himself. He should have come long before now. He had no way of knowing, but he guessed it was at least three in the morning. All he could hope was that every man was still alert, although they'd been in position for going on seven hours. None of the men, especially the three ex-prisoners, were trained to discipline, and it took self-discipline to force yourself to stay awake through a night that, with nothing to occupy your mind, must seem endless.

And then he heard a sort of muffled noise off to his right. It was a distant noise and he couldn't make out what it might have been. It was a kind of a thud, but it was not a sharp thud, more of a muffled sound.

He was turning his head to look over at Calvin when he distinctly heard the sound of horses coming. There was the creak of leather and another clink of a horseshoe. He strained his eyes into the night, looking toward the opening between the cars. He could see nothing.

A voice suddenly came out of the dark. It said, "You thar! You thar, Grayson! This here is Dick Hawser an' I'm comin' in. I got me a warrant. You damn well better not fahr on no peace officer er by gawd I'll hang you myself!"

Warner lay still. Perhaps Willis and Harvey could see them, but they were not to fire until Hawser and his party came into the target area.

Hawser called again, "Goddammit, Grayson, we be comin' in. You gonna answer me, boy? Or are you too ascairt?"

Warner debated. He didn't think the sound of his voice would be enough to give them an accurate target. Sound at night was difficult to place. He said, not too loudly, "Hawser, you better stay away from here. These are my lawful prisoners. You come back in the daylight. I ain't doin' no business with you half asleep. You ain't supposed to come out here in the middle of the night."

"I got a warrant, boy. Don't say nothin' 'bout the time. Jes' says I kin take them prisoners."

"Who's the warrant from?"

"It's a justice of the peace warrant an' it's plenty good for the likes of you. Now you get out of that stock car and walk toward me. Leave your guns where they be. This is the law talkin' to you, boy. You better damn well listen. I got plenty of men with me so your ass is grass, boy. Surrender them pris'ners er get kilt tryin' to keep 'em."

Before Warner could reply he heard a sudden, loud volley of shots from off to his left, Les's position. He couldn't tell how many shots had been fired because they'd seemed to come one right on top of the other. He was turning his head to look in that direction when Calvin said, "Oh, damn! Somebody's acomin'."

Warner swiveled his head toward Calvin just as a furious volley of shots, rifle shots, came from where Hawser's voice had been. He could heard the slugs whistling and crashing through the structure of the stock car. He was trying, however, to look to his right, when Calvin began scrambling to his knees and trying to back out from under the car. He made a grab for Calvin, trying to push him back down, and caught sight of a dim figure running toward them. He was no more than fifteen yards away and he was carrying a rifle. Even as the rifle bullets went off over him and part of his mind distractedly wondered what the shots from Les's end had meant, the rifleman saw the movement Calvin was making and dropped to one knee and fired twice, rapidly levering in a new shell after each shot. He wasn't firing at the boxcar. He was firing at Calvin's white shirt under the car.

Warner had his hand on Calvin's back, trying to push him down, when he felt and heard the first bullet strike. Calvin said, "Oooooh," and his body gave a little shiver and he began to fall from his hands and knees down to his belly.

Warner could see the man clearly. He was up and advancing, the rifle held at his hip. He fired again and Warner heard the bullet strike Calvin. It sounded as if it had hit him in the thigh.

Because Calvin was in the way Warner couldn't swing his rifle around and bring it to bear. Instead he dropped it and pulled out his revolver. He extended his arm, aiming over Calvin as he slowly sank to his chest on the blanket. The man was only eight or nine yards away, but it was a difficult shot because of the way Warner had to twist his body around. The man dropped to his knee for another shot as Warner thumbed the hammer back and fired. It was not too dark for him to see the bullet spin the man to his left, the rifle falling out of his hands. Before he could fall Warner shot him again, knowing, this time, that he'd taken the man dead in the chest by the way he went straight over backward and lay motionless.

But there was no time to waste on anything, not Calvin, not the man he'd just shot. Without pause Warner swung to the front, dropping his revolver and taking up his rifle. It was clear what Hawser's plan had been. He'd sent two men to flank him and locate his position by his gun flashes. Now they would charge. He hunkered low, showing just as little of his head above the rail as was needed to fire his rifle.

He did not so much see them as become aware of them in the blinding flashes as Willis and Harvey fired at almost the same instant. In that flash of light he saw three mounted men running toward him. He had time to squeeze off one shot at the rider in the middle as the blackness closed in and then was relit as Harvey and Willis fired again. In that flash he could see that the horses were riderless. He could hear one of them screaming, and there was no sound like the screaming of a horse. It always had sounded to him like the frightened wails of a woman. He yelled, "Hold your fire! *Harvey, this is Warner! Hold your fire! Hold your fire!*"

And then it was very quiet. His ears were ringing with the sound of his own gunshots. It was a moment before he could hear the moan. A man was saying, "Help! Help! I'm shot to pieces. For gawd's sake, he'p me."

He took a moment to feel for any sign of life in Calvin. There was none. He gave the boy a sad pat on the back. He had panicked. He had seen the man in plenty of time. All he'd had to do, from the protection under the car, was swing around and shoot him. Instead he'd lost his head and tried to rise up and then panicked in the close quarters. It had cost him his life.

Warner came out cautiously from under the car. He called to the two on top of the boxcars, "This is me, Warner. I'm gonna make a light and see what has happened here."

He heard the Hondo sheriff call, "Be careful, Warner. I don't thank they's anybody playin' possum, but you never know."

Warner went first to check the man he'd shot. He knelt by him and, by striking a match, could see that he'd hit the man in the left side and the middle of the chest. He was dead, but Warner nevertheless removed his revolver from its holster and picked up the man's rifle. He moved cautiously back toward the cattle car. He yelled to Harvey and Willis. He said, "Something happened down Les's way. I don't know what. Keep an eye in that direction. I figure four are down, but that's one short."

Then there came a far-off yell from the south end. It was Les. He called, "Mr. Grayson, Mr. Grayson! Kin I come in? I got one here!"

"Come in, but be careful! You might want to wait until I get a light lit!"

He climbed the ramp of the car and rummaged around until he found a kerosene lamp. The moans and pleas of the wounded man continued. He knelt down and pumped the lamp up and then lit the wick. Light instantly revealed splinters of wood everywhere the rifle shots had passed through. Warner trimmed the wick and then went slowly down the ramp, holding the lamp well away from his body. He didn't know how bad off the wounded man was. He said, into the darkness, "Who are you? How bad you hurt?"

The voice was faint. "Name's Ferris. I'm a depity. I thank my shoulder is shot plumb off."

"You got a gun?"

"Mister, I don't want to fight no more. I'm bleedin' to death. I don't know if I'm near a gun. I think my laig is broke. Horse went down with me under it."

Warner hated that, hated having horses get hurt in men's gun battles. But there was no help for it. If a man that was shooting at you was riding a horse, the horse very often got hit.

Warner hesitated about going to the man. He was not a risk taker and he did not know who the man was or how bad he was hurt or what he was capable of doing. He said, loudly, "Harv, you and Willis come on down. We'll come at this fellow from both directions."

The man's voice was getting fainter. He said, "Fer gawd's sake, mister, I ain't got no gun. I swear it. If I had the stren'th I'd drag myself over into your light so's you could see."

Warner could hear the sounds of Harvey and Willis coming down from the boxcars. In a moment Harvey said, "Warner, we be here. I can kind of see the men on the ground. I got a shotgun trained right on the one I think is wounded. You thar—make some kind o' motion."

Warner waited.

Harvey said, "He's the one. He moves I'll blow him to bits."

"All right," Warner said. "I'm coming." But before he moved he happened to glance behind him toward the east. To his astonishment he could see the sky beginning to lighten. He fumbled his watch out of his pocket and was amazed to see that it was nearly six o'clock. Dick Hawser had not held his patience all night as Warner had thought. He'd probably gotten a good night's sleep and then arrogantly figured to ride out before dawn and get the job done.

All of a sudden Warner felt very, very tired. For him it had been an all-night fight. He started forward, toward the wounded man, holding the lamp high.

14

The wounded man's shoulder, his right, was nowhere near shot away. He'd caught a heavy load of buckshot in the shoulder and his right arm and in his neck and the side of his face. And, indeed, his left leg was broken just below the knee where the barrel of the horse had pinned it against the ground. The man was in pain, pale, even by the dim glow of the lantern, and sweating. Les had arrived and Warner sent him to the cattle car to bring back a bottle of whiskey. They gave the man a drink and it helped his color some, but it was clear he was bleeding to death and needed a doctor badly. Willis said, "Judgin' from whar he was hit he was on my side an' this is some of my work." He got down on one knee and helped pull the man's shirt off. He said, "Maybe I can bind up some of the worst places he's lettin' out blood till we can git him to a doctor."

Looking at him Warner thought they had better get him some help pretty quick or it wasn't going to matter. He felt a certain amount of pity for the man, but not much. Looking closer he saw, though his features were somewhat changed by the fear and the pain, that it was the young deputy who'd visited him only the day before and had gone back to look at his prisoners. It seemed funny to think of it as less than twenty-four hours past. It felt more like a week. The man, in his present state, might have been more deserving of sympathy, but Warner didn't have a hard time remembering that only a few minutes earlier the man had been sending rifle bullets his way with the intention of killing him.

He turned to his right, not taking the lantern away from Willis and his work. The sheriff was kneeling over a body. Warner edged closer as Harvey turned him over. It was Dick Hawser. He had collected a load of buckshot in his left side and back, but there was a large bullet hole through his shirt in the middle of his chest. Warner supposed that it was Hawser he'd hit when he'd fired his lone shot at the group charging from the front. But he neither knew nor cared if it was his bullet or Harvey's buckshot that had killed the man. He noticed Harvey going through the sheriff's pockets. He said, "What the hell you doing, Harvey, robbing the dead?"

"Hell no," he said. "The son of a bitch claimed to have a warrant. I ain't finding no warrant, justice of the peace or any other kind."

Warner said, tiredly, "Save your time. He never had a warrant. I already had that fixed. He was trying to bluff his way in without a fight so he could massacre the bunch of us. Calvin's dead."

"Awww, hell!" Harvey said. "I'm right sorry to hear that. He wasn't a bad kid. A little slow and kind of harum-scarum."

Warner told him what happened. Then he said, "I guess maybe I should have held him out of the fight. Sent him off somewhere."

"You couldn't know he'd lose his head and act like that. Like you say, he had his man dead to rights. All he had to do was use the gun. And he'd told you he'd been around guns all his life."

Warner said, "Yeah, but I don't think the right end." He sighed. "Well, too late to change things now." He looked to his right. A few feet away the third man was lying on his stomach, his arms akimbo. Warner could see where the buckshot had taken him in the side of the head and the neck. He said, "Looks like you got two."

The sheriff said, "This one"—and he poked Hawser—"was still agoin' until I seen a flash from your end and he come off his horse backward. I'd say you got the biggest part of him."

It had become light enough for Warner to see the three horses that had been carrying the men. They had run off fifteen or twenty yards and were standing, their heads drooping, their reins dangling to the ground. One horse was pawing the ground with his feet and Warner reckoned that was the horse that had been hit and screamed. Maybe he'd only been peppered and the shot could be dug out. He reminded himself to have a look when he got time.

Then it suddenly dawned on him how late it was getting. Morning was coming fast and they had very little time. Either being up all night had dulled his brain or he was still thinking about the gun battle. He sure as hell hadn't been tending to business, that was for sure.

He said, urgently, "Harvey, put on your badge. Then go over there and borrow one of those horses. We ain't got time for you to go for the pinto. Then ride like hell for the mayor's house. It's right off of downtown on a side street. Anybody you see ought to be able to tell you where it is."

The sheriff looked startled. "You want me going to her *house?* At this hour?"

"Goddammit, Harvey, we are late already. She's expecting you. Tell her we got dead men out here and does she want to come out here and give a judgment or does she want us to bring 'em into town for the whatever you call it."

"Inquest?"

Warner pointed his finger at Harvey. "Yeah, that. How they died. Tell her I won't move a thing until I get word from her. They'll have a buckboard for you. Bring that back. And ask her husband, Muddy Roads, to come out here anyway, whether she comes or not. I got to talk to him."

Harvey was looking around. He said, "Where the hell is Otis Quinn?"

Warner took a quick look back. "I don't know. I'll find out. You have got to go like hell. I've got a bunch of business to get straightened up before nine this morning. Now get going."

He turned as the sheriff started for the horses, suddenly conscious of the shortage of time. Les was standing right behind him. Warner said, "I heard gunshots from your end. What happened?"

Les was a bit pale. He said, "I had me a man trying to work his way around the piece of train I was guarding."

"Goddammit, what happened?"

Les swallowed. He said, "I had to make a good bit of commotion to get the feller to shoot at me. You 'member you said they was to shoot first."

"But shots had already been fired."

"Oh. Yeah, I reckon they had. But he shot about that time." He put his hand to his ear where a little bit of blood was showing. "Son of a bitch missed me 'bout an inch. Hit a journal er somethin' an' a piece of the slug done near taken the lobe off my ear."

Warner stared at him. "I heard at least three shots."

"Oh, yeah. Then I shot him. Twicet." He looked around. "Where's Otis and Calvin?"

Warner told him. Les looked down and scuffed the ground with his boot toe. "I thought he'd be safe with you. I knowed he didn't have no business being in no gunfight. But where's Otis?"

Warner said, "I guess we'd better go see. The man that killed Calvin had to have gotten around Otis, though I didn't hear a shot. You don't reckon he'd run, do you?"

Les shrugged. He said, "You've knowed him pert near as long's I have, Mr. Grayson. He had a lot of mouth on him, more'n what's generally good fer a body, but I cain't see him runnin' out on you, knowin' you was dependin' on him to hold that corner an' not let somebody blindside you."

They started down the track, walking between the fence and the line of freight cars. Warner glanced over at Les. He said, "You still look a little green around the gills."

Les grimaced. He said, "It tuck me a little harder'n I thought. It wadn't something I'd like to do as a regular thang."

Warner said harshly, "You ain't supposed to like it. Nobody said that. But you're not supposed to let some bastard shoot you just because you don't feel like defending yourself. What did the sheriff tell you?"

Les lifted his hands in a kind of helpless gesture. "Said if you didn't shoot them they'd damn sure shoot you, you even hesitated. But he got so damn close!"

"You sure he's dead?"

Les looked uncomfortable. "Well, if he ain't, somebody come along and give him a new haid."

"You shot him in the head?"

"Hell, he was raight there, Mr. Grayson. I shot what was closest. We was nearly wearin' the same hat."

Warner saw the pinto and the Andalusian just ahead. They veered over to the horses and Warner took the Andalusian on lead and handed the pinto's reins to Les. "Too near to mount up," he said. "Just up here at the end of this line of cars."

They found Otis half propped up against the wheel of one of the boxcars. His eyes were closed and his body was slack. His hat was bashed in and they could see places where blood had seeped through. His revolver was still in his hand.

Warner knelt quickly by his side and put his ear to his chest. He listened a moment. He said, "He's still breathing. But I don't know for how much longer."

"Lord have mercy!" Les said. He'd lifted Otis's hat off and was staring at the bloody mess that was the top of his head. He said, "Somebody knocked the living shit out of him. Looks like he was hit with a sledgehammer."

Warner took a quick look. "Or a rifle barrel." He looked at the pistol in Otis's hand. He said, "All he had to do was point it and pull the trigger." He looked around, trying to decide what to do. He said, "We got to get him to a doctor 'cause he damn sure ain't going to get better back here. Bring up that pinto horse and we'll load him across the saddle and lead him back to camp."

They got Otis's limp body balanced across the saddle, though the pinto wanted to shy away from the smell of blood. Warner got him calmed down and then mounted the Andalusian. "I'm hoping that the sheriff is on the way back with a buckboard right soon. We can get Otis into town in that. Right now I'm going down to take a look at your work. You lead the horse back to camp and then you and Willis ease Otis down onto the ground. Be damn careful with him. For all I know his skull might be cracked and his brains leaking out. So don't jostle him. He ain't got many to lose."

He rode down to where Les had been stationed and looked at the dead deputy lying on his back. He had two bullet holes in his face, one right in the middle of his forehead. His arms were outflung and a revolver was still in his hand. Warner could see that the hammer was cocked. Yes, Les had given the man a fair chance, a hell of a fair chance. Warner thought to himself that *he* seldom let friends get as close as Les had let the deputy approach, much less an enemy.

He left the scene as it was and rode back to the camp. He looked at his watch. It was five minutes of seven. The time made him terribly anxious. He found Willis and Les sitting by the two wounded men, having a drink of whiskey. They offered him the bottle and he took a distracted sip as he stared toward the gate, looking for the sheriff to come back with the mayor and Muddy.

Les said, "Somethin' gnawin' on you, Mr. Grayson? Looks to me like we pretty well got the crop in. I was thinkin' of maybe makin' some coffee."

Warner said, "You might end up leaving it, Les. We still got the last of the corn to get in. The big ears, the prime cut. We're nearing the end of a long road, but you ain't to the end until you get to the end."

Les looked confused. He said, "What's left? You said the sheriff was part of the bank robbery. He don't look like he'll be robbing many others."

Warner looked down at the red-faced man, who was no longer red-faced but gray. Flies were buzzing around his wounds as they were the other dead man's. Dick Hawser didn't look like such a bully nor anywhere near as big as he had. Warner had noticed that before, how death seemed to physically shrivel men as if they lost weight and height and breadth as the life force ran out of them.

Then he saw what looked to be a buckboard zigging and zagging its way through the jumble of freight cars. An outrider seemed to be with it. He watched and then the buckboard rounded a curve around a boxcar, bumped over some rails, and then came on toward the camp. He could see Harvey driving with another man Warner didn't recognize beside him on the seat. Muddy Roads was trailing them on horseback.

The instant Harvey pulled up the buckboard Warner was at his side. He said, "Where is the mayor?"

But it was Muddy, who'd just ridden up, who answered. He said, "She's gone to get her constables in her buggy. She ought not to be more than ten minutes behind. Your sheriff"—he looked at Warner as if he hadn't mentioned he had a sheriff of his own—"your sheriff said you had some wounded men so I figured we'd better pick up Doc Breckenridge on the way out here."

Warner looked around. The doctor was going from man to man, making sure the dead ones were still dead and finally settling on Otis and the wounded deputy. With Willis's and Les's help he was getting them into the buckboard. He said, "I've got to get these men back to town. One is going to bleed to death if I don't do something and I don't know how bad the other one is hurt. He may have a skull fracture, he may have a concussion. But I can't practice medicine in a railroad yard."

Warner told Harvey to take the doctor and his patients back into town but to get back as soon as he had unloaded them. He sent Les along to help with the unloading.

Muddy Roads had dismounted. He came to stand beside Warner, slowly looking around, and said, "We got any sheriff's department left?"

Warner shook his head. He said, "There are two more dead to the left and the right where they tried to flank us." He glanced at Muddy Roads. He said, "I don't know what you're thinking, Muddy, but it happened like I said it would. He tried to sucker us and he came to either kill all of us or put us in jail. We protected ourselves."

"Looks like you did a fair job of it."

Warner said, "If we hadn't, it would be us laying there."

Muddy put up his hand. He said, "You are testifying to the wrong Roads. The judge ain't here yet an' I ain't got no influence with her."

Warner said, "That ain't why I asked you to come yourself." He took Muddy's arm and drew him a few feet away. He said, "The main finish to this business is going to take place at the bank. I need you there. We are going through that door at the stroke of nine and we are going to lock it behind us. Then we are going to have an audit. All our own."

Muddy looked at him. "How are you going to do that? I don't know as that is in the bank charter."

"Never mind about that," Warner said. "What I want you to do is get about two more solid citizens, stockholders in the bank, and have them there. Can you do that?"

Muddy thought a moment. He said, "I reckon I can think of a few, but I don't know what I'd tell them."

"Tell them it's a special stockholder's meeting concerning the bank robbery and that it is vital that they be there."

Muddy frowned for a moment. He said, "Well, there's Roy Garret, he owns the stock auction barn. He's one of the more upstanding citizens. At least he ain't a hypocrite. He don't come to my place and then try and get me closed down. And Amos Mills. He's retired from the cavalry."

"Not too old, is he?"

"Not over forty. Got retired because he lost an arm. Used to be an Indian fighter out in Arizona or New Mexico. We call him Major Mills because I truly think he misses the army, God knows why, and would still like to be serving. He's a good man. One-armed or not I wouldn't care to tangle with him."

Warner said, "It's passing seven-thirty. I'd appreciate it if you'd head on back to town and advise those two and caution them not to speak about it to anyone else. And then make sure that they are at the bank before nine o'clock."

Muddy studied Warner's face for a moment. He said, "I hope to hell you know what you're doing. By my actions I am joining in with you on whatever scheme you have in mind. Remember, if you're wrong you'll be leaving, but I'll still have to live here. So will my wife."

Warner said, "My grandfather was a great believer in arithmetic. If two and two didn't come out four then he knew something was damn sure wrong. I'm of the same turn of mind."

They had walked to Muddy's horse. "And you think we've got a situation here where two and two aren't four?"

"I'll bet you another hundred-dollar bill on it. Give you a chance to get your money back."

Muddy stared at him for a long few seconds and then put his boot in the stirrup. He said, "You ever come in my casino I'll have you thrown out." He reined his horse around. "I'll get Mills and Garret."

"And tell them to keep their mouths shut."

Muddy nodded and then rode away.

It was about ten minutes before the mayor arrived. She came in her buggy, bumping along over the tracks right behind Harvey returning with the buckboard. He led her straight into the middle of the camp and Warner went over to help her down.

Even though she had been called at the crack of dawn she looked as if she'd spent all day getting ready. Her light auburn hair was swept back and held in place by a bejeweled pin; her trim figure was held tightly by a lavender bodice and a deeper-colored skirt. She was wearing thin black pigskin gloves. As she looked around she slowly removed her gloves and then stepped toward where the two dead men lay. She stopped a moment to study Dick Hawser and then his deputy. She turned and said, to Warner, "Mr. Grayson, you appear to have a dead sheriff and deputy here. Are there more?" The marshal she'd brought stood behind her, watching and listening.

He realized she intended to conduct the inquest as if no previous conversation on the subject had ever occurred between them. As long as just results occurred he was ready to play it any way she wanted to. He said, "Yes, ma'am, Your Honor. There are two more dead deputies and one wounded deputy that's been taken into town with the doctor."

"Yes," she said, "I saw him as we were getting ready to come out. There was one of your men with him. A prisoner of yours, I believe."

"Yes, ma'am. There are also two more dead deputies. I can show them to you. There is also a dead man that I was considering my prisoner."

"You say 'considering.' Something change your mind?"

"Yes, ma'am, Your Honor. Since I've come to this city I've come to the conclusion that the men I was holding might not be guilty. But I needed time to prove it. The sheriff did not appear willing to give me that time."

Willis and the sheriff and Les were standing by, listening intently. The marshal was a young man holding a rifle,

wearing a Buster Brown suit with a bow tie. He stayed close
to Martha.

She suddenly turned to Harvey Pruitt. She said, "Sheriff,
even though you are not a duly constituted officer in this
county your experience is valuable. Did Sheriff Hawser
announce his intentions in a lawful manner?"

Harvey glanced over at Warner. He said, hesitantly,
"Wall, ma'am, that kind of depends on what you mean. He
shore picked a hell of a time. Somethin' like five in the
mornin'. Acted like he expected us to be asleep."

"I'm asking you if he announced himself in a lawful
manner. That's a simple question, Sheriff. I'd like an
answer."

Harvey glanced at Warner again, looking uncomfortable.
"He said he was Dick Hawser. He never called hisself
'sheriff.' Said he had a warrant and he was come fer the
prisoners. He was mostly talkin' to Mr. Grayson."

She glanced briefly at Warner. "But he said he had a
warrant?"

"Yes, ma'am. Mr. Grayson ast him what kind of warrant
and he said he had him a justice of the peace warrant. I
don't thank Mr. Grayson believed him."

She looked around at Warner again. "Oh? Mr. Grayson
didn't believe him. You're a sheriff?"

Warner was beginning to get uneasy about the overly
official way she was conducting the inquest. He said, "I told
him to clear off, that I didn't want to deal with him when we
were half asleep."

"Were you half asleep?"

He didn't answer, but gave her a look. He couldn't
understand what she was up to. Was she having sport at his
expense or trying to make it look as if she were doing her job
thoroughly? Or was she taking a serious view of what had
happened, even though she'd known his plans in advance?

Harvey said, trying to get her attention back to him, "See,
Mr. Grayson didn't believe he had a warrant. He figured he
was doin' what he'd threatened to do, come in and take the
prisoners and maybe do us all harm."

Martha said, "But you're a law officer. You may be out of
your county, but you are still a law officer."

"Yes, ma'am," Harvey said. "But the prisoners belonged

to Mr. Grayson by the bounty law. An' that's gospel. Besides, Mr. Grayson is a law officer also."

She swung around on Warner and for the first time he saw a hint of amusement in her eyes. She said, *"Mr.* Grayson is a law officer? You never cease to amaze, mister."

Warner said, uncomfortably, "I'm the captain of the Nueces County Sheriff's Mounted Posse."

"My, my," she said. "And I'll bet y'all cut quite a figure at parades and holidays and such." She turned back to the sheriff. "Who fired first?"

"Oh, they did, ma'am. No doubt about that. And several times. We defended ourselves as best we could. We lost two men. One dead and maybe one gonna die."

"Your Honor," Warner said, "one proof is that they tried to flank us. While Dick Hawser was holding my attention he sent a man to our left and to our right. He should have had us cold."

She looked at him, the faint amusement in her eyes. She said, "But you had taken steps."

"You damn right, Your Honor. Dick Hawser never left no doubt in my mind about his intentions. We fought in self-defense and we were in defensive positions because I expected something like this ever since my visit with him when he'd been antagonistic about my interest in the bank robbery. He threatened me then and he carried it out this morning." He looked at her, wanting to say, "Martha, we ain't got time for this. We got a bank to be at by nine o'clock."

As if reading his mind she turned to her town marshal and said, "George, write down that the justice of the peace finds that the death of the sheriff and this deputy . . . do you know his name?"

The young marshal had gotten out pencil and a pad. He said, "Yes, ma'am. This was Joe Bowden."

"Well, write down that the court finds they both died by misadventure."

Harvey said, "What does that mean?"

Martha said, "It means they killed themselves by ignorance." She glanced at Warner. "It means they went up against a situation they had not familiarized themselves with. That's a misadventure. It killed them."

After that Warner walked Martha back to where Calvin still lay. He said, "We haven't moved anything or anybody except the wounded men. We were waiting on you."

She looked down at Calvin and shook her head. She said, "I guess you could say this one was murdered."

As they walked toward the man who had killed Calvin and whom Warner had subsequently killed, he said, "Martha, hurry up if you can. I got my surprise at the bank planned for nine o'clock. It's nearly eight o'clock now."

She gave him a look, but then just glanced at the dead deputy. She said, "This one was killed in the commission of a crime."

In the end she didn't even go to see the other one, the one Les had killed. Instead she sent the marshal with Harvey in the buckboard to bring him back. While they waited she said, "What are you going to do at the bank?"

He said, "I done everything but tell y'all the other night. We know who robbed that bank and we're going in there and prove it."

She smiled faintly. "Who's we?"

"You and me and Muddy and a couple of other stockholders he's getting and Laura and a couple of my people."

She sighed. "Do you know what you're doing? I am not in the most secure position in this town."

"I was right about Dick Hawser, wasn't I?"

"That you were." She looked over at his body. "He won't be missed. But the bank is a different story. Are you sure you know what you're doing?"

"I offered to bet Muddy another hundred-dollar bill that I did. He wouldn't take the bet."

She heaved a sigh, her bosom moving. She said, "Oh, hell, in for a penny, in for a pound. What do I do?"

"Be outside that bank door at a quarter until nine. Get Laura on your way in and have her there. Tell her I'm running late. I've got to see about that man of mine at the doctor's. And bring a head full of arithmetic."

"Arithmetic?"

"Yeah. We are going to be doing some counting."

She finished up the inquest by declaring the man Les had shot had also died by misadventure. She found the wounded deputy guilty of criminal trespass and fined him fifty dollars and thirty days in jail. Then she declared the inquest closed.

As he was helping her into the buggy he said, "Bring both your marshals."

"Why?"

He said, "Well, my office as a Nueces County peace officer might not carry much weight here. And right now it looks like you've got the only official law in town."

She looked at her marshal, George, and nodded. "That's true. It's a very nice feeling for a change."

She left in her buggy, leaving George to help with the bodies and make their arrival at the undertaker's official. Willis drove the buckboard and they went about picking up the bodies and loading them into the bed of the wagon. Warner stayed at the stock car and started making a pot of coffee. It hurt him to see Calvin's limp body being lifted in with the others. He called to Willis, "Don't put nobody on top of Calvin. Especially that son of a bitch that killed him."

When they were through they all took a cup of coffee with a little whiskey in it, even George, who was young and a little awed by what he'd seen. He said, hesitantly, to Warner, "Say, now that the shur'ff an' nearly all his depities is dead, who's the law around here?"

Warner took a sip of coffee. He said, "Why, son, you are. You and the other marshal. But, of course, the main law is the mayor. Keep that in mind when she gives you a chore."

"Yessir, I will."

When they were through the marshal and Harvey Pruitt got into the wagon seat, the sheriff driving. Warner directed him to take the bodies to the undertaker, see to Calvin's disposal, and assure the undertaker that he, Warner, would be around to pay for burying the young man. Then he told Harvey to stay close around the bank and be ready to join up when they began to gather around the front door.

Harvey said, "Do I bring a shotgun?"

Warner smiled slightly and said, "Naw, these are a different breed of crooks than we dealt with last night. This morning, I mean. You can leave the shotgun here. I'll be coming right on in behind you."

He directed Willis and Les to go up to the freight depot

and see if they couldn't find some tools. If they could they were to begin ripping down the barred wall that had turned half the car into a cage. Warner said, "I got to turn this car back in like I found it. Besides, we'll be riding it back to Hondo."

Willis said, "We don't need much more than a crowbar. Shorely they'll have one of them."

Before he mounted his horse Les touched him on the shoulder. He said, "Mr. Grayson, don't feel too bad about Calvin. Wadn't nothin' you could do. The way he kept gettin' into anythang that come his way it had to happen sooner or later."

Warner looked at him a moment and then nodded. "Thanks, Les." He put his boot into the stirrup of the Andalusian and swung into the saddle. He said, "You and Willis be sure you gather up all the guns got left around. They're worth money. And watch the camp."

"Yessir."

Warner was about to ride away, but he stopped his horse. He said, "You going to come to work for me, Les? If we ever get all this settled?"

Les's eyes widened. He said, "You bet I am, an' plenty grateful fer the chancet."

Now they stood outside the bank door, a mixed group of sexes and ages and motives and experience and occupations. Laura was standing by Warner. She had on a different outfit; a light blue skirt that ended above her ankles and a white shirtwaist with bunched sleeves. It left him wondering just how many clothes she'd brought and how many carrying cases. She said, "Is this the last? When this is over are we finally going to get out of this damn town?"

"I hope so," he said. "I'm going to take you home and hide you somewhere that will keep you from causing me any more trouble than you ordinarily do."

"Ha," was all she said.

Half an hour earlier he'd stopped by the doctor's office to ask after Otis. The man was conscious though woozy. The doctor had said he was almost certain Otis hadn't gotten his skull cracked, but he had a dandy concussion. The doctor had said, "Man must have a remarkable head for it not to be broken. Whoever hit him left a dent in his skull you can lay two fingers in."

Otis had tried to apologize, but it had been difficult because he was slurring his words a little. He said, "I be mighty sorry, Missa Grayson. But'chou was raight. I coulda shot him. Had him. Jus' couldn't pull tha trigga . . . couldn't pull it. Hit me. Hit me with rifle. His eyes. Couldn' pull trigga."

He'd patted Otis on the shoulder and told him not to worry. Then he'd given the doctor a ten-dollar bill for his care and started out of the office. But he'd stopped and turned back to show the doctor his side, pulling up his shirt. He'd asked the doctor if his stitches were ready to come out yet.

The young doctor had looked with horror. "They should have come out two or three days ago! They are going to be hell to work out of there. Here, get up on this table. I'll give you some laudanum. It'll help some but I'm afraid you are in for a very unpleasant experience."

Warner had quickly stuffed his shirt back in his pants. He'd said, "Doc, I got some bank business to tend to that won't wait. I'll come back when that is done."

The doctor had stood in the doorway and called after him, "The longer you put it off the worse it's going to be."

The time had crept to nine o'clock. Warner pushed forward until he was right in front of the bank door. He heard a key in the lock and then saw the window shade flick a little as whoever was opening the door peeked out to see who the first customers would be. Warner guessed it was the young teller, Wayne Goddard. The key finished turning in the lock. Warner put his hand on the doorknob. When he heard the key leave the keyhole he turned the knob and pushed it wide open so that the rest could crowd in behind him. He took four rapid steps into the bank, the move bringing him almost to the line of tellers' cages. He said loudly, "All right! Everybody stop what they are doing and hold real still. We are about to have an audit."

15

Five people stared at him and the people who came crowding in behind him to fill the small lobby. Harry Wallace was the first to find his voice. He was standing by his desk, one hand on the back of his chair as if he were about to pull it out to sit down. He said, "What the hell is this? What's going on here?"

Warner said, "I told you. We are having a surprise audit."

A man standing by the door to the president's office, whom Warner took to be Bob Thomas, said, "What kind of nonsense is this? You can't audit this bank! Is that you back there, Mayor? What is this all about?"

"It's a stockholders' audit, Mr. Thomas, and I recommend you cooperate."

Wallace said, angrily, "It's a damn bank robbery is what it is." He pointed at Warner. "I know this crook. He was in here the other day trying to hold me up for reward money."

"Want to bet I get it?" Warner said. He jerked his head. "Now, I want all five of you to get on out from behind there. I want you to come up here and sit on the benches in the front."

Thomas said, "By whose authority is this audit being called?"

"By me," Warner said. "I'm a special Deputy United States Marshal and we have some questions about your so-called robbery." He hoped Laura and Martha were able to keep the smiles off their faces at the lie. "Now get the hell out from behind there! Move!"

Wallace said, "Like hell I will." He suddenly put his hand to the handle of a desk drawer and started to open it. In the same instant Warner drew his revolver and cocked, aimed, and fired it in one motion. The bullet hit the drawer, slamming it shut and scattering wood splinters. Wallace jumped back and began to curse. Warner said, "I reckon I'm going to have to come get y'all out of there."

The spinster lady, Miss Bainbridge, put a hand to her throat. She said, "Oh, I feel faint."

Behind him the mayor said, "Wayne, you'd better bring her out here and both of you take a seat on a bench."

Wilbur Crabtree was standing just to Warner's left, close enough for Warner to reach out and touch the man's turkey neck that stuck up out of his high, stiff collar like an old piece of hairy rawhide. He said, "They'll be trouble over this, mark my words."

But Warner thought he looked more than a little worried and scared.

From where he was standing Bob Thomas said, "Wayne! Go get the sheriff. We'll put a stop to this soon enough."

Warner said, relishing it, "The sheriff is dead. So are his deputies."

It was as if he had suddenly clubbed all three across the face with a board. If they didn't all take an involuntary step backward they seemed to. Warner could hear the sudden breath Wilbur Crabtree took. Warner said, "So now come out from behind there. I don't want you near the books or the money, savvy?" Over his shoulder he said, "Muddy, will you put out the closed sign and make sure all the shades are pulled? We want this private."

Bob Thomas took several steps forward. He said, "Mayor, is this true? About the sheriff?"

"Yes, it is, Mr. Thomas. And I strongly advise you to do as Mr. Grayson is telling you. This is a legal investigation and if you impede it you can face criminal charges."

Warner glanced back at her admiringly. She could certainly sound like a whip cracker when she wanted to.

Harry Wallace said, loudly, "This is a goddamn bank robbery is what it is!"

Warner said, "Well, you'd be the expert, Harry. But this time you're wrong. This time we are fixing to *catch* us some bank robbers."

Bob Thomas said, "I don't know what this is all about, but it is a mistake."

Warner said, "No, not paying me my reward was the mistake. You got greedy. You didn't read your man, Mr. Harry Wallace, even though I gave you the chance. Now we are going to find out. I give you one more warning to come out of there."

Behind him the mayor said, "Mr. Grayson, are you prepared to shoot them if they don't?"

"It's something I can say I'm looking forward to."

"Then I had better handle it." She spoke to her deputies. "George, O'Dell, go back and escort the three officers up here and seat them on a bench. Keep them on the bench and out of our way."

They came reluctantly, but they came. When they were seated the mayor looked at Warner. "Now what?"

Warner said, "I want Mr. Goddard to go behind the cages and get all the books and all the ledgers and I want him to show you, Mayor, what the cash balance was at this bank at the close of business yesterday. How much cash Mr. Crabtree and Mr. Thomas and Mr. Wallace said there was. Is that right, Mr. Goddard, did they do the counting? And did they not enter that amount in the ledger?"

The young man nodded. He was pale but more from confusion than anything else. He said, "Traditionally it is the job of the head cashier. That would be Mr. Crabtree. Usually the tellers are held late to help, but they don't do it that way here."

"Didn't you find that strange? Miss Bainbridge, you are not going to faint. Didn't you both find that strange?"

Mr. Goddard shrugged. He said, "This is my first job. I had no way of knowing. But it let me out early so I was glad."

Miss Bainbridge swallowed and summoned the energy to whisper, "It was contrary to the practices we'd used in the past. Before Mr. Wallace and Mr. Thomas. But they were the officers so we did not argue."

Warner motioned. He said, "Mr. Goddard, go get those ledgers and lay them on Mr. Wallace's desk and then make sure the safe is open as well as the tellers' drawers."

Bob Thomas made as if to rise, but Harvey Pruitt, who was standing next to him, pushed him back. It didn't stop him from saying, "I protest! This is a violation of the banking laws."

"So is what you did."

From the back Roy Garret, the auction house owner and stockholder said, "What the hell is going on? What are we doing?"

Muddy Roads said, "I don't know any more than you do, but I'll bet you a hundred-dollar bill that *Marshal* Grayson does."

Garret said, "No bet, Muddy. You taken enough of my money through the years."

Warner said, "Now, Mayor, I want you and the two other best money counters to go back there and, with Mr. Goddard's help, locate every bit of cash in this bank, and it won't be hidden. It'll be right where it's supposed to be. I want you to take that money and split it up amongst yourselves and count it. Then I want you to compare it to the cash balance from yesterday. If all is on the up and up the two figures ought to match."

Before anyone could move, Harry Wallace jumped up and shoved George aside and started to bull his way toward the door while he felt in his pocket with one hand. He had the derringer almost clear of his coat pocket when Warner took two quick steps and hit him over the back of the head with the barrel of his pistol. He dropped down to his knees and then slumped forward. Warner reached down and picked up the derringer and put it in his boot. He said to the two constables, "Reckon you better search Mr. Thomas. Might also give Mr. Crabtree a patting down. Have them both take off their coats. It's getting a little warm in here, anyway. Miss Bainbridge, don't put your hand to your head like that. You are not going to swoon."

They propped Harry Wallace in a corner. Bob Thomas was looking paler than Miss Bainbridge.

Warner said, "Now, Mayor, I figure you and Mrs. Laura Pico of Corpus Christi, Texas, and Muddy Roads are the best counters. If you'd go on back and get started I would appreciate it. Mr. Garret, I'd like you and Major Mills to go back and watch over their shoulders. Mr. Goddard, you may also watch. Miss Bainbridge, you may go home."

It took almost an hour and the tension was thick in the bank. Even though Warner felt almost certain, especially after Harry Wallace had tried to bolt, he still could not help a twinge of worry from time to time.

Harry Wallace had come to and now sat on the bench in sullen silence. Bob Thomas, too, was silent. He leaned forward, staring at the floor.

Finally the mayor stood up. She was standing at Wilbur Crabtree's desk. She had a piece of paper in her hand. She said, "We've got a final figure we all agree on. We each counted our own pile and then we switched and counted what the others had counted. Wayne, who is more familiar than we are, agrees we've come up with a correct amount."

Warner said, "And?"

The mayor said, "The cash on hand is thirty-five thousand three hundred eighteen more than the cash balance showed from yesterday."

Warner heard Bob Thomas behind him sigh and say, "It was too good to last."

Muddy said, "Warner, how the hell did you know?"

"Because there wasn't any other place to hide it. It was the safest place. As long as no one else was counting it, why move it? Just say you had a bank robbery and let it go at that. The only other place it could have been was with Jake or Darcey."

"But how did you know it was a fake? The robbery?"

Warner shrugged. "Because there were no insurance investigators and they claimed to have insurance coverage. They said that to keep the public from panicking. They knew there was no reason for the depositors to panic. They had plenty of money to cover withdrawals. Besides, by claiming to buy the insurance they were able to pocket another five thousand dollars." He pointed in the direction of the mayor. "That's why that overage is thirty-five thousand and not thirty."

Behind him Harvey Pruitt said, "I'll be a son of a bitch."

The mayor said, "O'Dell, you and George take them on over to the jail and put them in a cell. Don't let them get away from you."

Warner said, "I got one more piece of curiosity to satisfy and I think Mr. Crabtree can help me." He suddenly turned and took the scrawny man by his arm and jerked him up and led him around the tellers' cages. He said, "Harv, come on with me. Major Mills, you and Mr. Garret might want to help our young marshal get those two prisoners bedded down. Mr. Garret, I notice you are carrying a sidearm. Don't let either one of them get close enough to make a grab for it."

Warner was heading for the president's office, still pulling Mr. Crabtree along. The mayor said, "Warner, what are you going to do?"

"I told you, satisfy my curiosity. I won't be long."

He and Harvey Pruitt took the cashier through the president's door and into his office. At Warner's direction the sheriff locked the door. Warner pushed Crabtree back against a wall. The scrawny man was frightened, but he was still arrogant and trying not to show it. He said, his chin up, "You can't scare me."

"I'm not trying to," Warner said. He had noticed a window behind Bob Thomas's desk that led out onto a side street. It must have been on that very street that Otis and Calvin and Les had waited while Jake and Darcey had rushed into the bank and tied up Wayne Goddard and made it look like a robbery. He said, "Harvey, does that window open?"

The sheriff stepped over and tried it. "Yep," he said.

Warner stood studying the scrawny man. He judged Crabtree to be in his late forties. With his coat off he was in a white shirt with sleeve garters and some kind of cotton pants and high-topped shoes. He had a high, starched collar and he was nearly bald on top. Warner said, "Crabtree, I know how y'all faked the robbery. I know about Jake and Darcey coming in and tying up Goddard and then you and Thomas and Wallace acting like you'd been held up. But I want you to tell me all the details. I got a feeling there's a hell of a lot more to this than I know or can guess. You been at this bank considerable years and then all of a sudden you take part in a bank robbery. How come?"

Crabtree held himself stiffly against the wall. He said, "I will not open my mouth to you, you Philistine."

Warner kept on studying him. He said, "I hear you got your own key to the front door of the church and that you are powerful strong for tellin' folks about being sinners and such."

Crabtree said, "It's nothing you'd understand. A man like you."

Warner looked at him, thinking. His grandfather had always told him every man had his weakness. The trick was in finding it. He'd said, "With some men it's fear of being hurt. With others it's their dignity or their pride or their wallet or their family. It can be a lot of things, but be sure that every man has that soft spot and if you hit it he'll sing you his song."

Warner said, "You realize that I am a hell of a lot bigger and stronger than you are and I could hurt the hell out of you."

Crabtree pulled himself closer to the wall. He said, "I ain't afeared of a sinner like you."

Warner thought a minute and then looked around at the sheriff. Harvey raised his palms as if to say he didn't know what to do with the man.

"Take off your clothes."

Crabtree first looked as if he hadn't heard right and then he looked horrified. He said, "I will not!"

Warner said, "You are a fine one to talk about sinners, Crabtree. Don't you reckon the Bible take a pretty dim view of robbing a bank and stealing other folks' money?"

"I had nothing to do with it."

"Take off your clothes."

"I most certainly will not! You'll not put me to that indignity."

Warner reached into his pocket and pulled out his big clasp knife and opened it. He said, "You take 'em off or I cut 'em off."

"You wouldn't dare!"

"Harvey, come over here and take hold of the reverend

while I shear him like he sheared the sheep that deposited with him."

The sheriff came over and took the scrawny Crabtree in an iron grip. For a moment the older banker struggled and then saw it was no good. Warner came over and began cutting buttons off Crabtree's shirt.

Harvey said, "Hell, that's too slow. Just rip it up one side and down the other."

Crabtree broke. "No, no!" He was almost sobbing. "These are quality goods! You would cut them up, you heathen."

"Then get 'em off. And be quick about it."

It took time because Crabtree tried to do it and still preserve his dignity. Finally he was down to a pair of long johns.

Warner said, "Little warm for that kind of underwear, ain't it, Reverend?"

Harvey said, "Don't josh him, Warner. Little runt ain't got much meat on his bones to keep him warm."

Warner said, "Let's get the shoes and the underwear off. Help him if you have to, Harvey."

As he unbuttoned his top Crabtree said, tremulously, "What are you going to do?"

"Throw you out that window," Warner said matter-of-factly. But something else had taken his attention. On top of Thomas's desk were two ink pots, one red and one black. While Crabtree was slowly unbuttoning his long-handled underwear Warner took Crabtree's handkerchief and wrapped it around his index finger. Then he took the top off the pot of red ink and dipped his finger in the ink. He turned around and, in large letters, wrote SINNER across Crabtree's forehead.

The cashier flinched and tried to pull back, but his head was against the wall. He said, "What are you doing? What are you doing to me?"

Harvey laughed. "Looks to me like he's labeling you like a jar of preserves."

Warner said, "Get that top off him."

When Crabtree's chest and stomach were bare Warner soaked his makeshift brush again and wrote SINNER in even bigger letters across Crabtree's chest and stomach.

"What is it? What are you doing to me?"

"Getting you ready for public display. Turn him around, Harv, so I can get at his back."

He wrote the same word in two places on Crabtree's skinny back. The cashier was almost in tears. Warner said, "Now let's jerk off his bottoms and his shoes and fling him out the window."

But Crabtree was almost frantic. "What have you soiled my skin with? What, what?"

Warner looked around. There was a bureau on the other side of the room. He thought he saw a big hand mirror lying on it. He walked over and got it and thrust it at Crabtree. He said, "Here, look for yourself. Not only are you going out the window naked, but with the mark of Cain on you."

Crabtree just stared with horrified eyes. He slumped against the wall. He could see it on his face and on his chest and stomach and Harvey kindly told him it was on his back, too. Harvey said, "You planning on painting his pistol with it?"

"You can. I ain't touching the nasty thing." He put out his hand and took hold of the top of Crabtree's underwear bottoms. He said, "Let's get the rest of it and heave him out the window."

Crabtree broke down. He sank to his knees, dropping the mirror, putting both his hands to his face. He said, moaning, "No, no, no, no. I'll tell you, I'll tell you everything. I'll confess every sin. You have labeled me rightly. I am a sinner. I will tell you everything."

Warner said, "Then start talking, and don't leave anything out."

Crabtree began to talk, still in his kneeling position, the words coming out, sometimes muffled with sobs, so that Warner had to ask him to repeat himself. But what Crabtree had to tell was nothing like Warner had expected. It was far bigger in scope than he could ever have guessed. It was plain and simply a plan whereby Thomas and Wallace and Crabtree were well on their way to embezzling their way into control of a string of banks. The first had been in Ennis, Texas. Thomas and Wallace, Crabtree said, had pulled two fake robberies there, one to get the money to gain controlling interest in the Ennis bank, and the second to obtain the funds to buy their way in as officers of the bank in Round Rock. They had left the cashier, who had been part of their original plan, in charge as president in Ennis. He'd hired new officers. The plan in Round Rock had been the same; once they left for the next bank Crabtree would become the president. Crabtree said, "You can't work it without the cashier because he's the one generally does the counting of the money."

The last robbery had been to get the money to buy the majority interest in a bank in Gonzales, Texas, a town near San Antonio.

Warner and Harvey looked at each other and shook their heads. It was far beyond any plan they could have guessed. Crabtree said they had come into the bank and it was a long time before they began to talk much to him. The way it was explained no one would get hurt. The bank would continue to go on, the despositors would still have plenty of money because money was always circulating, and there'd be plenty of money for loans. When they had finally broached the subject to him of being an officer in a string of banks he'd been overwhelmed. It was like a dream come true. He'd be the president of the bank he'd labored so long and so hard for. And he knew what a good job he'd do. He'd raised his head. "And no one would be hurt. Can't you see that? The way money circulates in a bank no one would ever be the wiser. And I counted the money. I deserved it. I was owed it. I'd be a more important figure in the town and my church would benefit. Don't you see? I was doing good."

Warner shook his head again. He pulled Crabtree to his feet. He said, "Now you got to go out there and tell the rest of the folks."

He looked frightened. "Oh, I don't want to do that!"

Harvey said, "You're proud of it, ain't you? Looks like you'd want folks to be proud with you."

Crabtree's face settled. He said, "Yes, yes, that's right. But I must have my clothes on. I must have my dignity."

"Oh, you'll have that," Warner said. "And a few more things, besides."

They had to help him get dressed. Crabtree seemed a little dazed, a little unsure of where he was and what he was doing. When he was ready they opened the door and took him out so he could tell his story to the others. By now he seemed quite proud of it.

His shirt covered the words Warner had lettered on his chest and stomach and back, but there was nothing they could do about the SINNER that stretched across his brow. The ink was indelible.

Just before he went out the door Crabtree said, wistfully, "Less than a month. That was all. It was arranged. Bob and Harry had it handled. Less than a month and I would have been president."

"What are you talking about?"

"Taking the money from here and buying into the bank in Gonzales. It had to be done before the stockholders' meeting, don't you see. And it would have. It would have been so nice." He wiped his palm over his brow and looked at his hand. He said, "My hand is still a little red. I thought it would be gone by now."

Warner said, "No, I think you'll have that particular color on you for a long time."

"But red means you've gone in the hole, shown a deficit."

"It also means you and Bob and Harry have caused some to be spilled. But you're right about the hole. You put several folks in one so you could be president of the bank. Now get on out there and tell the people what a hell of a fellow you are."

After they had heard Crabtree's story with a mixture of shock and astonishment, and after Harvey Pruitt had taken Crabtree over to the jail to join the others, and Wayne Goddard had made a big pot of coffee and they were all sitting around cooling out, Warner got up and said he wanted to make a point. He said, "Now this might not be the appropriate time to bring this up, but I'm short of time and I've got you all here together."

The mayor said, "By all means, *Marshal* Grayson, make your point."

He gave her a look, but went ahead with what he had to say. He said, "Now I got started on this because I saw a reward poster advertising a bank robbery at this bank." He pointed at the floor. "This bank right here. And that bank, this bank, offered a reward for the arrest of the five men believed to have robbed this bank. It offered five hundred dollars a head for these men, dead or alive. Well, I had reason to believe I had those men in my possession, four alive and one dead at the time. So I set in to collect that reward. I'm not going to burden you with all the trouble and time and money I spent trying to collect that reward. Some of you already know it. But I am going to point out that I caught the five men that did rob this bank. Only two of them turned out to be part of my original five. That would be Clinton Darcey and a man named Jake. They lie buried in graves in Hondo, Texas, and I can prove that they were the ones who came in and tied up Wayne Goddard and made it look like a robbery. Well, so far as that goes, Crabtree has already confirmed that. He's even confirmed that Thomas and Wallace used Darcey on their first holdup at the bank in Ennis.

"So I caught the five robbers. Two are dead and buried and the other three"—he pointed in the general direction of the jail—"are under lock and key.

"My point is that it wasn't Thomas or Wallace or the both of them and Crabtree who advertised that reward, it was this bank, the Mercantile Bank. I caught your robbers and I recovered your money, five thousand dollars more than you thought you'd lost. So I am putting in my claim for that reward." He sat down.

They stared at him for a moment and then Roy Garret said, "Marshal Grayson—"

Laura laughed. "He's not a marshal, federal or otherwise."

Warner said, "It seemed like a good idea at the time. I wanted to speed matters along."

Mr. Garret bowed his head. He said, "I understand. I also understand your point about the reward and I don't think there's a stockholder who will argue your claim." He half smiled. "Outside of them in the jail. But the point is we ain't exactly organized right now. We've got to get the books audited by a real bank accountant and elect officers and get the bank running again. I'm sure you can see that and be patient a little longer."

Muddy Roads stood up. He said, "Roy, I don't think all that is necessary. We owe Warner the money. He done us all a hell of a good turn. Remember, he saved us over thirty-five *thousand* dollars. I figure me and you and Amos and a few other stockholders can get together and since the other big stockholders are in jail and can't vote we'd represent a majority. I don't see why we can't get Warner a check this very afternoon." He looked over at Garret. He said, "When you come out to my place and you win you expect to be paid right off, don't you?"

Garret said, "I don't know. Been so long since I won I can't remember." He waited for the laugh to die down. "Yeah, I see how it could be done. And I'd be in favor of it."

Muddy said, "When are you planning on leaving, Warner?"

He shrugged. "I don't think I can get out today. I've got to arrange for a stock car to be hooked onto a train headed for San Antonio."

Garret said, "There's a mixed freight and passenger train leaves tomorrow at one P.M."

"Then I guess that's the one I'll be on." He looked across at Laura. "That is, if it suits Mrs. Pico."

She gave him a sweet smile. She said, "Why, Mr. Grayson, you know I am amenable to any plans you care to make. After all, who am I to argue with the hero of the hour?"

Martha Roads laughed.

Muddy said, "While we're talking about paying . . . " He walked over to the tellers' cages, where Wayne Goddard was busy assembling the money for storage in the vault. He said, "Wayne, I know the bank is closed, but I want you to cash me a draft."

Warner was glowering at Laura for her sarcastic little statement when Muddy walked over to him and held out a hundred-dollar bill. Warner glanced at it blankly. "What's that?"

"It's the hundred-dollar bill I owe you from the bet."

Warner waved his hand. "Aw, forget that. I was joking."

Muddy said, "Well, I wasn't. I don't joke about betting. If they'd had an insurance policy you can damn well bet I'd've taken it from you."

Warner shrugged and took the bill and put it in his shirt pocket. Roy Garret said, "Mr. Grayson, you don't know how much good that does me. So far as I know that is the first bet Muddy Roads ever lost."

Muddy looked over at him. He said, "I got a hundred-dollar bill that says that ain't so. You want to bet?"

Roy Garret just put up his hands. "Hell," he said, "I've got to get back to work. I nearly lost my part of thirty-five thousand dollars this morning and that scares the hell out of me."

Now they were on the train heading for Austin. Laura had insisted that Warner ride up front with her in the chair cars. Back in the train the stock car was rolling along carrying the pinto and Warner's Andalusian and Willis and Harvey and Les and Otis. They had preferred, as Warner generally did, to ride in the stock car.

Warner had wired ahead to Austin and, during the three-hour layover there, he'd be meeting with a deputy U.S. marshal about the robbery in Round Rock as well as looking into the past robbery at the bank in Ennis. He had some hope that they had offered a reward in that case also and, if they had, he knew right where the culprits were.

In his pocket was the check for twenty-five hundred from the Mercantile Bank. A thousand of it belonged to Laura because they were partners and that was her half, because he'd told Harvey Pruitt that, as soon as they got to Hondo, he was going to cash the check and give him five hundred dollars. The sheriff had protested that their original deal had been for three hundred, but Warner had said, "That's right. But I figure things got about two hundred dollars' worth more complicated."

He'd given Otis fifty dollars, enough to tide him over while he and Les sold the extra horses and guns that Warner had deemed were theirs. Otis had insisted on coming, though he was still weak and woozy and the doctor had recommended against it. But Otis had said he'd started this matter and he was "by gawd gonna finish her." Which was an example of just how woozy he was.

Warner had had his stitches taken out when he'd gone in to visit Otis, and the doctor had not exaggerated. In spite of the laudanum, he'd arrived back at the hotel suite weak and pale and sweating. When Laura had found out she'd been furious that he hadn't let her be there. She'd said, "That could have been serious! You needed me there to look after you."

He'd said, with what little strength he had left, "Oh, don't lie. You wanted to be there to see if I'd yell and scream. You are the meanest woman God ever made."

They'd had dinner at the Roadses' house and it had been a pleasant meal and good conversation. Muddy had said, "Warner, you was shore right about taking the sheriff out of the picture. When Thomas and Wallace found out he was dead they folded their tent. But how the hell did you figure him to be involved?"

"He had to be, Muddy. Oh, I don't know if he was privy to the inside particulars, but they had to make it clear to him they didn't want to have much of an investigation. I'm sure that the facts of that will come out when the proper authorities, the Marshal's Service, I'd imagine, investigate. But I knew I couldn't go into that bank and have my way if the sheriff and his deputies came barging in. Besides, I'd already scared Wallace enough so I knew he'd put the sheriff on us and we were going to have to fight one way or another. I stirred him up so I could pick the time and the place and make my preparations as I did."

Muddy had shaken his head. He'd said, "I told Major Mills, you know, the one-armed cavalry officer, about how you laid all this out and he asked me to ask you if you'd been an army officer. He said you ran it like a military campaign."

Warner had laughed. He'd said, "Well, it may look like that in hindsight, but, believe me, I was doing an awful lot of guessing along the way."

Muddy had thought about that a moment. Then he'd said, "Naw, I don't think so. Suckers guess. Men who make their living at what other people call gambling, but which ain't if you know what you're doing, call it playing the odds. I make my living that way so I recognize it when I seen it. Odds said that since no insurance investigators hadn't come prowling, then Thomas hadn't taken out no insurance. I should have seen that. We all should have. But it was only you that did.

Same thing with the money. It wasn't anywhere else so it had to be in a place where it wouldn't be noticed. I reckon if you want to hide money a bank is the best place for it." He'd shaken his head. "Naw, you wasn't doin' much guessin'.""

The train was rattling and rolling along. Warner had a piece of paper on his knee and a stub of a pencil in his fingers. He was peering down intently at a column of figures. Laura glanced over at him. She said, "What are you doing, Warner?"

Without looking up he said, "Trying to figure out if I actually made any money on this damn bank reward adventure." He glanced up at her. He said, "I'll tell you one thing—you insisting on that high-priced suite at the hotel didn't help matters one damn bit."

She said, with some heat, "I went to Round Rock on your express orders. Or have you forgotten? And it was easily the last place I wanted to be."

"Did that mean you had to sleep in the most expensive set of rooms in the whole damn town? I *asked* you to go to Round Rock and have a look around, but I never said nothing about no damn suite. In fact, I never even heard the word before."

She said, "Where was I supposed to sleep? In the street?"

"There's other places between a suite and the street."

She tossed her head. She said, "Any comfort I might have got out of it was thrown out with the cat when you set in to *bargain* with the management. I never felt so cheap in my life. Besides, mister, you used that room three nights."

"Yeah, for your gratification and satisfaction."

She turned and gave him a glare. "Now, *that* is a laugh. *My* gratification and satisfaction. I'll remember that the next time you come sniffing around. Besides, this wasn't about the reward money. You know it and so do I."

He looked at her, his mouth open. "It wasn't about what? Wasn't about the reward money? Are you crazy?"

"It was another one of your righteous adventures. Oh, I know you far better than you think, Warner Grayson. Here was a wrong that needed righting and off you ride. You don't fool me."

He briefly thought about the conversation he'd had with

Calvin when they'd been lying under the cattle car awaiting the arrival of Hawser and his deputies and how unsure he'd felt. And how scared. He started to tell her about that, but decided it would be wasted. He said, "Woman, you have got hold of the wrong end of the rope. I never chased down money so hard in my life. That was the slickest money I've ever tried to lay hands on. Was like trying to grab a greased pig. And then you come along and tell me I wasn't after that slick money. That makes me so damn mad I feel like throwing you off this train!" He glared at her. He mimicked her. He said, "Here was a wrong that needed righting. Hell and damn and hell again. You are loco, woman."

She turned to face him. They were only inches apart. She said, gritting her teeth, "I wish we were at home and in bed. I'd make you sit up and beg. Who do you think you are talking to?"

He pushed his face closer until their lips were only an inch apart. "I think I'm talking to the one who would be doing the begging. And soon as we get near a private bed I'll prove it to you."

"I'll prove something right now," she said. "I'll prove you weren't doing it for the money but for that hero picture you've got of yourself. Learned from that grandfather you're always talking about."

His face got hot. He said, "I ain't got no hero picture of myself. I told you I did it for the twenty-five hundred!"

"Oh, yeah?" She lifted one eyebrow. "Then how come you didn't stop and take the money when I offered it to you?"

He stared at her for a second, trying to think what to say.

She said, "See? There's the proof. I offered to give you the money if you'd quit and go home. But you wouldn't do it."

"Aw . . . you didn't mean it. You were trying to fool me. If I'd've given it up, I'd never seen a dollar off you. I know you better than that. You're tighter than Dick's hat band when it comes to money."

She said, "I would have paid you." She nodded her head. "I swear it. Every cent."

He cocked his head and looked at her. He said, slowly, "I mean that much to you?"

"Of course. I thought you knew that."

"Noooo," he said. "No, not really. And I'm even suspicious of it right now. Soft words are not your style."

She said, "What soft words? You're worth that to me as a partner in the horse business. Where would I find another one like you? And what did you think I was talking about?"

His face got hot again and he glared at her. He said, "Why, you—" Then he stopped and the glare slowly turned to a small smile. He said, "No, I don't think so. I don't think it had anything to do with me as a partner. No, indeed. I think the lady made a slip." He was grinning openly. He said, "I knew you cared, but not twenty-five hundred dollars' worth."

Now it was her turn to flush. She said, flustered, "Don't kid yourself. How dare you think such a thing? Ours is strictly a business arrangement."

"Oh, sure." He started laughing out loud. "Yeah, business arrangement, bed and all."

"That's different!" she said. "One has nothing to do with the other. You are setting yourself mighty high, mister!"

He kept laughing and she suddenly started beating him on the chest with her dainty fists. She said, "It was only as a business partner!"

He grabbed her wrists, still laughing, and brought her across the seat to him and pulled her lips to his. She held them there for a second and then jerked her head back. She looked around the chair car to see if anyone had noticed. She said, "How dare you! In public like this."

He said, "What do you care, brazen huzzy like you? Try and buy a man off from doing what he thinks is right." He started laughing again.

She sat up, putting a hand to her hair to make sure it wasn't out of place. She said, "Just shut up, you. How much of that slick money, as you call it, did we end up with?"

He was still laughing. He said, "Oh, no. You don't get any. Because you lied. You said you were trying to protect me as your partner. But that wasn't true."

She launched herself at him. She said, "We'll just see who

gets what from whom." She put her hands on him, slipping them under his shirt.

He said, alarmed, "Laura! Stop it! Can't you see we are in public?"

She put her face up next to his ear. She said, "What do you care, big, brave hero like you? Now, how much did we make?"